CHARACTER

T0130876

F. Bordewijk

CHARACTER

a novel of father and son

translated by E. M. Prince

Elephant Paperbacks
IVAN R. DEE, PUBLISHER, CHICAGO

CHARACTER. Copyright © 1938 by F. Bordewijk.. Copyright © 1966 by
the Council of Europe. English translation copyright © 1966 by Peter
Owen and E. M. Prince. This book was first published in the United
States in 1990 by New Amsterdam Books and is here reprinted by
arrangement.

First ELEPHANT PAPERBACK edition published 1999 by Ivan R. Dee,
Publisher, 1332 North Halsted Street, Chicago 60622. Manufactured in
the United States of America and printed on acid-free paper.

Library of Congress Cataloging-in-Publication Data:
Bordewijk, Ferdinand, 1884–1965.
    [Karakter.   English]
    Character : a novel of father and son / F. Bordewijk ; translated
by E. M. Prince. — 1st Elephant paperback ed.
        p.   cm.
    ISBN 1-56663-227-7 (acid-free paper)
    I. Prince, E. M.   II. Title.
PT5816.B7K3713   1999
839.3'1362—dc21   98-45232

To my children
Nina and Robert

CONTENTS

CONTENTS

In view of the difference between Dutch and English legal practice, it has not always been possible to find an exact English counterpart to some of the terms used in the original.

For example, there is no distinction in Holland between solicitor and barrister. An *advocaat* can be either, or as very often, both together. The same difficulty has arisen with the various types of law-court occurring in the text.

I therefore crave the indulgence of any learned readers who may find room for criticism in some of the English terms used.

TRANSLATOR

A sadder and a wiser man
He rose the morrow morn

S. T. COLERIDGE

No

During the dark days around Christmas, in a Rotterdam maternity ward, Jacob Willem Katadreuffe was assisted into the world by a Caesarean. His mother was an eighteen-year-old servant-girl, Jacoba Katadreuffe, called Joba for short. His father was a bailiff, A. B. Dreverhaven, a man in his late thirties, renowned for his ruthlessness towards any debtor who fell into his hands.

The girl, Joba Katadreuffe, had been with Dreverhaven, a bachelor, for only a short time when he succumbed to her innocent charms, and she to his strength. He was not the type of man to yield; he was a man of granite, with a heart merely in the literal sense. He only yielded that once and he capitulated more in respect to himself than to her. Perhaps even, had she not possessed such exceptional eyes, nothing would have happened. But it happened after days of pent-up anger over a grandiose plan he had conceived, set in motion, then seen wrecked before his eyes because the money-lender backed out at the very last moment. Later than that even, when withdrawal should have been no longer possible, after the money-lender had pledged his word. There was no scrap of proof, no shred of evidence, and Dreverhaven as a man of the law knew that he could do nothing about the broken promise. With the man's letter in his pocket – a letter very carefully worded but at

9

the same time an obvious refusal – Dreverhaven had come home late. He had felt it coming; lately, whenever he rang up, he was told the skunk was absent. He knew it was a lie; he sensed it. Then that evening the letter had arrived, the first and only thing in writing, and there was nothing to catch hold of. So cunningly drafted, there must have been a lawyer behind it.

Dreverhaven returned home, seething inwardly, and in a suppressed fury he made himself master of Joba Katadreuffe. The girl was not by nature one to yield : she had a strong will, but still she was a girl. What happened to her was on the borderline of rape, but not actually so, and she did not so regard it.

She stayed on with her employer, but no longer addressed a single word to him. He was naturally taciturn; it did not worry him in the least. It will turn out all right, he thought : if anything happens I shall marry her. And he, too, kept silent.

After a few weeks she broke the silence :

'I'm in the family way.'

'Oh well,' he said.

'I'll be going away.'

'Oh well.'

He thought : it will all turn out all right. Within an hour he heard the front door close, not emphatically, quite normally. He went to the window. There was the young thing walking away with a bulging wicker basket. She was a sturdy girl and was not weighed down by it. He saw her go as the evening began to grow grey; it was the end of April. He turned back to the table where the remains of his dinner lay. He stood for a while, meditating, a broad-shouldered, heavy man, a solid head on a short, thick neck, a black felt-hat on his head. It will turn out all right, he thought, dubiously all the same. Then, without a word, he went off to the kitchen to do the washing-up, himself.

The girl, Jacoba Katadreuffe, made no attempt to communicate with him. She found work as a temporary help, and when her pregnancy could no longer be hidden, she simply said that her husband had deserted her. During this period she was not badly off, always plenty to eat and comfortable quarters. Up to the last moment she was sufficiently provided for at the houses where she was employed. She did not have to go to the employment exchange, where they would have made enquiries and discovered her unmarried state. She worked well; she had an iron constitution; she was recommended from the one to the other. For the last months, to avoid any embarrassment, she worked where there were no children in the house.

She had reserved a bed in the maternity ward in good time; although indeed young she was by no means ignorant, and she was provident by nature. She had also chosen the right moment to take to her bed, and was able to have a little rest. A sensible girl, without relations or friends, a girl who did not have to be taught anything, who knew it all. This Joba.

Right up to the end she felt remarkably well. The fresh face with its firm teeth and eloquent eyes completely captivated the nurses who, after all, were used to so much. And this in spite of her seriousness, her silences, her abrupt way of talking. They asked her what she would call her child. Jacob Willem. And if a girl, just Jacoba.

They pointed out to her that the father was obliged to provide for it. She answered promptly, and pathetically:

'The child will never have a father.'

'Yes, but we don't mean with a father's rights, we only mean that the father must provide for your child.'

'No.'

'How do you mean, no?'

'I don't want it.'

They told her that when they let her out she could go to the Mothers' Care, to Child Welfare.

Her small, reddened hands, plump, child-like, strong, lay motionless on the coverlet. Her dark eyes were stern; she clearly did not want any of it. The nurse's irritation quickly disappeared she found the girl too nice, and sensed signs of breeding in her obstinacy.

She confided in no one. Her one companion, grimly inquisitive, fished about the father. The companion had the idea, though she could not say why, that there was a rich man in the case. Joba answered:

'It's no good, the child will never have a father.'

'Why not?'

'Because.'

The birth went far from smoothly. The doctor was surprised. Such a thoroughly healthy girl. But there it was. At last he decided on an operation: Joba was taken along.

The doctor already had plenty of experience in this field. However, it was a case he never quite forgot; in his medical circle he often referred to it, even years later. Under his instruments he saw the stunned girl fading away. In an hour she had left adolescence behind; he feared for her heart, but the heart remained sound. The invalid just slowly withered, like a flower in poison-gas. Far from confident, he hoped that she would pull up again. But no. All she preserved from the ruins of her youth was the grim, serious air of breeding.

He came every day to sit by her.

'You can't work to start with, you must talk to the father.'

'No.'

'You must do so for the child's sake.'

'No and no and no.'

'Very well,' he soothed her. 'You must, in any case, have your child officially registered.'

She let him explain, and gave her consent. It was the first yes.

She knew that it was a boy but she did not ask for the child. By that she certainly forfeited some of their affection. They did not realize that it was not in her character to ask for the smallest favour, not even that of showing her her own whelp.

In cases of this kind the child seldom suffers from the birth. The nurse brought it on the third day.

'Look, Joba, what eyes the little fellow has.'

They were her eyes, brown, almost black. The child had a black tuft of baby-hair.

'You can already make a parting in his hair, the nurse joked.

The child lay petulant and impatient by its mother. On the beds to the left and right other women came to lie, and again others.

'I should like to leave,' Joba said.

They let her out after three weeks. She went and shook hands with all the nurses, with her small, pale, withered hand.

'Thank you,' she said to each one, 'thank you.'

'Remember what I told you,' warned Doctor Merree. 'The addresses of Mother Care and Child Welfare have hung above you for so many days you ought to know them.'

'No,' said Joba, 'but thank you.'

Youth

It was not difficult for the bailiff, A. B. Dreverhaven, to follow the mother's movements. Tracking down people went with his profession, and he knew his profession inside out. He learnt, after a few days, that the mother was living in one of the poorest streets near the slaughter-house. She was no longer Joba, she was *juffrouw*[1] Katadreuffe.

A letter came for her. On the envelope was the printed address of Dreverhaven's office. Inside the envelope was just a half sheet of paper with Memorandum printed at the top in large letters, together with the address. The letter consisted of a date and five words :

'When are we going to marry?'

It was unsigned. The writing was black, angular, gigantic. She tore it into little bits. The same day, the postman handed her a money order for a hundred guilders. The slip bore the same address in the same writing. She stood for a moment irresolute, but she was not one to remain irresolute for long. She had considered tearing up the money order, but she merely crossed out the address. 'Return to sender,' she wrote, and put it in the letter-box.

Dreverhaven was a man without heart, in the sense of a man without finer feelings. That he received no answer

[1] The Dutch word *juffrouw* is really the equivalent of 'Miss', but used to be applied to married women of the lower orders. (Trans.)

and that his money was just returned did not bother him in the least. He calmly cashed his money order. But he was not without some notion of responsibility; he possessed both a sense of duty, in a limited way, and the wish to do it. After a month, Mrs. Katadreuffe received another letter : 'When are we going to marry?' Also a money order, this time for fifty guilders. She treated these in the same way as before.

Punctually every month, Dreverhaven wrote altogether six of these memoranda. He never received an answer. The duel with the money orders lasted a whole year. The twelfth time she wrote across it : 'Will always be refused.' Whether that was the cause or not—the duel, anyhow, was over. Now *she* had conquered, but she had little satisfaction from it. All her life she retained a certain contempt for herself, not a feeling of inferiority but a defiant hatred of her sex in general. She was actually more angry with herself than with him for having given in to him; she was angry at being a woman. However well she got on with the neighbours, in the reserved manner of the respectable poor, she was not very popular with the local women as she was so often running down her sex. Her ruthless judgement on feminine weakness was known and aroused surprise. She lived modestly, but at times she could air her contempt with crudity.

'We women are only good for producing children, otherwise nix.'

The men liked her. She had aged and was wrinkled, with two lines of grim embitterment at the corners of her mouth; the once strong teeth, through the birth, deteriorated; small and upright, she gave the impression of fragility. But her eyes like coals appeared to attract the men; they did not notice the lines, the withered skin, the hair, neatly done but turning a dingy grey.

Once, at some friends, she met a *bokschipper*, in charge of a gigantic floating crane, hauled on its steel hawser from one dock to the other : he lived in the engine-room. He was a tough, robust, hard-working man; a deep, booming voice and movements in keeping with his character, just such a fellow as is only produced by Holland and the water. He was a little older than she was; he must, she thought, be about Dreverhaven's age. His name was Harm Knol Hein.

He wanted her to go and live with him, and they had hardly left the house when he asked her whether she had no wish to marry. He had been telling the company about his life aboard the crane. She loved the water. Here, in the big town, she was so far away from the huge network of docks; where she lived there was often a stench of bones and entrails, and of boiling blood from the slaughter-house. Yes, she did miss the water, and the fresh breeze coming from it.

He went on talking. She could live on the crane, and if the boss objected then he would take a room for her ashore, still near the docks, naturally. No, that wouldn't be any difficulty; he would fix it.

'I'll think it over,' she said on parting.

She only said it out of friendliness towards the crane-driver. She liked him and did not want to turn him down flat. But she had already made up her mind; it wouldn't work. She, such an old corpse, and that healthy chap—what did he see in her? No, it wouldn't do. She asked an acquaintance for his address and wrote her refusal in a few words. In this refusal lay a subconscious contempt for herself, for the whole female species.

She looked after her son well; she was a taciturn, stern, unyielding, strict mother, but she was good. She was not able to go out to work anything like as much as before. And the child made demands on her time; he was not strong, he had chicken-pox and measles, and with it all became temperamental and impatient. She had to leave him with neighbours for half the day, where he was brought up amongst the riff-raff; he did not get the training she considered right and therefore – believing in a firm hand – on coming home she was even stricter than really lay in her nature.

The first years gradually became more difficult. She had to move to a dilapidated little court where she found herself amongst the poorest of the poor. In the summer, the hovels were not clean; that, as yet, was her greatest vexation. Then the world war broke out with its rising prices and shortage of food. 1917 and 1918 were very black years for her.

But the child must not suffer from it, she said to herself, he has got to have the very best. But that best had far less food-value than the normal in peace time.

During these years she, now and again, got a little into debt. She could not always pay the rent every Monday, but she always managed to get square again through her extreme economy. She possessed no clothes for going out. As long as her working dress and aprons were absolutely clean, she was satisfied.

Young Katadreuffe also remembered these years as pitch-black. He sat with the smallest rascals in the lowest class of the poor people's school, a building in a dingy side street, such a street as gives the impression that it can never be warm there. One felt the same about the school. The building was frighteningly large, hollow and gloomy, but neither that nor his class-mates gave him so much fear as the rabble of the higher classes. Boys of the kind that lived in their court, who smashed street-lamps, cursed like grown-up drunkards; who, on leaving school, waited round the corner for the little ones and bullied them.

Once little Katadreuffe came home with his mouth all bloody. A lot of his top teeth had been knocked out, but fortunately they were his first teeth and were already loose.

In the Spring of 1918, when he was in the top class, two helmeted policemen came to put fear into the court, including him. But they were not after him. They searched all the houses and took four big boys, ringleaders, who had plundered a bread-cart the day before, in broad daylight. In a gunny-sack they found five whole loaves which they had not been able to dispose of.

His mother had kept him, as far as she could, away from the riff-raff, and for that reason he was naturally bullied and punched whenever possible. Now, with deep satisfaction, he saw four of the louts taken in charge.

His small, frail mother was treated with respect by the neighbours. She realized that she owed this to her eyes which could emit flashes of lightning, and she seldom had to make use of her razor-sharp tongue. Young Katadreuffe also learnt gradually to master his fears and to use his fists. He felt himself at one with his mother, on the defensive against the riff-raff. He had her eyes, which could likewise flash, and he had a quick temper. Once he went for a bigger boy. Like lightning, he landed a kick in the softest spot in his stomach. The attacker lay flat out on the ground, unconscious, in the middle of the court, for everyone to look at.

Mrs Katadreuffe saw it. She did not punish him, but she understood they would have to move. And that worked out all right. They moved at night. A hand-cart outside the entrance to the court was waiting for their few poor belongings. The remover, himself, carried the stuff out of the house. It often happened that tenants flitted overnight. It would then be a case of a woman leaving her husband, letting him come back to an empty room, or simply a matter of owing the rent.

Mrs Katadreuffe left without owing anything. She had wrapped up the rent neatly in a piece of newspaper, laid it in the window-seat on top of the rent-card in which the signature of the rent-collector was not once missing. A *lovely* rent-card it was, almost full, without a gap; a rent-card such as not many in the court could have produced.

Youth

That they had to move turned out to be a good thing. She had already been considering it, as things had begun to improve for her. She possessed a natural aptitude for handwork.

At the poor people's market in the Goudse Singel she had found an odd lot of wool of the most remarkably strange green. The saleswoman said that the consignment had been damaged and discoloured by sea-water. She got it cheaply, and had to owe the rent for one week, though she quickly caught up with this. She worked a wool-embroidery after her own design, a large indigo flower-centre, sprinkled with black dots, bordered with light-blue calixes, the rest of the canvas filled with the strange green as a background. The flower was placed at one corner and occupied a third of the whole surface.

She went to an embroidery shop, where the proprietress immediately bought her work for a large sofa-cushion. She received fifteen guilders, the amount she had asked for and, moreover, was requested to return when she had something new. One afternoon the cushion lay in the shop-window, priced at forty guilders. It was sold within a few hours. This period, just after the war, had brought greatly improved conditions to the country; there was a big demand for fancy goods and prices were high.

From now onwards, she lived from the shop and a lodger. She used up the consignment of wool with care; she knew the limitations of her talent; she possessed an inborn flair for unusual colour-schemes. Her handwork was always different and always successful. The colours that she juxtaposed did not always, in theory, go together, yet she harmonized them by choosing just the right shades. Even orange, the ugliest and most intolerant colour that there is, in her work had a beautiful effect. She designed the patterns herself. One of them looked as if it were Persian, but she found this on the whole too fussy and too uneven; also the colours were too loud. Sometimes the shopkeeper criticized her work, when it was beyond her old-fashioned notions. However, she seemed to have a better feeling for public taste than the shopkeeper.

This was the time when she moved from the court to a street near the cattle-market. It was a far better neighbourhood than the court, and better than her first place near the slaughter-house. The live cattle sometimes smelt, but there was not the continuous stink of offal; this air had something healthy about it. Herds of cows lowed up at the house-tops; in streams of rippling wool the sheep came, filling the street from side to side.

It was during the same period that she began to seek company amongst her neighbours, because every woman occasionally needs to talk. But she could not get on with these respectable poor, as they disapproved of her contemptuous remarks about the female sex.

She appealed to the men, but she was never familiar with them. She was careful not to arouse any jealousy, and this was something the women appreciated, as women, whatever their walk in life, are wary of anything that might threaten their marriage. They all regarded her as a respectable woman, seeing nothing reprehensible in her having an illegitimate child. This is unimportant to the working class; if the man leaves the girl in the lurch, then he is the blackguard and the girl just a poor wretch. That she did not

talk about her unwillingness to marry her seducer gave no
occasion for passing an unfavourable judgement.

Her new work was not physically tiring, but was all the
more so mentally. When she worked, her lined face sometimes took on an unhealthy, uniformly pale flush, the dark
eyes shining fascinatingly. Sitting in a bent position was
bad for her lungs and she began to cough.

The child was not strong. One could see immediately that
it was her child, mainly by the look in his eyes, the ardour
in them. He had fine teeth, but not so strong as hers had
been before his birth. The teeth were more irregular, and
chalk white. He seldom laughed, and had the same stern,
quick-tempered nature as his mother, but being a child he
was less able to control it. He made few acquaintances and
possessed no friends at all.

Young Katadreuffe had in the meantime finished at the
primary school. His mother did not have him taught any
trade : he would have to make his own way in the world
as she, herself, had had to do. He was errand-boy for various
employers; then worked in a bottleworks; but his health
suffered there, his complexion became sallow, so she let
him go back to being an errand-boy. During his adolescence
he had ten trades and thirty employers, and when he was
eighteen he was no more advanced socially than when he
had begun. She spent his wages exclusively on him, buying
his clothes; when he was older and earning a little more,
he got what she had left over as pocket-money. She did
not need his money as she was able to live off her own work,
and she also had a lodger, Jan Maan.

The latter was a fitter with quite decent wages. She had
answered an advertisement in the Rotterdams *Nieuwsblad*
asking for a room with full board. She got Jan Maan, and
they liked each other immediately. The room behind had
just become vacant so she rented it and now had the entire
first floor of the house; the front room with the alcove where
she slept, the cubicle occupied by young Katadreuffe, the
kitchen, and the back-room for the lodger.

Jan Maan was a fresh-looking, healthy fellow. He had had a quarrel with his parents over his girl friend : they ran her down, saying that a waitress from a lunchroom who had to live on tips could never add up to much.

Jan Maan was furious at this unjust verdict and stood up for his girl. That led to the advertisement in the *Nieuwsblad*. Later on, he had a row with the girl and broke it off, but he was not small-minded. All that they had saved up for the wedding he left with her, although he had contributed more than half of it. *Juffrouw* Katadreuffe found this a nice gesture, but she did not refer to it. She was, in this respect, a woman of the people; a good type, reticent, ashamed of revealing their true feelings. Jan Maan and young Katadreuffe became friendly; one was a man already and the other still a youth, but that did not matter. They were to remain friends for ever.

Mrs Katadreuffe did not need the lodger any more than she did her son's wages. She regarded him more as a reserve; should things not go so well, then it would all come in useful. In the meantime it did not matter whether she had to cook for two or for three, or if there was one more bed to make.

Between his eighteenth and nineteenth year Katadreuffe went for more than six months without a job. He hung about the house but gave his mother little trouble. Most of the time he sat in his cubicle reading. From his pocket-money he had gradually bought a whole lot of books, second-hand. Through inexperience he had paid too much for them as regards actual market value, though not the personal pleasure he derived from them. They were all solid books : botanical and zoological, the wonders of the earth, the wonders of the universe. His favourite was an old German encyclopedia with the last section missing. From it he learnt German; what he could not understand he looked up in a small, old German dictionary. In the end, he could understand German fairly well.

Although he was no trouble to his mother, and she commended his sober pursuits – to herself, never openly – it annoyed her that he got no further. He must get out, make his own way; she had had to do it. She felt certain there was a lot more in the boy; he would never be satisfied with manual work, but he must make his own way up; that he did not attempt to do so, and just sat reading a jumble of stuff without properly digesting it, annoyed her. Now he had been hanging round the house for half a year doing virtually nothing.

Then, up to his twenty-first birthday, he worked in a bookshop, in the storeroom, though, not the shop. This was the first job which had given him any satisfaction, as now there was no limit to what he could read. But he made no headway; he was still not earning enough to be independent, and continued to live with her.

Their behaviour towards each other was harsh. Yet he was not a bad son to her. On Sunday afternoons they always went for a walk. She wanted to make for the river, never anywhere else, so they went either to the Park or to the Oude Plantage. They looked across the water, saying little, their silences at times bordering on enmity.

For a long time he had known that he was a natural child and what his father's name was. But he did not show the slightest wish to meet his father. He knew where his office was, but he had always instinctively avoided it and even the very neighbourhood. Once, on a walk, he said to her :

'He ought to have taken care of you and me.'

'Yes, but I didn't want him to.'

'And he could have married you.'

'Yes, he was willing to, but I wasn't.'

'Why on earth not?'

'That's my business.'

'Not mine by any chance?'

He got no answer. After a moment he asked :

'Is he married?'

'Not as far as I know.'

She said it with indifference, but she was lying. She knew very definitely that he was unmarried. The important things in his life she knew by instinct, as he knew hers through investigation.

But neither was aware of this. Dreverhaven and the woman, each in their own particular way, possessed those taciturn natures which hide their feelings, must always hide them. The woman had more sentiment, being a woman, but her outward show was just as hard.

A Bankruptcy

A few months after Katadreuffe attained his majority, something awoke in him. He visualized his future : poor jobs, subordination, periods of unemployment, and when his mother would no longer be there, not enough to eat. He was, after all, not in the world for that. He now thought for himself what his mother had so often thought but had never wanted to say to him. To begin with, he wanted to be a free man. There was in the Hague a small tobacconist's to be had for 300 guilders, 100 for the goodwill and 200 for the stock, according to the information supplied by Jan Maan's acquaintances.

Katadreuffe bought the business with an advance from a small money-lending bank, the People's Credit Company, which used to place minute advertisements in the papers. He did not consult his mother; he just told her that he had given up his job at the bookshop and was moving to the Hague the following week. She gave no reply when he told her. That made him angry.

'You might say something for once.'

'Do as you please,' was all she said.

It was worse than no answer. He remained angry with her. That Sunday he shut himself in his cubicle, away from everybody, even Jan Maan. He savoured his future triumph over her, once he had found his way, gradually acquiring larger and larger shops and finally returning from the Hague, rich. That would be better than manual labour day after day. In his naïveté he never wondered why the bank had advanced the money so readily, even though the interest was very high. Later, when he knew more of the world, he still wondered at the easiness of it; still later, when he discovered who owned the bank, no more.

He moved with the few contents of his cubicle to the Hague. The affair was a fiasco. He had not the first idea of conducting a business. One could not say that the tobacconist shop had run to seed under its previous tenant; it had never been anything. It was unfortunately situated in a back-street in the poor neighbourhood by the fishing-harbour. The fisher-folk, who had had to move on account of slum clearance in old Scheveningen, now lived in the district. There were already two other tobacconists' in the street, much better-looking than his.

He lived for five months on the stock; he did not buy any more, just used up the stock; and all the same had scarcely sufficient to eat, ending up owing the rent. Then, at night, he moved out, just as years ago he and his mother had moved from the court. But this time there was no money lying on the window-seat for the landlord. His few bits of furniture and his books went back to Rotterdam in a lorry on night service. That took the last of his money.

The following morning he moved back into his old cubicle. His mother said nothing; she had seen it coming and only failed to understand how he had held out for five months. Without a word, she examined the emaciated figure of her son from top to toe. She was thinking how his rather weak physique needed good nourishment—she had always given him the very best. Their eyes flashed angrily at one another, but no more. She gave him some thick slices of bread with plenty of butter : he swallowed them without a word.

After about a fortnight, a paper arrived from the District Court. A lawyer, a certain Dr Schuwagt, applied in the name of the People's Credit Company for his bankruptcy. He showed it to his mother.

'Look at this.'

'Deal with it,' was all she answered.

He had vaguely hoped that she would help him. A mother always helps her child when necessary. But no, and he was much too proud to ask. He was sorry enough that he now had to live on her again. Fortunately he had not told her anything about his expectation of riches, of his intention to show her that he was capable of other things than she was. How she would have chuckled. That was lucky!

After all, the debt was not insurmountable. If she had been willing to help him, it could have been paid off in instalments. But she would not do so. He must manage, himself, just as she had had to. And she had another subconscious motive, the innate providence of a woman of the people who has been able to save a little and who will only hand it over for really important things, the marriage of her child, or her own death with a proper funeral and something left over for the child to inherit. No, she would not draw on her book at the Savings Bank in the Botersloot for this, and getting involved in instalment payments was even less in her line.

Katadreuffe let it all ride.

He did not go to the court: he refused to do that. They must come for him here and sell his bits of books. He would not admit to himself how this would break his heart. His mother sensed it; particularly as regards the books she shared her son's feelings, for deep down she was very much a mother. Nevertheless, she did not raise a finger to help him; he must find his own way.

Jan Maan was the one who wanted to help him, but Katadreuffe refused this categorically, and in the battle of magnanimity which followed he was the winner. Jan Maan had just found a new girl; they were saving for their marriage, and Katadreuffe would under no circumstances accept responsibility for interfering with their plans.

And so, confound it, he was declared bankrupt, with an announcement in the paper, and was called on by his trustee, Dr de Gankelaar. The latter brought a bailiff with him to make an inventory.

When Dr de Gankelaar and the bailiff came, Katadreuffe was out and his mother was at home alone. A gentleman bustled up the stairs and behind him came a broad-shouldered fellow, no gentleman, just a man. *Juffrouw* Katadreuffe stood at the top of the stairs unsuspectingly. The gentleman said he was the trustee. The man behind him had now come up to the landing and merely from his silhouette, seen from the obscure landing against the light of the staircase, perhaps also just by instinct, she recognized the man she had not seen for twenty-two years : Drever-haven. She felt herself grow white as a sheet, and quickly drew back into the darkest corner. A moment later she had regained her self-control. With incredible will-power her face even regained its usual colour. Her voice was perfectly normal as she invited them in, and she offered them a chair each at her table, the gentleman and the man. She had summed him up in the fraction of a second : an elderly man, but a healthy man, a formidable man. Something like pride was aroused in her by the fact that her seducer had been *this* man and no other, that she had never wished to accept anything from this man, neither marriage nor money. She sensed that the grey-haired, silent, powerful fellow remembered her and knew that she, the mother of his child, sat opposite him, in her own home, created from her own work, without his help. For she knew well enough who this Dreverhaven was, bailiff, true, but also an execu-tioner for all debtors who fell into his hands. Woe to the tenants behind with their rent who were ejected by Drever-haven ! The Law is something sacrosanct to the people; those who do not fear God or their parents still always fear the Law. The Law in its full inhuman severity and Drever-haven were one. Many people feared Dreverhaven; they

had often discussed him in her presence. Where he knew
hundreds, ten thousand knew him, at least by name. But
she knew more than most; he was not married, never had
been.

It was strange. For he had come in after the trustee; as
is proper, the man takes second place to the gentleman.
But he filled the whole room and the gentleman scarcely
existed. And she could not feel vexed that whilst the trustee
had, on the landing, uncovered his head as becomes a
gentleman who is calling, if only on a woman of the
people – Dreverhaven sat there with his black felt-hat
pressed down on his head, in her very own room. For she
felt that Dreverhaven was such a man as would not un-
cover even before God, only before the Law. And she remembered how, in his own house, he always used to walk
about with his hat on, sat at table with it on, just such a
black felt-hat as this one.

In the meantime, she heard herself talking to the trustee.

'No, sir, my son possesses next to nothing. He has been
living with me for the last couple of weeks, but the place is
rented in my name. All this, although there's not much of
it, is mine. He owns only a few books and what would
they be worth? But naturally, the law must take its course.'

'Where are they?' came the voice of the older man.

The same voice, deep, powerful, of twenty years ago – yes,
even more impressive than then.

She pointed with a steady finger in the direction of the
cubicle. For the first time he looked her in the eyes and
then in the direction of her calmly pointing hand. The
small, piercing eyes looked into the large, dark ones, which
still had their fire. Remarkably fine eyes for an old woman,
but she was not old, only aged. The lines of embitterment
round her mouth had gradually given way to the softer lines
of age. She was forty. He went out without a word. She
heard him open the door of the cubicle. The trustee was
speaking :

'I shall summon your son to come to me. I must talk to

him, myself. Let him bring along a list of his creditors and his books, if he kept any. What he owns will have to be sold, but I must first have the valuation. The bailiff will look after that.'

He paused, looking at her. He found her different from what he had expected, aloof, not unlikable.

'Well, we'll see what we can do.'

The meaning of these last words eluded her, but she did not ask him to explain. He stood up.

'Now I must go. So I'll write to tell your son when to come to me. I think *meneer* Dreverhaven must have finished.'

He opened the door of the cubicle. There was no longer anyone there.

He had not heard Dreverhaven go away although she had. While they were talking no sound had come from the cubicle. The trustee looked around him and his eye fell on a big rack full of books, some self-bound and others with worn covers. He walked up to the rack, took out a book here and there glancing at the titles.

'Hm,' he said every now and then.

She stood stock still beside him, studying the man very closely. A real gentleman, an educated man, a young man, friendly, well-bred. An intelligent face. Very fair hair. An athletic type, with easy movements. The trustee for her son.

'Hm,' he said again, and then affably took his leave.

Façade and Office

A few days later, Katadreuffe received a letter. 'From the Trustee' was written at the top of the envelope. The only address the envelope bore was that of Dr A. Stroomkoning, Boompjes. The letter-head included several names, in this order: Dr A. Stroomkoning, barrister, solicitor, average-adjuster – Dr C. Carlion, Dr Gideon Piaat, Dr Th. R. de Gankelaar, Dr Catharina Kalvelage, barristers and solicitors.

Dr Stroomkoning's name was printed somewhat larger and separated from the others by a line – he must be the chief. The trustee was the last but one, and there was also apparently a female lawyer in this office. A large office. Under the list of names was printed: 'Please address your reply to the undersigned.'

Katadreuffe felt himself at once drawn into the world of big business. There was something fascinating about that phrase; he could weave dreams around it. Each of these five lawyers had his own department. But he had no need to send an answer, he was merely given notice to appear. 'I request you to come to my office at 10 a.m. tomorrow. Please bring with you books and documents, also a list of your creditors with details of the debts.'

Katadreuffe had only three, the People's Credit Company, the Hague landlord, and Jan Maan, from whom he had

31

borrowed altogether thirty guilders. Jan Maan had strictly forbidden him to breathe a word about it, but Katadreuffe did so none the less, fearing in his ignorance that otherwise the debt might be cancelled or something. With this short list and the contract for the shop – this was the only document he had and he had never kept any books – he went off the next day to the office.

He was a little too early, having still ten minutes to wait, and walked irresolutely past the door. At a glance he had seen the five name-plates, an exact enlargement of the letterhead, Dr Stroomkoning's being the largest.

He turned round, a few houses further on, zig-zagged across through the traffic and walked back on the other side. There, in a small open spot between some crates, he stopped and looked up at the office. A tall building, narrow, once an old private house he could see at a glance. Curtains in all the windows; you could discover nothing of what went on inside. But the door stood wide open. Behind it a short flight of stairs led to the first floor, on a rather low level, with tall windows. And then in front of it all the row of yellow, brass name-plates with coal-black letters. From here he could only see them now and again, just a glimpse between gaps in the traffic, but he saw them sparkling in the sun like pilot-lights.

And he watched the traffic. Close to him was the slow traffic with the unwieldy, towering trailers, the fast traffic moving in the middle in both directions. Around him stood crates and bales, behind him the ships, greedily loading or lavishly discharging. He stood still amidst an overwhelming business activity, with only a few cobble-stones available to stand on. And the office with the five suns nailed to the door was included in this activity. He saw people going in and coming out; even the suns were active. Though so calm from the outside, inside it must be buzzing.

Then something in Katadreuffe awoke. The real thing was not to become a small shopkeeper, it was *this*. All he knew, and from the encyclopedia he knew quite a bit, much more than other young men of his class and age, was *nothing,* as it did not lead to *this.* He did not ask himself exactly what he meant, and what he meant was not precise. However, quite definitely, he knew two things : begin at the bottom and get away from his mother. These two things belonged absolutely together. He could of course begin at the bottom from home, but he felt he would not be able to climb up from there. He *had* begun at the bottom, and again and again. Twenty-one years of failure, but it did not matter. He was still so young, and now he would do it much more quickly. And he would do it alone. Away from mother. Mother and son as far apart as they could possibly be. He loved her and she him. But they did not get on together. For the first time in his life he probed himself so deeply that he was surprised at possessing such depths, and this profound penetration also gave him an insight of her. What he now realized for the first time she had long ago realized; for a long time she had wanted him to go out into the world, but not as an adventurer like in the Hague business. 'Do as you please,' she had said, and therein had lain her assessment of the Hague adventure. She was far shrewder than he but, after all, she was older. Now he would go his own way; *he* wanted it and *she* wanted it. And he wanted to be in this house.

It was a decisive moment in his life; later he would realize it was a moment such as few others could match in importance. Just now, all he realized was that he wanted to get away from his mother and work in this house. He completely failed to see the absurdity of his desire; he had quite forgotten that the only thing bringing him to this house was an order to call, as a bankrupt, on his trustee.

He asked a lad for Dr de Gankelaar, giving his name, and was told to wait. The front room on the first floor was the waiting-room. There were quite a few people sitting there. The double doors into the room beyond were open. That room had three small windows, high up, looking out on to a light-shaft. From that room another open door lead

to a third room on a lower level. He could see little more
of the third room than a strange, ochre-coloured light. He
sat in the window-seat with his back to the street and the
river, and from here he had the whole front part of the
house in view. The house went still further back, as he had
just seen from the awe-inspiring, marble corridor.

In the second room the typewriters hammered away, and
every now and then the telephone rang, served by an invisible, high-pitched, but hoarse, masculine voice. At small
tables in the middle two men of striking likeness tapped
away, certainly brothers, possibly twins. A dark-haired
young girl, with her back towards him, who from there
looked small and plump, was also typing. The lad he had
spoken to ran hither and thither, in and out of the room.
Several times he saw a man walk past the others with
papers, which he distributed; this man had a rather arrogant appearance, being good-looking in a way which all
men find repellent and many women also. He was obviously
a boss. Once, just for a moment, a man appeared, with
gold spectacles, rather bald, who spoke to the boss. Could
this be Dr Stroomkoning? He seemed rather young to be
at the head of this formidable office. For it suddenly became overwhelming, and Katadreuffe had made no mistake;
here they worked!

Ever and again sounded the loudspeaker from the house-
telephone, also served by the hoarse, high-pitched voice. The
voice called:

'*Juffrouw* Sibculo to Mr Piaat!'

The brunette got up with pencil and pad. She was, in
fact, small and plump, with a rather short neck. She went
off, coquettishly patting her curls with one hand for the
benefit of the staring clients.

Katadreuffe observed those waiting. Three men were
talking together round a small table in the corner. Very
likely they were here on the same business; they smoked
cigarettes and talked in lowered voices round the table. At
the large table in the middle a gentleman sat alone, every

now and then picking out a paper from the untidy heap of periodicals, opening it, thumbing through it in a bored way, and picking up another. A young woman near Katadreuffe, on a chair against the wall, who for a long time had been sitting looking at his fine eyes, spoke to him:

'We have to wait a long time, don't we? But they're always so busy here.'

He only nodded.

'Do you also want Mr Piaat?'

'No, Mr de Gankelaar.'

A lady came in with bleached hair, dressed smartly and strikingly, but of heavy Rotterdam build. She sat down on the only upholstered seat, of faded wine-red velvet, as if this were reserved for her. Everyone looked at her, except the man at the large table in the middle.

'She's sure to go in first,' said the girl in the know. 'Anyone with a certificate of lack of means has to wait. Otherwise . . . I can't complain about Mr Piaat. I've been having a lawsuit with my husband for over a year. But he is working for me, I mean Mr Piaat; he's doing his best, I can't say otherwise.'

Then Katadreuffe saw in the clerks' office a thick-set figure, stout without undue corpulence, broad rather than tall, a man with a huge felt-hat crushed down on his head. The hat had suffered much; the man was carelessly dressed. His broad, black trousers slopped about. Although it was summer he was wearing a shabby burberry. It was open, and the coat of his jacket underneath also, as though he could not button the coats over a chest like a plateau. He kept his hands in the pockets of his burberry. Papers and envelopes were protruding from all his inside pockets. They pointed forward threateningly, like the banners of an army on the war-path. In the corner of his mouth was stuck a cigar, unbelievably long in its cigar-holder, slanting slightly upward. Like a warship with one gun cleared for action.

Katadreuffe was at once extremely fascinated by this rare

apparition which, after a couple of vigorous strides, stood still in the middle by the twins, looked around, and asked for everyone to hear :

'Where is Rentenstein?'

A small, piercing, grey eye revolved, also taking in the waiting-room, passing over Katadreuffe without stopping.

'Do you know who that man is?' asked the young woman importantly.

'No, who is it?' he asked, very curious.

'Fancy not knowing that ! That's Dreverhaven, the bailiff. Dreverhaven. Don't you know him? Half Rotterdam knows him. See that you keep out of that bloodhound's clutches. The people below me once had a to-do with him when they hadn't paid the rent. I shall never forget the terribly mean way he treated those people. I hope never to see a scene like that again in my whole life. Threw all their stuff into the street, literally threw the lot.'

His father. There, in the other room, his father was standing. *This* then was his father. This was the man his mother had never wanted to marry. Otherwise his name would be Dreverhaven and not Katadreuffe. Now he was called Katadreuffe; Katadreuffe, Dreverhaven's son. But it wasn't his father at all. It couldn't be, that was just impossible. He felt nothing for that man, just a fellow, as far as he was concerned. *If* he felt anything about him it was, at the most, a relief that he had never had anything to do with such a father. He had not understood a lot of what the girl had gone on to say, but he had caught the word 'bloodhound'. Yes, you could see that; a fellow like an animal.

And he had no time to analyse his feelings. This impression, fresh and intense, kept his thoughts, as far as he could express them in words, on the surface. He did not realize that already then, at that first moment, he was permeated by an awe which his superficial thinking regarded just as bestiality – that he *really* thought : is this my father? What a fellow, what a chap!

'Have you got to deal with him?' asked the girl, inquisitive. She was struck by his sudden pallor.

He did not hear her. Through a haze, he saw Dreverhaven in the second room, standing near the head clerk. They were standing together, their backs towards him. Dreverhaven had laid his hand confidentially on the shoulder of the slim, handsome man. They were talking confidentially. The light from the high windows fell on them. In spite of the shadow from the pressed-down hat light fell on his father's cheek, moving slightly as he spoke. His dazed eye might play him false, but it appeared as if the cheek were surrounded by a silvery tinge, an aureole.

The young lad was standing in front of him without his having noticed it. He now tapped him on the arm.

'Will you come with me?'

A Friend

Katadreuffe's only friend was the fitter, Jan Maan. When, after breaking off his engagement with the girl from the lunchroom, he made peace with his parents, he still stayed on with Mrs Katadreuffe. She called him Jan and he called her mother simply, just like his friend. Nobody suspected them of any illicit relationship; the word mother excluded any suspicion of that kind. The two got on well together. There was not even the slightest breach in their mutual affection, never expressed and scarcely conscious, when Jan Maan gave clear signs of communist sympathies. He was a healthy young man : his features were far less attractive than those of her son, but at first sight appealed more. He wore his very fair hair brushed back, his eyes were a faded blue, he kept himself very clean. Often he came back from work without having had time to smarten himself up. But he never went in to her like that, always washed and changed, and put on a good shirt. She then liked not only his outward appearance but also the smell of him, the clean smell of unscented soap from his hands with the well-brushed nails. Even more, the smell of his skin, hardly a smell at all, so subtle and fresh, just as water smells yet has no smell – that was the effect it had on her sensitive nerves. There was nothing sensual on her side, just something pleasant. She was not sensual by nature; she had been fresh like that. But she could not understand how it was that anyone so amiable and gentle as Jan Maan always had to be quarrelling with those nearest to him. For now, once more, there was trouble between him and his parents, over his new girl, a sales-girl in a general store. The parents had been disparaging. Couldn't be much, a girl like that, where thousands of people of all sorts were wandering round the shop all day long. From that continuous contact with all kinds of strangers something would stick, no doubt about it.

He naturally took her side and so was seething with rage against his parents. As regards the girl, she wasn't so wonderful, say eighteen carats. They met every other day, so as not to get bored too quickly, and on Sundays of course.

When, at table, Jan Maan began to talk about Lenin Ulyanov, Mrs Katadreuffe was not vexed. She merely could not understand how anyone so good-natured could feel attracted by that ragtag party. But later on she had other thoughts. And once she said straight out : she herself wasn't interested in politics, but every party must have something good about it or else it couldn't possibly continue to exist. It was against human nature for people to openly organize for the purpose of doing harm. She had in mind, in the first place, Jan Maan, who was becoming more and more a convinced communist and yet remained the best fellow in the world. But his theories did not go down well with her.

Young Katadreuffe was by nature a rebel : the communist creed ought thus to have appealed to him. He was also the right type for it, in the best sense. He could, on the platform, have made a good spokesman for an elevated kind of communism – but he was too intellectual, too calculating to give way to his deepest feelings. He could not have kept any policy separate from his own personal case; his ambition might have endured belonging to a party, but not the materialism going with it. The teaching of Lenin did not open up any future for him. In his half year of unemployment his lack of activity drove him a little in that direction;

he had often joined Jan Maan at meetings in the Caledonia building. A good speaker could for a moment carry him with him, but then as soon as some ragamuffin or other got up and ranted some gibberish about his creed, he felt again that it was not the right one, for *him*.

They were, none the less, great friends. Many an evening they sat smoking in his cubicle. They never smoked in their common mother's room, as she had a dry cough, particularly when she sat bending over her work. She had never had to say anything about not smoking; out of instinctive consideration for her they abstained. In the cubicle Jan Maan smoked a lot of foul-smelling cigarettes, Katadreuffe more moderately; he was moderate in all things. It was then he tried to pass on to his friend some of the things he had learnt from the encyclopedia and his other books. He did not understand Jan Maan not feeling the same need to learn; the fellow knew disgracefully little, particularly for a communist.

Jan Maan listened dutifully, but absorbed very little. His thoughts were on the Party or his parents with whom he was quarrelling. Katadreuffe sensed this but still persisted. It was a good exercise for himself. In the evening, after dark, he took him to the market. They stood there among the cattle stalls. Katadreuffe pointed to the moon, the planets and constellations. Dutifully, his friend looked up, thinking all the time of the Party or his girl, with whom he was likely to have a fresh row as things had not been going too smoothly of late. Before his two official engagements he had had quite a few girls. That didn't count; he had merely gone out with them, yet every time it had ended in a row.

That afternoon, when Katadreuffe came home, his mother was once more sitting working by the window. His place at the table was still laid, his sandwiches ready for him. He was deep in thought. She had seen him like that before, but not often. She noticed it now. He was quite calm, a controlled calm. Whilst he was eating he dwelt all the time on one theme.

'That bankruptcy will work out all right.'

'It's a large office there.'

'Dr de Gankelaar isn't the boss, Dr Stroomkoning is.'

'My bankruptcy will be washed out. Lack of means they call it.'

'That Dr de Gankelaar's a fine man; he's going to help me.'

'I can keep my books.'

'Nothing will come of the bankruptcy.'

'By chance I saw my father there. They pointed him out to me, just like that. I naturally pretended he was a stranger. As a matter of fact, he *is* a stranger.'

'Do you know how much my books were valued at?' he asked, addressing her directly for the first time.

'No,' she said.

'Fifteen guilders altogether. You can't force a bankruptcy on that, Dr de Gankelaar said. So it will be washed out.'

He got up before he had eaten half his sandwiches.

He went to his cubicle.

Three things she had picked up : his father – that 'help me' – his books. But she asked no questions and did not go after him.

Katadreuffe stood in his little room. He looked at his books. He only now sensed their silent companionship, after fearing to lose them and their having been saved by a simple miracle. By the miracle of their small worth. For him they meant a hundred times more than their official value. In *his* eyes their value was not diminished; they had been undeservingly insulted, rather. But, taking everything together, it was all right like this.

Then he felt he ought to have told *her* a little more, about the other matter. But he could not, he just wasn't able to talk about that and why he was going to leave her for a second time. He did not know why, but he just couldn't do it.

However, he found complete silence was not possible. In the evening he said :

'Come out with me, Jan.'

They walked together round the market. At first he did not say much. They walked in step, the same height, Katadreuffe just a little slimmer, still in his best suit in which he had visited the trustee that morning. First he spoke of the impending end to his bankruptcy, in fits and starts, like with his mother in the afternoon. Then he said that a whole new life lay ahead of him, at least – he added modestly – he believed it did. From that moment he went on talking without a pause. He only omitted the meeting with his father and what he had said to his mother about it; but he told his friend what he had not told his mother, that he probably had a new job, clerk in the trustee's office, or rather in the office of the latter's chief, Dr Stroomkoning.

When he had finished, all Jan Maan said was :

'We'll have a drink on that. My treat.'

Katadreuffe answered :

'All you can think of is just advancing me money; I shouldn't accept it. *I* ought to be treating you, but I haven't a penny left. And *she*'d be the last person I'd ask for some.'

In a pub by the cattle-market they sat, each with a glass of beer. They never referred to the mother other than by 'she' and 'her'. This was no disparagement; it merely stressed the fact that they did not share any other woman, whoever else there might be in their individual lives.

Jan Maan said :

'I suppose she doesn't know yet, otherwise I'd surely have heard.'

'No,' said Katadreuffe abruptly.

And then, in explanation :

'I wanted to tell you first.'

Jan Maan's nature was uncomplicated. He did not understand, and merely said :

'But you must tell her at once.'

'Of course.'

'She'll be sorry you are leaving home.'

'I'm not so sure of that.'

The hostility in the words was somewhat softened by his tone. Neither were remarked by Jan Maan, who was used to his friend's strange utterances. Already the considerable disharmony between mother and son had often shocked him. Two such singular people who hit it off so badly without actually quarrelling. He found that strange; he was a peaceable type, but when he had a row he preferred to have it out in the open. In recent years, he had tried to ignore the painful relationship between them; he turned a blind eye to the small jibes with which, at table, they so often sought some small-minded satisfaction, and would begin, in a natural way, to talk of something else. But Katadreuffe was quite ready to acknowledge, in retrospect, his mother's right judgement.

'In one thing she was right. I should never have gone to the Hague. That filthy hole is nothing for us Rotterdammers.'

Jan Maan had ordered a second glass. Katadreuffe would not have another.

'True,' he remarked soberly, 'but all the same it led in a roundabout way to your new job.'

He thought for a moment.

'After all, when you look at it, it's a terrific stroke of luck that you pulled it off. I'd have said that you might have got a job almost anywhere except just where they knew you were bankrupt. How you fixed that I still don't understand. A job with your trustee! You must have had an almighty nerve.'

Katadreuffe gave his rare smile, which made him look so much younger.

'Yes, Jan, I know you think I've got a nerve. And yet it isn't quite that. I was thinking about it this afternoon. And do you know what I believe it was? I'm a crazy sort of chap, I sometimes have a presentiment. And I had one when I was standing in front of that house; I had the feeling that there my future lay. There was a job waiting for me in that house. Of course I didn't know it, and yet I felt it.'

'We'd better call it a day now,' said Jan Maan. 'You look tired. And tell *her* straight away.'

Katadreuffe nodded. That's hardly surprising, he thought. When you at last know you're on the way, when you can at last see your future, that's what you do feel.

But, at home in bed, he realized that an additional cause of his tiredness was the discovery of such a father.

Knowledge up to T

This is how it happened.

On his way through the house to his trustee he had moved as if in a dream. He was not dreamy by nature, but the sight of Dreverhaven had given him a shock. Dreverhaven was someone always on the war-path; why then should he not be so to a son whom he had never met, a son moreover, weakened by those wretched months in the Hague, and the fear that the bankruptcy would rob him of his books. The moment of deep heart-searching on the quay in front of the house had sapped his vigour. But he still had some energy left. Standing before the door of the room, he was able, with an incredible effort of will, to put aside everything unconnected with the imminent visit; he was even able to force his face to resume its normal colour.

The trustee sat at his desk. He looked up and saw before him a young man of strikingly handsome appearance. He was a man interested in people. The small bankruptcy was nothing, absolutely nothing; but he remembered the skinny little woman with the fiery eyes, whom he found a difficulty in placing in any normal category; and he had never had to administer an estate consisting solely of books. Moreover, books of that type went with the house even less than the mother with that neighbourhood. What would the bankrupt be like? And he saw at once that he, too, had something special about him. He was very like his mother, particularly in the look of his eyes. He had put on his best suit for the visit; De Gankelaar noticed that at once. And he took good stock of him.

The young man's features were dangerous in this respect, that the slightest trace of obsequiousness would have made him unbearable to anyone of sound taste. He no doubt knew that he was good-looking; that he gave no sign of knowing it saved him, completely. He was correctly dressed —in his best suit—but simply, not a single detail of his dress demanding attention. One could see at once he had other ambitions than that of trying to ingratiate himself. But, at the same time, there was a lack of warmth in his fine eyes. They shone with a pure ardour, but the fire was not warm. Just as snow can sparkle or glow red, though one knows all the time, can *see* that it is cold.

'Sit down,' said De Gankelaar.

The thin file of the bankruptcy was lying in front of him; he opened it and did not let it be seen that he was somewhat put out.

Katadreuffe saw a young man, four or five years older than himself, with an athletic figure, a high forehead, unruly fair hair combed back, small brown eyes, strong cheek-muscles. The mouth was rather large, not very handsomely shaped, the teeth were irregular but nice and white; his wrists protruded from broad, clean cuffs, with a signet-ring on his hand. Someone who in the summer must spend a lot of time in the open air, but who didn't tan easily; there were just a few freckles on the white skin around the nose, but not unsightly.

'You are obliged to answer my questions truthfully.'

He again looked up from the file, his eyes searching, but at the same time friendly.

'Have you brought your business books?'

'No, I never kept any.'

'Then the list of your creditors.'

Katadreuffe handed it over. The trustee looked at it, and

made the usual enquiries regarding any other assets besides the books already noted down; money, outstanding debts and so on. Katadreuffe answered that he possessed nothing but what had already been recorded.

'I had a talk with your mother. Is your father still alive?' asked the trustee.

Katadreuffe merely answered :

'I'm called after my mother.'

'Oh !'

De Gankelaar realized that in all innocence he had asked an embarrassing question, but the young man's mien did not alter. Yet he gave no further explanation. De Gankelaar dropped the subject. He asked him to explain his debts in greater detail and Katadreuffe told him about his unsuccessful Hague adventure. It was all very ordinary and did not interest the trustee; he had merely been struck by the mother and by the books. And now by the bankrupt.

A man came in, the same one whom Katadreuffe had seen below, with the gold spectacles and rather bold. He must also be a lawyer. Carlion? Piaat?

'Just a moment,' said the trustee.

They spoke in low tones at his desk; then the other went away. He resumed :

'I shall recommend to the court that the bankruptcy be annulled on account of lack of means. Your books are valued at fifteen guilders. In such a case it does not pay to pursue the bankruptcy. The costs, even, would not be covered, not by a long way . . . How did you get hold of the books?'

'I bought them bit by bit.'

'Do you know German?'

'I can read it. I have read a lot of the encyclopedia.'

'What are your plans for the future? Are you going to stay with your mother? Can she keep you?'

'She certainly can as she earns good money, although just after the war it was better than now. She does handwork for a shop here, and it has to be something special. I can't judge it. I sometimes find it nice and sometimes strange but I am, of course, no expert . . . But I would prefer to get away from her; I want to become completely independent of her and live on my own. She also would prefer that. She has had to make her own way and she wants me to do the same. She doesn't actually say that, but I sense it.'

'I want,' continued Katadreuffe in one breath, 'to get into an office – see how far I can get. I don't mind what or where,' he was careful to add.

But at the same time he looked straight at De Gankelaar. Didn't he want to understand? The answer was disappointing as it went back over the old ground.

'Have you taught yourself German?'

'Yes. I only went through primary school.'

'And after that?'

'Then all sorts of things. Errand boy, in a factory, storeroom boy. I didn't get on there; that kind of work doesn't suit me.' The trustee just nodded.

'I wanted to learn more and so I bought the books and taught myself quite a lot. I think I must have a good memory. I'm not trying to pretend I'm a scholar but I know more than most people of my class.'

Once again he looked straight at De Gankelaar.

'Most of it I learnt out of the encyclopedia, but I don't know much after the letter T. It ends there, it's not complete. And it's old, so on many points out of date as well as incomplete; that I fully realize.'

De Gankelaar liked that. He had half expected something pleasantly appealing like this. He smiled and Katadreuffe smiled back.

'A cigarette?'

'Thank you.'

He, himself, lit a pipe. The conversation was for a moment interrupted by the telephone. While De Gankelaar spoke into the mouthpiece Katadreuffe looked around the room, a small room at the front with one window, sunny, overlooking the busy water, with a plan of the docks framed behind glass on the wall. De Gankelaar, during the telephone conversation, kept looking at his visitor. And he asked himself whether he could get him a job here. A youngster like that ought to be given a chance. When he had replaced the receiver he continued his train of thought out loud.

'Listen, I won't deny that the books interested me. Perhaps – I don't know – but perhaps you might be able to get a job in an office.'

He paused, thinking that if this boy had aptitude he could develop into an excellent solicitor's head clerk. He continued :

'It is a pity that you are not somewhat better grounded. Can you type?'

'Certainly. As a store-room boy I also had to type addresses for my boss, and sometimes invoices.'

'And shorthand?'

'A little,' lied Katadreuffe, now desperate.

'Then we'll give you a trial. Is there a typewriter free?' he asked through the house-telephone. 'I want one for a bit.'

There appeared to be two machines free. Miss Te George was with Dr Stroomkoning at a meeting in the conference-room; Dr. Piaat was still dictating to Miss Sibculo.

'Remington or Underwood?' De Gankelaar asked Katadreuffe.

It was all the same to him. The boy brought the machine upstairs. De Gankelaar dictated a long legal clause out of his head. Katadreuffe did not know any shorthand; he got none of it down correctly and could not read a word back.

'If you would dictate it once again, a little slower?' he asked.

Then, the second time, using his own abbreviations and with the help of his good memory, he succeeded in getting down something legible to him, and the typing he accomplished neatly and without a mistake.

'That should be all right. The rest will come with practice,' said De Gankelaar.

Katadreuffe thought so too. De Gankelaar said :

'I'll see what I can do for you. You must go back to the waiting-room for a bit.'

Katadreuffe found his way back. He had not for a moment doubted that he would get a job, here, in this office. It was simply a matter of making a good impression, and in that he had apparently succeeded. At the same time, he realized that the decision did not rest with Mr de Gankelaar – he could and would be merely his advocate. He went back to sit in the waiting-room; he was now the only one there. He did not ask himself how late it was. It was lunch-time. He didn't feel hungry; he waited.

The door leading to the ochre-yellow room was closed; in the general office the hoarse voice on the telephone could be heard now and again; the typewriters were silent. The two men who looked so alike ate their sandwiches out of a piece of paper, a cup of coffee standing by each of them.

In the meantime, De Gankelaar was conferring with the head clerk, Rentenstein; the man with the self-satisfied, arrogant appearance.

De Gankelaar was a man of moods, inclined naturally to melancholy, which he chased away with athletics; in his spare time he went in for all kinds of sport. He was governed by impulses. He had made up his mind that Katadreuffe should be his own typist. Everyone here had, as far as it was possible, his own clerk, who took dictation and typed. Miss Te George belonged to Stroomkoning, Miss Sibculo worked for Carlion and Piaat, but could not manage it all. The Burgeik brothers would then help her out. One of them also did De Gankelaar's work, the other Miss Kalvelage's. The latter had the elder and better of the brothers, but neither of them worked very fast : they were youths from the islands south of Rotterdam, with a limited outlook and slow fingers, willing and accurate, but they would always remain in a subordinate position. There was a tremendous lot to do in the office : the practice began to overshadow many of the larger ones in the port. The Bur-geiks had a lot of copying work, and in that they were at their best. Consequently De Gankelaar had lately been get-ting his memoranda and even his letters behind time. Some-one else was certainly needed, and he would have liked to have his own man, part time if necessary, but someone who was always available for him. For the rule of this office, where otherwise there were not many rules, was that one could use another's typist but that he to whom he was offi-cially allotted had precedence.

Thus De Gankelaar wanted to have Katadreuffe as his official typist. He made his proposal first to Rentenstein. Actually, he couldn't stand Rentenstein; he found him affected, and also he didn't trust him. Rentenstein looked after the police-court work and was, besides, head of the office, but was not responsible for direction and organiza-tion. Rentenstein was, moreover, always having private chats with Dreverhaven, from which he was not likely to come to much good. But Rentenstein was officially in charge of the staff. De Gankelaar did not want to by-pass him; he respected everyone's place, although in the end Stroomkon-ing would have to decide.

De Gankelaar ascribed to Katadreuffe more virtues than he could justify. Rentenstein, at first, thought it was risky to take on someone who was bankrupt, having a lower middle-class suspicion of bankrupts. But, on the other hand, he recognized that the office could do with someone else; every increase in the staff added, moreover, to the import-ance of his own position. He possessed the vanity that goes with a weak will.

'What would we have to give him? Sixty guilders to start with? He certainly seems to be worth that.'

'We must first ask Mr Stroomkoning.'

'Of course, is he free?'

'No, he mustn't be disturbed.'

'Oh. Is he in conference?'

'The big meeting of the margarine syndicate.'

'Not over yet?'

'No. Ask him this afternoon – perhaps he'll have a moment to spare then,' said Rentenstein.

De Gankelaar looked at his watch.

'Good Lord, it's one o'clock already. Now my coffee will be cold. I'd forgotten all about the time . . . But I'll just ask him on the telephone.'

'He doesn't want to be disturbed on the house-telephone, either.'

'Oh well. I'll try it – we'll see.'

He was a creature of impulse. He wanted now at once, at this moment, to make sure of Katadreuffe. He had a crazy fear that the boy would slip from his grasp, that by the afternoon he would perhaps have found something else. Such a fellow would surely be successful anywhere. He, himself, recognized the absurdity of his thoughts but he could not wait – he picked up the receiver.

After speaking for a few seconds he hung up, in the middle of a sentence.

'Mr Stroomkoning agrees.'

'He's very easy-going in such matters.'

'Yes. Now all we've got to do is to fix the salary. What do you say to sixty guilders?'

And he called Katadreuffe upstairs again. For the third time Katadreuffe walked along the marble corridor; he no longer needed any guide, he knew the way, he already felt at home.

At the end of the passage, and of the same width, were seven stairs, heavily carpeted, leading down to a massive eighteenth-century door. The door opened. By the light of a huge chandelier, through a thick haze of cigar smoke, he could see a number of men sitting round a long, green table – a lot of flushed faces. At the head of the table sat an elderly man, with grey hair like an untidily ruffled lion's mane. A loud and excited male voice repeated three times, stressing the first syllable :

'Absolutely, ab-solutely, ab-solutely.'

Someone shut the door. A tall, slim girl went by. There was plenty of room on the staircase. Yet he stood still. Miss Te George gave him a quick glance as she passed him. Under her arm she carried a pad; there was something dreamy and smiling in her features, her free hand playing absently with a silver pencil. He noticed the simple, eloquent nobility of those slender hands. He merely noticed it, and then at once dismissed the encounter from his thoughts. He registered things quickly and accurately, but besides this gift he possessed that other one of keeping, in all circumstances, his aim clearly in view.

He turned to the narrow side staircase which curved upwards to where De Gankelaar had his room.

A Beginning

De Gankelaar remembered that Katadreuffe, besides wanting a job, was also looking for a room. Of course there
were more than enough to be had. But good, cheap accommodation with decent food was not to be found so easily.
Perhaps Rentenstein would know of a place. But Rentenstein seemed to have gone off to eat. And on second
thoughts De Gankelaar felt Rentenstein was not, after all,
the right source of information. He therefore sent for the
concierge, who occupied those upper rooms of the house not
in use for the archives. He asked him whether he knew of
any solution. The concierge, Graanoogst, gave Katadreuffe
a quick glance and then asked if he could fetch his wife.

A little later, husband and wife came along together with
the proposition that Katadreuffe should come and live with
them for twelve guilders a week. Katadreuffe went with
them to inspect the room, but he did not forget first to
express his thanks to his trustee 'for everything'.

The following day, Katadreuffe moved into his new
home, bringing his few possessions on a hand-cart. His
mother had let him take her bits of furniture from his
cubicle, as at the time he went to the Hague; and she had
packed his clothes in a suitcase.

At Graanoogst's request, Katadreuffe arrived after office
hours. It wouldn't do to bring along his bits and pieces

under the eyes of the gentlemen and their clients. Kata-dreuffe had understood. Together, they quickly carried his scanty possessions up the stairs.

Katadreuffe had reckoned that with a salary of sixty guilders a month he could afford this price for his board and lodging, provided he need not pay weekly but at the end of each month, to start with. Also, if he couldn't quite manage it, he would rather make the strictest economies in other things than turn down this offer. For many reasons it suited him extraordinarily well. The presentiment of a change in his life which he had momentarily had on the quay the previous day, with the accumulation of good things happening to him that same day, had become an unshakable certainty. Under the happiest auspices, he took possession of his new home.

The apartment he entered was an extremely sombre in-side room, right at the top of the house. It was already furnished to some extent, but poorly, with just the bare necessities. There was an old-fashioned cupboard-bed to sleep in. The room was large, but it had only one window which did not let in much light. The window looked out on to an air-shaft, not the broad light-shaft above the sky-light of the yellow room, but a small, narrow gully between the window and the wall of the bank building next door. That wall was quite a bit higher than the lawyers' office. Katadreuffe could only see the sky by opening the window and looking straight up. Below him, the shaft disappeared into the oncoming night.

There was no means of heating. Graanoogst said that in the winter he would put in an oil stove. Being an inside room, it was not in itself cold. Katadreuffe supposed he would always have to use artificial light here, but he wouldn't be there much, except in the evenings and on Sundays. He was to have his meals with the concierge and his family.

None the less, he found the room gloomy, particularly once he had arranged his things, which stood there strangely lost. He had had to pile up his books in a deep, musty wall-cupboard, since he had given his book-rack to Jan Maan on his departure. It was perhaps a curious present, but Katadreuffe had meant it as a silent hint that Jan Maan should furnish it and get down to studying, himself. The wallpaper was something between green and grey, dully insignificant, and a great contrast with all the wallpapers at home which, although also cheap, owed their individuality to his mother's sense of colour.

He found the cupboard-bed very disagreeable. He had never slept in such a rabbit-hutch, always in a normal bed with room to move about. There were two doors to this *bedstede*, with little holes in them. The occupant, obviously, was meant to close the doors and obtain sufficient air through the holes. Further, a red tassel hung from the ceiling at the height of his stomach, on a heavy red cord, badly moth-eaten. And above his feet a shelf was fixed, on which former generations had placed their chamber-pots, but which now did not serve the slightest purpose.

Katadreuffe had said that he absolutely must get rid of the doors, the tassel and the shelf. Graanoogst had promised to do this and to put up a curtain to hide the gap. But he had had no time to do so on that first day; the bedstead remained unaltered. It gave out the same musty smell as the cupboard.

Katadreuffe suffered from depression this first evening in the now silent house. He heard no sound from the others living there; and as he was not yet acquainted with the whole house and everything appeared on a magnified scale, they seemed to be unapproachably far off. He had brightened up the walls as best he could with a few prints, but the room remained inhospitable, dour, and musty in the modest light of the electric bulb hanging above the table. He had gone to sit under the light at the table, with his back intentionally turned on the bedstead, but the presence of the dark gap, though invisible, had a disagreeable effect on him. He felt tired, depressed, and also hungry. He had nothing with him to eat. He sat for a while staring in front of him, reflecting that it was absurd to begin his plan to work by doing nothing, and yet unable to come to action. At last he got up and pushed the window up as high as possible. He leant out and saw a small square of sky which, in this reduced extent, looked just as dull and discoloured as the wallpaper, for it was only late evening, not yet night. If he had not seen a star, the sky might just as easily have been overcast as clear. The star only faintly twinkled; perhaps he knew it, but without anything to guide him he could not place it at all.

He came back into the room, dissatisfied with himself, and then opened the door. The passage outside was dark; a few steps descended and then the passage continued. He heard no sound of human activity, saw not a chink of light. The Graanoogsts' little daughter had naturally long since gone to bed; both of them perhaps as well. All right then, he would go and sleep; tomorrow would be another day.

Whilst he was undressing he noticed that he had omitted to unpack his suitcase, which stood in a dark corner by the bed. His clothes, his night things, his washing things were in it. He looked into the deep wall-cupboard. There was a shelf in it on which he could put his underclothes. There were hooks on which to hang his outer garments. He unpacked the suitcase and discovered amongst his underclothes two new shirts. They were a present from 'her'. He laid everything neatly on the shelf, and his Sunday suit on a coat-hanger he hung on a hook. He had always been neat in his dress. Like Jan Maan, he had an innate need for cleanliness, always presentable linen, his collars and ties good in style and colour; but, with his slimmer figure and finer features, he had never worked hard at his appearance, in contrast to his friend. The two new shirts from her were very much to his taste.

He at once began to think of her; the hard hand that had often chastised him, but also cared for him up till now, always without many words. The care and the blows had always been accompanied by very little talk on her part. She could act more easily than talk. Now too. She had not said much, but there were the two new shirts of a shade he liked to wear. What had she answered when he had told her about his job and his leaving her?

'Oh well,' she had said.

It wasn't much but sounded better than 'Do as you please'.

It was neither commendation nor disapproval, just an attitude of wait and see.

He was his mother's child, not his father's. His father had only come into his life incidentally, for a few seconds, and that had scarcely touched him. If he had been a tenant behind with his rent and his father the bailiff who ejected him, his emotion would have been more violent, his impression deeper than now. At the moment he was not thinking at all of his father. He did not have a warm nature but something drew him, in spite of all, almost against his will, towards his mother. Feeling that, he became annoyed with himself and began to belittle the value of her present. It was certainly a nice present, but a few words with it would have been nicer still. And actually, he would have preferred the words without the present.

He again had the old feeling almost of enmity. He just wouldn't put up with it; he wouldn't breathe a syllable about the present, merely act as if he hadn't noticed it. The old opposition welled up, the result of the dourness of their characters, in spite of so much resemblance, in fact, just because of so much resemblance between them.

But he had begun to think of something else. He quickly dressed again, and until midnight he was busy dictating to himself from a book and writing it down in a shorthand of his own invention.

The following morning, from six o'clock until breakfast-time, he typed out his stenographs in the general office.

The First Months

Katadreuffe surpassed himself; that was not difficult, as in the past he had never achieved anything much. And it fell out as he had supposed : at his present age he understood things so much better than when he was younger and everything went more quickly.

He also surpassed De Gankelaar's expectations, and that was more difficult, as he, from only the vaguest reasons, had promised himself a great deal from his protégé; and he was a type to have taken it amiss had Katadreuffe not come up to his standards.

He did not surpass his own expectations, as an ambitious man is never satisfied with less than reaching the aim he has set himself, and Katadreuffe's aim was high. But he went about it in a thoroughly systematic way; he took care in the first place to make a proper job of the work for which he had been engaged; for from this place in this office he must rise high; if he lost this place his growth would be at once arrested. Within a few weeks he could type with the best, owing to his practice in the early morning and late at night, on Saturday afternoon and Sunday. At the same time he practised shorthand; he had bought a textbook, but he retained his own abbreviations, so that it became a mixed system and no one but himself could read it. Although shorthand was more difficult to learn than typing,

59

after a little he was also reasonably proficient at it. By his watch, he controlled the number of words he could take down per minute; he gradually brought it to quite a considerable figure, and as he was dictating to himself, it went still more quickly when De Gankelaar was dictating, as his attention then was undivided.

There was, after all, nothing magical in this. He had quickly overtaken the Burgeiks. There was not much merit in that, as these country lads would never get very far. De Gankelaar spoke in praise of him, and the office soon recognized that the new hand gave a lot of promise. Only the head, Dr Stroomkoning, from his throne, remained oblivious of him. The latter had nothing to do with anyone beyond his colleagues, his own secretary and the head clerk. He had already forgotten Katadreuffe's existence.

As regards his work Katadreuffe had only one worry. He did not like making mistakes in punctuation and grammar, and was not sure of his spelling. He felt humiliated when De Gankelaar corrected an error in these matters. Yet it was not his fault; in the primary school one cannot learn more than the principles of the difficult business of writing correctly. Through his considerable reading he was further advanced than the top class of the primary school, but he made mistakes, sometimes bad ones. He bought a couple of secondary school text-books, worked carefully through these, and soon had no more reason to blush over knowledge of his mother tongue than the average educated Dutchman. Indeed, when De Gankelaar now and then gave him a written opinion or a summons to type, he could discover faults in them—more faults of syntax than of words—that he, himself, would not now make.

The humiliations at the beginning had been very painful to him, for in this kind of way he was very sensitive, and the knowledge that he probably knew more than anyone in the office about erysipelas or poliomyelitis, for example, or Van Scaliger, or the magnetic pole, did not help him. On the contrary, his ignorance on essential points was, in his eyes, all the more mortifying. But this was soon a thing of the past.

Having surmounted this worry, he was still not satisfied. He was no all-round shorthand-typist yet, by any means, as he knew no foreign languages. A lot of French, German and English correspondence went through the office, particularly English, admittedly dealt with in the main by Stroomkoning, who knew these languages; but also his colleagues, now and then, had to do some of it. In that case they waited until Miss Te George was free, as out of the whole staff, only she understood all three languages. Rentenstein knew enough German, but he was fully occupied with the police-court practice, at least so he said. Nobody except Stroomkoning, himself, could get him to take down a letter.

It happened occasionally with De Gankelaar that Katadreuffe had to make way for Miss Te George, and each time it made him feel miserable. He wanted to be first among the typists. He knew that it would be years before he reached her level, but one day it would have to happen, and he would take her place in Stroomkoning's room. Incidentally, the organization and the ways of the office he had very quickly assimilated.

Stroomkoning was the old lion with the ruffled mane whom he had noticed at the head of the meeting in the conference-room on that first day. He was tall and broad-shouldered, untidily dressed – he did not give a thought to his outward appearance. But with that head it wasn't necessary; his head was everything. Broad and grey, with a sparse, bristling, white moustache, like feline whiskers; the green eyes, small, narrowed like a beast of prey's; the voice a gentle, distant yet powerful growl. He did little now in the actual practice, his colleagues pleading and attending courts of enquiry throughout the country. He looked after the more important affairs, contracts over commercial interests, meetings of important business men, arbitration over disputes that they did not want to drag into the courts. He knew nothing about organization of the office. leaving this to Rentenstein. He had a villa just outside Rotterdam, on the Bergse lakes. He was married for the second time. Iris, his very beautiful wife, sometimes came in the car to fetch him. Formerly, he used to drive himself; but as he had so often run into all and sundry, his attention on his affairs and not on the road, he gave it up, leaving her at the wheel, sitting next to her fashionable figure in his shabby suit, bare-headed in the open car, while his mane waved in all directions and his whiskers bristled. Small and blonde, Iris Stroomkoning reminded one of an elf, but she was a sporting type, very muscular. Stroomkoning was amused by the gossamer sleeve and the biceps beneath it, which she could turn into a ball of steel, like an athlete.

He had two children by her, of the slight build produced by men who having passed their climacteric allow themselves the luxury of a second family.

He had many foreign connections, particularly with England, being in continuous contact with the office of C. C. & C. – Cadwallader, Countryside & Countryside – and was always going to London. Every steward of the Batavier and Harwich Lines knew him. Of late he had often flown over.

He withdrew himself more and more from the mass of affairs dealt with by his office. His original principle, formulated when he first engaged a colleague, was always to receive the clients himself, even if the clerical side had to be done for him by his colleague – that principle he had been forced to abandon long ago. To that colleague was added a second, then a third; old faces disappeared, new ones arrived; now he had four lawyers in his office, and in many matters they acted quite independently. Carlion was a specialist. He was allotted all the practice dealing with inland water transport. In the room which he shared with Piaat large maps of all the rivers and canals hung from an iron stand. Also, as with De Gankelaar, a plan of the docks hung on the wall behind glass. Piaat, too, was a specialist; he dealt with the criminal practice.

In those days, Stroomkoning had had the good idea of lunching with his colleagues at half past twelve in the conference-room, the one with the ochre-coloured walls, the third room of the suite. During lunch they were able to discuss the important cases. At half past twelve, as he used to say, the lawyers' exchange was open. There were often lively debates. However, as the practice grew, he was less sure of his time, arriving too late and, in the end, not at all. He would take half an hour off to go to lunch in a restaurant in town; then clients often went with him, or waited for him there. The colleagues kept the exchange going, but one or another of them was constantly missing, at the law-courts or out of town.

The one with the golden spectacles and rather bald was Carlion. A dry-as-dust man from the North, with a very precise manner of speaking. He had been in Java for four years and still retained an even, light brick-red colouring. He enjoyed a reputation for excellence. No doubt he had a very decent salary; how much no one knew. For Stroomkoning, himself, paid his colleagues out of the main cash account, of which he alone kept the books. The subsidiary cash account was entrusted to Rentenstein. There was no difference in principle between the two accounts; what the colleagues received from clients or contesting parties, or what was paid out to these, passed through the subsidiary cash account. As regards the turnover of the main account, no one had any idea, except perhaps Miss Te George, but she never talked about the business.

The telephones in the general office stood in a corner behind the sliding-doors, which always remained open. It had been a surprise to Katadreuffe to discover a girl back there, sitting under a lamp. The high, hoarse voice belonged to her. She looked boyish, and was extremely cheeky. But she never forgot a message and Stroomkoning, who had long since forgotten about her, had at one time discovered that her voice was cut out for the telephone. He used to say : a thin, girl's voice didn't sound right on the phone – you must have a man's voice. Such matters were not unimportant; the first impression of an office was obtained via the telephone. A small, piping voice or a bad accent gave rise to thoughts : that's not the place for me. A man, therefore, with a refined bass. But when Rentenstein introduced him over the telephone to the sounds produced by Miss Van den Born, it was settled at once. Yet this girl would never have been Katadreuffe's choice. She had no accent, but her voice had the coarseness of the common people. Moreover, he found her, for her age, annoyingly emancipated; an Eton crop with a parting, sloppy unfeminine clothes, saucy eyes and a saucy nose with wide nostrils, whether laughing or sneezing; a nose which, no doubt when small, she had often wiped on her glove. She had, from the start, categorically insisted on being called *juffrouw*, and not by her Christian name; but Rentenstein used the familiar form[1] with nearly everyone. She was a type that, according to Katadreuffe's judgement, did not go with an office of standing. He found his chief's choice unfortunate, but perhaps the latter had never even seen the girl. She was not the only thing he did not like. Indeed, the organization also left much to be desired. Stroomkoning had not the time and Rentenstein not the talent, and so the office had the slovenly air of a post-war practice which had grown too quickly.

The Burgeik brothers did not bother Katadreuffe. They were, of course, people he would never understand. Seen more closely, they were still brothers, but no longer showed that striking likeness. There were a few years between them, and one could tell it. They were broad and square-built, with thin, short, black hair and square faces. The elder had two fingers missing from his right hand, but that did not interfere with his typing. One saw at once that they were respectable, solid, very dull people, the elder having a little more in him. They were country boys; they would

[1] 2nd person singular.

always be gauche, never smartly dressed. Their powers of endurance were great; they were never ill; they were best at the soul-deadening copying work. But Katadreuffe did not understand them, and no one understood them. They kept themselves to themselves. They were completely lacking in humour; when the others laughed they merely looked on. But sometimes, when there was nothing much to laugh at, the younger one would give a broad smile, quite silently, and his brother would take it up and, without a sound, sit shaking on his chair. It lasted a moment or two, and then they both resumed their work with straight faces. At times it appeared idiotic, and yet if one observed closely, one could see that they were far from simple. Stupid, in the sense that they wouldn't be receptive to much book-learning, but not unintelligent. But they had set faces, they wore masks; one couldn't get near them : they wore the masks the countryman wears when in contact with the townsman, whom he regards as his enemy. The town would never get a grip on them; they would never allow that. Katadreuffe, gauging them with his sharp intelligence, in so far as it was possible for a townsman to do so, often asked himself whether this exhibition was not quite wrongly judged as crazy, whether perhaps there did not exist reasons of a very intricate nature for this display of hilarity. He never succeeded in fathoming it.

There were two office-boys. The one who had spoken to him on his first day was known only by his Christian name, Pietje. He seldom sat down. He conducted the clients, carried papers about, ran from one room to the other, took messages. He had a delicate, girlish appearance; fine, yellow child's eyes, and ugly, brittle little teeth. He looked as if he had consumptive tendencies. Katadreuffe had picked up a certain social sense from Jan Maan, and he felt that the child had to run about too much.

The other was a robust youth named Kees Adam, a few years older. He ran messages of a more important nature, going to the law-courts with files and that sort of thing. It was also his job, together with Miss Van den Born, to file the office papers. He fetched money from the bank; he brought money, sometimes large sums, from other offices here or to the bank. The larger the amount the prouder he was. He was hoping one day he would be attacked, and displayed a knuckle-duster with which he was keen to show his prowess. His father had a garage in a side street. He spent his Sundays tinkering with a motor-cycle he was assembling. He sometimes managed to reach the end of the street on it, with deafening reports and a blue stink, until the neighbours cursed and complained to his father.

The First Months

Katadreuffe very quickly found the explanation of the chance meeting with his father here on the first day. Dreverhaven had for years been bailiff for the office. Right at the beginning, Stroomkoning had had another, but the serving of a writ of attachment on a ship had forged an unbreakable bond between them. It had been a famous case; even after so many years it was raked up now and then in the lawyers' chambers at the law-courts. The case had enhanced both their practices; from an ordinary lawyer, an ordinary bailiff, they had become celebrities, each in his own sphere, each for a short time; but the fame had had its consequences, attention had now been focused on them.

In the office, too, the story was sometimes passed round. Rentenstein liked to highlight the glory of both, not forgetting his own, although he had played no role in this affair. It had occurred before his time, but he knew how to tell it to look as though he had been closely associated.

Katadreuffe had seen Dreverhaven again in the office, on several occasions. The first time, he had passed him in the corridor; it had been quite a shock, but had happened before he was aware of it. After that, he was prepared; he wouldn't give anything away. And that was easy, as whenever Dreverhaven showed up in the general office – the black felt-hat on his head, the cigar in the corner of his mouth like a gun, the voice whose very sound proclaimed a powerful chest – on those occasions father and son did not look at each other. Did his father know him? His mother had never said so; he had never asked her, and it seemed unlikely. How should Dreverhaven know the names of the clerks here? He only ever asked for Rentenstein; he stood talking earnestly, but in low tones that could not be overheard, by the high windows with his back to everybody and everything. Why should Rentenstein have told him the name of the newcomer? It didn't seem likely. Otherwise, he would have quickly noticed it in Dreverhaven. But then he remembered that he himself did not give anything away; no, that was no proof. And in the uncertainty whether his father knew him or not he was inclined to the latter. He had no grounds for a definite opinion, but he believed it to be so.

What he did realize now was that Dreverhaven had made a list of his belongings. On a certain day, after he had been some months in the office, it had occurred to him : if you are bankrupt, a bailiff comes to make an inventory of your things. Dreverhaven was the bailiff for this office. Had he done that to his things? Had he been to the house?

After office hours, he went to look for the file in the steel cabinets. It was no longer there; it must have been removed to the archives in the attics. In the index he found the number of the file, and the file itself under the rafters. He looked through it. Yes, Dreverhaven had assessed him. There, in the memorandum was : 'Bankruptcy J. W. Kata-dreuffe. Books, generally in poor condition, encyclopedia incomplete, value f. 15.' The writing jet-black, angular, gigantic. Otherwise nothing : no signature. Katadreuffe stood with the paper underneath the low beams of the attic, in the yellow light of an electric bulb. Musty and dusty everything smelt here, a real archive atmosphere. Drab and dreary, the shelves with enormous masses of paper stretched out on all sides, around him, above him, and beneath him. The rows ran away from him, turned a corner sharply and came back again towards him, not inanimate, but as if they had never possessed a soul. The memorandum was in keeping with the surroundings and the surroundings gave emphasis to the memorandum. In the midst of this fusty, eternal decay, the note was like something bursting with life.

For the first time, he was aware of the terribly suggestive power that can lie, if only very rarely, in a handwriting; of what power lay in that writing. This was the writing of a Caesar, and it was the writing of a bailiff. What a hand! When he compared it with his own scribble! He then realized that in this respect he was sadly lacking too. His characterless letters carried the stamp of his school writing. He had not stayed at school long enough to develop his writing, whether to a fine hand or an ugly one, at least to something definitely his. He had for years hardly handled a pen. His writing still had that clumsiness, drawn rather than written, of the early beginnings. There was a lot he still had to learn. To start with, he could improve *that*. His signature was like nothing on earth. Begin again, right from the bottom, even if he would never be able to develop such character in his writing. But just wait; he would show them that his future did not depend on handwriting; he still had other shots in his locker.

He took the small file back with him to his room. Nobody would ever ask for it again, and it would not be able to compromise him there. He hid it in his cupboard, placing his father's note on top. He had never owned anything of his father's. Then he took it out again, and that evening, he sat at his table staring at it. He couldn't get down to work.

He began to feel the chill of the deathly still, clammy room. He got up and lighted the oil stove. The concierge's wife knocked and brought him his tea. He quickly placed a book over the paper. Alone once more, he paced thoughtfully about the room. His father had called on him at home; 'she' had not mentioned it; that's what had happened. That she did not want to have anything to do with her seducer, that was her business; he could appreciate that all right. He had never reproached her for leaving him illegitimate and never would. For that he was too generous. And he did not regard it as shameful. In the first place, it was not his fault; moreover, and really in the first place, the world now thought differently about these things than formerly. The world was no longer so narrow-minded as fifty years ago. He had indeed been ashamed – if only moderately so – of his bankruptcy; after all, for that he could only blame himself. That he was a bastard didn't matter a bit; he wouldn't shout it out from the house-tops, but if it were necessary, he would state it boldly; he was much too proud to lie about it. Should he succeed in life, all the greater the honour. But why the confounded silence of his mother? Why did he have to discover his father's visit in this way? What was behind it all; why was he not to know of it? She went too far, by God, she went too far. He would have to bring her to her senses one of these days, and without mincing his words.

Katadreuffe did not realize that he was glad merely to be angry with her again : in small matters she grieved him, deeply offended him.

Unaware of it, he had a great curiosity in everything concerning his father. He would never ask her anything about him. However, in the office, he cautiously brought the conversation round to Dreverhaven. When Rentenstein mentioned something about the famous ship's seizure, it sounded quite natural for Katadreuffe to ask for details.

Stroomkoning had only been established a few years, his practice not yet amounting to much when suddenly an important claim on an Italian ship came into his hands. The ship lay in the Rijnhaven and was on the point of sailing. With the authority from the president of the Court to seize the vessel, he rushed off to his bailiff. He was out. But, hurrying along, a few houses back he had noticed Dreverhaven's name-plate, and the latter was at home. Together, they dashed to the dock; Hamerslag, Dreverhaven's clerk, with them as a witness. On the way, they had to pick up a second witness, a fellow who was always at home, as Dreverhaven knew for certain. And so he was. This fourth man in the taxi was a horror who, for a moment, left Stroomkoning speechless. At every corner the creature wobbled in his place, with his head lolling forward on its long, spineless neck, drunken, idiotic, or dead. But Stroomkoning could spare neither the time nor the attention for closer examination. They arrived at the quayside. The ship was just turning out of the dock into the Maas. From then on, Dreverhaven took charge – it was a seizure; he was on his own ground. A motor-boat heaved up and down nearby. With the promise of a good fee if they caught up the ship, the boatman set off after it. It was already growing dark, with bad visibility, that afternoon in late November. The silhouette of the unlighted ship and its black smoke showed up against the western sky. They were gaining on it quickly : the vessel was scarcely under way.

'Right up to the bow,' said Dreverhaven to the boatman. 'And then stay there.'

Nothing more. Stroomkoning kept silent. He would be desperate if they failed to stop the ship, but something in that Dreverhaven, told him they would succeed. He asked no questions.

Then, just by the bows of the ship, Dreverhaven stood up, so that the crankly little boat rocked in the swell from the larger one.

'Catch hold of him,' cried the boatman, who did not understand what was happening.

Already, with a cry, Dreverhaven had toppled over into the Maas and lay roaring like a police-siren.

Stroomkoning had grasped it immediately. He stood up, waving and shouting in every language he knew :

'Man overboard ! Man overboard !'

High up, on the ship's rail, heads appeared, looking down. Something was splashing there alongside – to be sure – a chap was lying there, roaring madly. Dreverhaven, floating on his broad coat, in a few strokes was the first to reach the rope, hat crushed down on his head; and climbed streaming on to the deck, the others after him.

The captain, a dark, common, little fellow, saw his mistake too late; none of his crew had fallen overboard. He gnashed his teeth, he foamed at the mouth; but there stood Dreverhaven in front of him, leaking all over the deck, the broad bailiff's ribbon with the badge of office hanging round his neck – the captain couldn't keep his eyes off it – and the writ of attachment, taken from Stroomkoning, held between two fingers, well away from him so that the water wouldn't spot it.

But to hell with it! The captain was here on his own ship – what did he care for any papers or any damned Dutchman! But then he saw Stroomkoning (who had guessed the sort of people he had to deal with) playing so happily with his revolver, go off up to the pilot. Whereupon a fellow like a nightmare hurled himself at him and he was aware of a head like a lump of rock on a thin neck towering above his captain's cap, and an open mouth into which an Italian skipper could easily disappear.

The vessel turned about. Already Dreverhaven's imperturbable clerk, sitting on a packing-case, was, by the light of an oil lamp, recording the attachment on the stamped papers. They let go the anchor; the monster was left as guard; and Dreverhaven went back home in a taxi to change his clothes.

I must have him from now on, and no other, thought Stroomkoning. And what most astonished him was that iron constitution. For he had stood for over an hour, soaked through, on deck in the November night breeze; he wouldn't go into the cabin. And when, the following day, Stroomkoning rang up to ask how he was, the answer came at once in the deep bass :

'No, sir, I've not had to blow my nose once more than usual.'

From that time dated the relationship between these two. The office was a fine client for Dreverhaven. In later years, they also did business together, handled by Stroomkoning in the main account, or still more mysteriously, in his private books which he kept at home. Rentenstein, to his vexation, never found out about them. Dreverhaven was a man given to flashes of inspiration and reckless acts. For that reason he had an extraordinary appeal to Stroomkoning. And so Stroomkoning did not sufficiently keep his distance; for a lawyer, he was too intimate with one who was a bailiff and who very soon earned the reputation of terrible harshness towards debtors. But Stroomkoning, himself from lower middle-class origins, did not see it. His father had been water-clerk; it didn't bother him being intimate with a bailiff, particularly one like Dreverhaven. So they did business together, often outside the normal law practice; pure gambling deals, in which they won a lot and lost a lot. He also liked Dreverhaven's lack of scruples; he was, himself, not too scrupulous. His office had become important and commanded regard, but the regard was more for the volume of the work than its quality. He did not belong to the highest class of lawyer and he never would. The bar knew it; they would never elect him to the Supervisory Board. He realized that and used to say :

'All jealousy on the part of people I've left standing.'

He said :

'I'd really like to know the clients that used to go to them who are now on my roll.'

For that matter, he was indeed not one who sought honours; he wanted to work and to make money. He worked hard and made money proportionately. And his colleagues liked him; they liked his *bonhomie* and his simple ways.

The First Year

With the adaptability of youth, Katadreuffe soon felt at home in the new world of the office. But during the first months he confined himself to observation.

He was struck by the importance of this world. He was not one to renounce his own milieu; for that he was too proud. But he was forced to acknowledge that what he experienced here was something different. He was still only at the beginning; he was looking at the world of the great ones from below. But there was more in this one than in his former world, which was drab by comparison. He didn't forget that he came from the old world, though; and he found it unfair, unreasonable, unjust that the two existed side by side. After all, everything stemmed from the people; why could not this difference be done away with? Why was it possible for only a few individuals to climb? There lay consolation in the fact that they usually sank down again, if not themselves, their descendants – a consolation, also, that he belonged to the climbers.

He had never been in contact with anything like this. He had been surrounded by the working class, except in those years in the court when it had been the very dregs of humanity. In the factory, in his many jobs as errand-boy, always just the common people. It had been a little better in the bookshop; then his boss had been at least something of a gentleman, but he hadn't picked up anything from him, only from his books.

Now take the two people who were closest to him. His mother was certainly an exceptional woman for her circles, yet she had not been able to free herself from them. Jan Maan's performance fell short of what he was capable of achieving. In spite of their friendship, Katadreuffe was able to pass clear and sharp judgement on Jan Maan. A fellow with good brains who, with the Party and his girls, came to a dead end. The book-rack, Katadreuffe's present, remained as unfurnished as his brain-pan. Behind the curtain was a collecting place for everything; underclothes, tobacco, rubbishy detective stories, inflammatory pamphlets about Lenin. 'She' just left it all like that; she had given up trying to bring order into it. All was now over with the girl from the general store. For the second time he had, in vain, saved for a home and generously left the whole lot to the girl. He had made it up with his parents, but he remained living with Mrs Katadreuffe; from her place he would move into his own house, well and truly married, or else he wouldn't move. He supported his parents financially. He could not get down to educating himself : he could listen to what his friend had to tell him but he had no wish to climb with him. And Katadreuffe, on the one hand very ambitious and on the other humble, did not realize that he was more talented than Jan Maan, although the latter was indeed able to get more out of life.

The office world was an entirely different one; from there he had contact with the world of individuals. This was partly due to Rentenstein's lack of organization. On every available occasion they chatted, except for the two brothers who continued to work. The story of the seizure of the ship had aroused admiration for his father, and at the same time, envy. That was his nature : he was big in big things and small in small ones. He would never blame his mother for his bastardy; although it was his affair it was also hers, and hers in the first place, as she was the elder. Only once, during a walk, had he questioned her, when she had said she didn't want to marry Dreverhaven. He had then asked her whether it wasn't his business, but when she had remained silent he had never again touched on the matter.

After the story of the attachment he felt proud of his father, though he did not show it. He could hide his feelings well, but he felt proud, something of that kind might be expected from such a man. However, upstairs in his room, he had a pusillanimous feeling of jealousy for this man who had been so splendid whilst he was only just beginning, an insignificant typist. But it also awakened his ambition to emulate the man, to surpass him.

In the office, he came to see not only Stroomkoning but also the other lawyers. As at one time he had filled his mind from his library, continuing to do so now in the evenings from his lesson books, so he trained his eyes and ears to assimilate his whole environment. But he never forgot that the achievement of his aim lay in his work.

He felt a dislike for Rentenstein, which was not yet mutual. He quickly saw that Rentenstein was a man who liked to take the line of least resistance. The police-court practice was not particularly large, and what he did besides this and keeping the subsidiary cash account Rentenstein alone knew. Dreverhaven, who had long tête-à-têtes with Stroomkoning, had short ones with Rentenstein. He did not grasp what the two were whispering about : De Gankelaar had told him straight out that he did not like the intimacy between Dreverhaven and Rentenstein.

'An extraordinary fellow,' said De Gankelaar to Katadreuffe, referring to Dreverhaven, ' – but I would rather he wasn't our bailiff. He's a chap you have to watch out for. He probably wouldn't steal himself, but he seems the sort of person who would egg others on to do so. And Rentenstein, between ourselves, is spineless.'

Rentenstein, moreover, looked it. Circles under his eyes, which had something peculiar about them; thick, smooth, gleaming hair, though there was always dandruff on his collar; a handsome face with regular features, but the colouring too pink and effeminate; a slim figure, but with something girlish and soft about it. In addition, he was flirtatious with the female members of the staff.

Katadreuffe also felt a dislike for Miss Sibculo, a coquettish, flighty girl who could find time enough for love affairs. De Gankelaar had even asked himself whether engaging such an unusually handsome and charming young man, who left Rentenstein far behind, would not be a disturbing influence in the office. For De Gankelaar could not help feeling that the calm arrogance of his protégé, with his quiet politeness, would be more to the taste of the girls than the affected mannerisms of the senior clerk. Miss Sibculo had, in fact, immediately and openly lost her heart to Katadreuffe, but after a few months his reserve had cooled her off. And there it remained. For the other two girls he presented no danger. Miss Te George, herself calm and correct, his elder by a few years, was moreover not a person to indulge in office flirtations : the husky girl, Van den Born, was completely preoccupied with herself. The main point was : Katadreuffe was not looking for love, flirting or fun. If at first they found this attractive, it would end by repelling them.

He never let them see what worried him. But because of her falling in love, he disliked Miss Sibculo all the more. He was chaste by nature and the posturings of the plump little figure with too short a neck were almost physically abhorrent. When he saw the little white fingers tapping her curls, he looked in the other direction. She worked for two of the lawyers and could never manage it all, but yet found time for arch looks and graceful poses. Her eyes were certainly nice, but she made too much use of them. At quiet moments she would give a deep, melancholy sigh. When she laughed her face was full of dimples and, none the less, far from pretty. She was really just a little nonentity who could only type neatly and quickly. On the face of it, one would have expected her to be all over Rentenstein, but viewed more closely, the latter seemed to be merely what La Fontaine describes as '*un homme qui s'aimait sans avoir de rivaux*'.

In spite of his natural coolness, Katadreuffe felt a real liking for De Gankelaar, the man who claimed to have 'discovered' him and who was busy continuing to discover him. De Gankelaar had one great fault for which Katadreuffe, in spite of his own industry, made excuses because he was De Gankelaar : he was definitely lazy. Of them all he did by far the least; not that he worked slowly but in spasms, between times smoking his pipe, dreaming, or holding forth to Katadreuffe. He was the most thoroughly educated of all the colleagues, with the possible exception of Miss Kalvelage. He had a philosophical trait in his character; his musings were often tinged with melancholy, and this he drove away with his sport. He earned least of them all but he didn't care; he appeared to have private means as he went in for expensive games. Miss Kalvelage, the latest legal addition to the office, earned a higher salary than his, as Stroomkoning knew quite well what his colleagues were worth : he did not often pass comments, but he paid according to deserts. He really ought to have given De Gankelaar a hint to take himself off but, out of vanity, he was glad to keep him attached to the office. De Gankelaar was of an aristocratic family; his father a *jonkheer*[1] from the Hague. However, he would never use his title.

Katadreuffe had often less to do for De Gankelaar than he would have liked, but from the latter's unbosomings he picked up a thing or two.

De Gankelaar liked to display his inertia. He used to lie back in his chair with his feet on top of the desk; yet his attitude was never really unseemly, always away from Katadreuffe, and having a certain athletic grace. And he could comment gracefully on his laziness.

'When I lie like this with my legs crossed, then I can

[1] The lowest order of Dutch nobility.

sometimes spend an hour wondering whether I should leave them so or vary it by changing them over.'

'On Sundays I don't work, obviously, but I get no satisfaction out of that. It is only nice to be lazy when others have to work. That's why I'm lazy on weekdays, particularly on weekdays.'

He aired his views frankly on every subject to Katadreuffe. He spoke out openly about the staff, his colleagues, his chief; he cared little how another would take this. He was also frank about himself. He said :

'What does it matter if I am risking my position here? Without this job I shan't starve. No, if your living depends on it and yet you play cat and mouse with it – assuming you're the mouse – that's another matter; that's meritorious. But what am I doing here with my dilletantism?'

Katadreuffe thought for a moment; he more or less understood. He answered :

'You aren't, I believe, really suited to this work.'

They knew each other too well for De Gankelaar to take offence. He said :

'Thank God for that. Being a lawyer means action and reaction, big talk about everything, and yet close as a clam. But I was born with only one interest – people.'

Keeping his legs on the table, he filled a fresh pipe; it was to be a lengthy dissertation.

'And just remember, Katadreuffe, that I fully realize I have dedicated myself to a study that will never end, full of blanks with enormous question-marks. What is a human being? I don't know, but the fellow interests me. Not you or I, but that mug, Man. What does that mean? When I look at you or Stroomkoning or myself or Miss Kalvelage, there are four objects called human beings in our language. But why, why, in Heaven's name? I see four objects that have nothing, nothing in common. I see in each one a thousand facets and, each facet being different, I see four thousand differences. Sometimes my brain just won't take it in – a : that we never see people but only facets of them, b : that every facet is different, c : that we still hang on to a standard conception – Man . . . Now don't tell me that Man is a rational creature – I understand that still less – and then, moreover, you are at once faced with four different meanings of reason . . . Have you ever heard of Diogenes who came by day to the crowded market with a lighted lantern to look for Man?'

Katadreuffe knew the story.

'That fellow,' said De Gankelaar, at last changing over his legs on top of the desk, ' – that fellow, according to my layman's opinion, was one of the very greatest philosophers. Not so much because he is the father of cynicism, although I must admit that makes him attractive to me, but for his truths in a nutshell, particularly for his words : I am seeking Man. For, Katadreuffe, it isn't right to dismiss that saying as a piece of effrontery. That fellow thought much further and more deeply. He was looking for Man : he knew well enough *where* he must look, if there was such a thing – but he didn't know exactly *what* to look for. His only hope of discovering it was with the lamp of his knowledge.'

Observations like this enlarged Katadreuffe's mind, but they did not deflect him from his aim. Whenever he had been working hard and could not sleep, he used to reflect on what had been said.

Yes, what exactly was a man? You only had to look at this office to fail to find an answer. With the exception of the two brothers the differences were enormous, and more so amongst the lawyers than amongst the staff.

Katadreuffe could then understand that they rightly spoke of the grey masses; that the individual really only began in the privileged classes. To them was given the opportunity to expand, and they all grew in one and the same direction. He saw the formidable significance of deep knowledge. Deep knowledge meant expanding enormously, showing a thousand facets.

Katadreuffe, himself, was still a character in formation. He had undergone a late growth after adolescence. He had some striking qualities and talents but he was far short of being a complete character. Without realizing it, his personality was less formed than that of Jan Maan, but he gave greater promise. A child of the people, but with possibilities, with considerable knowledge, though haphazardly assimilated, too variegated and often out of date. A hodge-podge which, with iron determination, was trying to form a whole.

One of his virtues was the will to learn wherever he could, but never to accept things uncritically. It was true; no two people were alike. Take Dr Gideon Piaat, the quick-witted pleader in criminal cases, who so often raised a laugh in the court-room; a short fellow with a large head, a child's face with spectacles, restless, often exuberant in his gestures. How different from his room-mate, the dry-as-dust Carlion. And he had a weak heart: once he had fainted. He had a simple nature but he was so fond of his Christian name that he had to use it in full, all the time, everywhere. And the female Doctor of Laws, Miss Kalvelage, who sat in a small room on the first floor, just below De Gankelaar's office. A sharp little rapier, that one. Still young, in no way feminine, hardly any figure, a skeleton crowned with a skull; thick, dark hair, cropped short, which had already begun to go grey. A slight frame, almost charming in her round spectacles, when the eyes of changing amber grew so big; a highly aggressive little creature who pleaded with a harsh voice and a tongue like a lancet.

And yet, thought Katadreuffe, what De Gankelaar says sounds all very well and is no doubt true, but not only in the case of human beings. When I talk of a table I mean something different than when 'she' talks of a table. When you think of it, all people talk at cross-purposes. And in this way he began to think for himself and to discriminate.

He turned on his side to go to sleep. He now had a divan-bed; the dismal cupboard-bed was no longer in use.

The First Year

Things had not been going so well of late with his mother, but he did not realize this and she did not mention it. The tubercular tendency which her lungs had so far resisted began to gain ground in her frail body, but that could go on for many, many years. At the same time, it was impossible for her to cut down her handwork; on the contrary, times were no longer so favourable and, in spite of working harder, her earnings were less than shortly after the war. Also, the shop was no longer so completely satisfied with her and she, herself, could see the justice of this. Her originality was gradually wearing thin; she began to repeat herself, noticeably. She still chose pretty colours, but the special combinations recurred too often to be striking. Her subjects were becoming exhausted, as although you could draw anything you could not work everything in wool. A divan-cover in black and yellow diamonds, starting large and diminishing in size, was certainly a nice piece of work for a modern sun-parlour. But one must not ask how long she had had to work on it whilst, at the same time, doing other pieces and her housework. But in the end she didn't really like it and the price she received for it seemed rather low in relation to the number of working hours and, on the other hand, too high for the final result. Secretly, she regretted having been deprived for so many years of that strange green. She had a vague notion that if she could find it again her inspiration would return, and every now and then she searched the markets. She once saw in a shop-window hanks of wool that appeared similar, but when she examined them at home, without the decay, the fading, the discoloration, there was no similarity at all. She put the wool in a tub with some salt, but the only result was that the wool shrank. No, she had had to pay dearly for that lot.

The only visits Katadreuffe made were to her and Jan Maan. But he was too hard at work; the Sunday afternoon walks he more or less gave up. Their relationship was better now; she had lost the restlessness she had had when he was at home, wishing, without saying it, to rouse her son to get on, get on, hurry up; as she, too, had had to do. It had been something indeterminate in her; an irritation at seeing the big lad reading and not getting anywhere; great expectations for that exceptional lad whom she, a girl of good stock, had brought into the world, who had for his father a fellow like none other in Rotterdam; expectations which threatened to become illusions. It was only a vague feeling she had, and yet it exasperated her when the boy didn't fly off up into the sky on wings which had suddenly sprouted from his shoulders. During the silent hours of work she often thought of this : she had these indeterminate fantasies, that she could not put into words; moreover, should she say anything, the brightness of the vision would be lost. It had sharpened their relationship, in an atmosphere laden with the everlasting, silent irritability, until the boy had felt his departure as a liberation. Not the Hague adventure, which was reckless nonsense – fortunately now a thing of the past – no, this other business. She had at last cut herself off from him, as it should be; renunciation lay in a mother's nature. To try and hold on to your child, that was a despicable softheartedness indulged in by ladies : a woman of the people kicked her son into the street. Kicked? – well, it wasn't far from it. But the child, naturally must be old enough.

For the time being she was satisfied. She did not know exactly what his plans were; he wouldn't be quick to wave them in front of her, she realized. And he didn't get that from any stranger; she, herself, was as close as an oyster. But she felt he was on the right road. He hadn't exactly *flown* up to the present, but she wouldn't ask the impossible; that flying had merely been the dream of too proud a mother. But *get on*, that he would certainly do – she felt it. She also noticed that he had changed. That office work could not take up so much of his time; he must be working on his own. She noticed he was paler, his body not so well-covered as formerly, though the light in his eyes was stronger and steadier.

And so she was satisfied, as although in many respects things were not so good, she still had Jan Maan. She desired just as strongly to keep Jan Maan as to lose her son. It was not only the money Jan Maan brought in; she liked him. Whatever tenderness she possessed – and it was not much – she expended on him. There was no trace of sexual attraction in her feelings for Jan Maan – that would be madness; the birth of her child had killed all that in her – but she was favourably disposed towards him, like a woman can be towards a man where no love exists; with a sublimated motherliness. She would never deter him from marriage – she was too generous for that. Though she could see he was a boy who would kiss a lot of girls and yet was unlikely to marry. His butterfly nature charmed her, yet it was the very thing she would have censured most sharply in her son. That he had on more than one occasion got together the foundations of a household and then broken it off, leaving everything to the girl, touched her heart. Now, he was probably without a girl; at least, every Sunday he walked faithfully with her to the Maas, the Oude Plantage, or the 'Hill' in the Park. So it should remain. She hoped she would never have her son at home again, but Jan Maan did not get his cubicle, neither did she use it to sleep in; she kept it free for her son.

However, the following summer, she refused to trespass on Jan Maan's time and so deprive him of his free day in the sun and sea at the Hook of Holland. The first few times he came home red as a lobster; his white skin burned so easily and gave him a lot of pain.

If he could get Katadreuffe to go with him, he did not go to the Hook. Once or twice he was successful in enticing his friend away from his work. He made a little canvas tent, and with this tied to his bicycle, he came in the early morning to call for Katadreuffe at the Boompjes. Then they walked together across the big Maas bridges, and it was not until they had reached the south bank that the modest and correct Katadreuffe dared to sit on the back, with Jan Maan toiling along until they changed places. It was quite a way to the extreme southerly point of the Waal-haven. In that out-of-the-way corner, adjoining the aero-drome, where no ships came, the current had formed a small beach.

There, Rotterdammers who did not go to the Hook, lay stretched out. They set up their tent; they stayed there the whole day on the hard, rough river sand, clammy with clay. They lay in the brackish water, or between the tents in the sun, amidst the scratchings of dreadfully worn gramo-phone records. Jan Maan liked to swim a good way out. Katadreuffe merely splashed about close in. He could just manage to swim but not for long; he liked to dry again quickly in the breeze. Here he felt at ease, amongst the people, his people; he belonged to them and it was not in his nature to deny it. There was seldom anything to bother him. The character of the Dutch workman is modest; nine keep themselves decent; only the tenth is vulgarly noisy, but he does not hold out long against the nine. Katadreuffe brought books with him and worked a little in the tent, but mostly lay, stretched out on his back, looking up at the sky, his Sunday handkerchief folded underneath his head. Although the girls noticed him, he paid little attention to them, unlike Jan Maan; he just lay there, his feet at the extreme point of South Rotterdam, that maze of docks, this Waalhaven being the most regal of them all, like an inland sea under the immensity of its own firmament.

Once they brought back lice from the camp, but 'she' immediately produced an efficacious remedy. Some petrol – dip your head in the petrol – then a couple of cloths round it and to bed. The following day, wash once or twice with soft soap, and they've gone. And so it was.

Once, on the beach, Katadreuffe let himself go, and told his friend of his plans. They were lying amongst the people; a strange small child had just made a sand-pie over Jan Maan's big toe; but they lay here as safely as if between four walls; no one paid any attention to their conversation. Katadreuffe on his stomach, the other on his back, their heads close together – thus the story was told. He was studying for his matriculation.

He was a systematic worker; he did not aim too high at once. He had, first of all, aimed at cutting a reasonable figure as a typist. And although there were certainly others who could produce better, particularly quicker work than he, his considerable ability was evident from the short time he had been learning. Taking dictation in foreign languages was still something for the future. That would right itself; he would have sufficient command of the languages when he was ripe for the exam.

Then, he had improved and increased knowledge of his own language. That had also gone quickly. Now he was improving his handwriting. It might be an ugly hand but it would be *cursive*, not the clumsy, childish writing of the people, but a writing from which one would at once recognize the educated man. He had, at last, a proper signature, his name without a break, simple, business-like.

As regards pronunciation, he was favoured from home. His mother, although sometimes coarse in her speech, spoke without any local accent. And so he had learnt to speak, and the ugly Rotterdam dialect of many school-children, even of some teachers, particularly in the court, had never got a hold on him. Once when he came home cockily using the common accent, his mother quickly smacked it out of him. And he explained to Jan Maan how extremely important for his career a pure, or at least a reasonably good accent was, thinking how his friend might easily improve himself on this point. And he said it so earnestly and with such good intention that his friend, who had something (not very much) of the Rotterdam accent and had only just now realized it, smilingly promised improvement although, in his easy-going way, he had no intention of doing anything about it.

Then there was another delicate terrain, that of the foreign words often used in the office. Latin terms and that sort of thing. You must particularly watch out for the right accentuation. It was different in *totaliter* than in *hectoliter*, different in *res nullius* than *luce clarius*; and then you had the Dutch *reus*[1] and the Latin *reus*. He was now busy on that; he had a book of foreign words and as they came up he ticked them off.

This was all partly in preparation for his actual job, partly those secondary marks of culture, without which you could not speak of a properly educated man.

He did not talk much about his studies in the narrower sense; that would probably be above the understanding, and certainly beyond the interest of Jan Maan. He told how he had bought a radio on hire-purchase. He wasn't interested in a note of music; only what there was to learn: the fundamentals of foreign languages were what he was now specially following – it was a magnificent invention. He also took correspondence courses, and in the winter he was going to evening classes at the People's University. And he was looking for an institute which gave correspondence courses for the matriculation.

When Jan Maan asked him what use all this was going to be, Katadreuffe said simply :

[1] Giant.

'Lawyer.'

Jan Maan felt he ought to sit up but he was, after all, too comfortable lying down. He merely opened his eyes wide, and then shut them quickly on account of the dazzling sky.

Katadreuffe went on to say that these studies ought not to cost too much, at least not for the moment. And, on De Gankelaar's recommendation, he had had a rise. He was now earning eighty-five guilders a month, almost as much as four times Jan Maan's weekly wage. But no one must for the time being know about these plans, 'she' in particular.

It was still summer when one evening he paid her a visit. He found her alone; Jan Maan had gone out on his cycle. He was glad of that. He sat down opposite her and laid fifteen guilders in the middle of the table-cloth. He said nothing; she just looked up and then again down at her work. She also remained silent. He played with his teaspoon, beginning to feel angry at her silence.

Then she opened her mouth.

'I would never take anything from your father, not marriage, not a penny.'

That was her way of accepting, and in her acceptance her thanks lay hidden. He felt that, and his anger subsided. When all was said and done, he was of the same mould. Talking was difficult and thanking doubly so. He had put the money on the table without speaking either. It still lay there.

'That's the first time,' he said.

He meant that in future she could reckon on it every month. She nodded.

Then, a little later, she again spoke.

'You've got a good head, Jacob; you can be grateful to God for that.'

In this manner she let him know that she understood he was studying in order to make progress, and he grasped it. But he did not understand that 'God'. Was she religious?

He had never noticed it, although she was from a Protestant family. Perhaps now that she was growing older . . . De Gankelaar had said that religion was actually a complaint of old age; it might be that.

He did not mention his plans. They sat for a while, saying a word now and then. They did not need to talk much; with a single word they understood one another. That was really their tragedy. They knew each other too well, had too much in common. They did not complement one another; they got on each other's nerves.

The question whether she could be religiously inclined had aroused his curiosity, but he would die rather than ask her. He looked at her; for years now she had been as white as a dove. Recently she had been wearing glasses when she did her handwork. Also she coughed a lot. Her colour was not pallid, but faded yellow. Her cheekbones shone as if polished by time. Something like ivory.

'You ought to rest a bit more, Mother.'

'I'll be all right.'

He did not know that her earnings had shrunk; she would never tell him; she would rather die.

He had another cup of tea and, after an hour, went back to his room, his work. The money still lay exactly where he had put it.

Outside, he again became angry with her. Why, as she now understood he had plans, didn't she ask about them? Twice during the winter she had been at his place and had never asked what he did with his spare time. He had never met anyone so pig-headed. But he would support her, with fifteen guilders a month for the time being.

He did it once.

Dreverhaven

The network of little alleys and streets east of the Nieuwe Markt is for the most part very gloomy. But one of them, too narrow for vehicles, is full of small shops, crowded with pedestrians, gay and lively. In this little street, the Korte Pannekoekstraat, were two shops almost opposite one another, which for more than a year had particularly attracted public attention. They both sold the same cheap, smart rubbish, mainly lamp-shades; their window-displays were remarkably similar, but the prices in the one shop were considerably higher than in the other. The dearer shop had the pretentious title: *Au petit Gaspillage* – the other was simply called The Competitor.

For more than a year a competitive war had been waged between the two shops, with provocative notices behind the windows, in which the one referred to their higher price as a proof of their greater reliability and the other to greater reliability in spite of lower prices. Sometimes the printed or written invective was of such a nature that the police had it removed. The dear shop and the cheap one, turn and turn about, copied each other's window-displays. But there was no question of any law-suit between them: both shops belonged to Dreverhaven.

The cheap shop was not actually so very cheap; it merely appeared so in contrast with the other. There was no real war; this battle was merely a form of advertisement. The cheap shop attracted a lot of people, the dear one naturally less, though now and then they had a customer who really thought he was buying more reliable goods here. The cheap one made a profit; the dear one a loss. Up till now the profit had been greater than the loss, but did not in the least justify the queer, complicated, risky set-up. Nobody else would have thought of starting anything of the kind, but Dreverhaven was just the man to find a deep, secret pleasure in it. For him it was more a question of the game than of profit. Yet the latter was by no means a negligible factor. Before long he would do away with the dear shop – the performance had lasted long enough – and the cheap one had presumably established itself sufficiently. Later on he would also get rid of that. In the meantime, he had had the fun of fighting himself.

His interest lay mostly in enterprises which had nothing to do with his actual profession; thus he lent money on very onerous terms. During the war he had, together with Stroomkoning, gone in for transactions in merchandise. He was the man who gave the tips, and Stroomkoning had great confidence in him and followed him. They had made a lot out of sugar but lost it all again, and more, on molasses. The worst knock they had had was in vegetable conserving when – as they called it – peace broke out, though before that they had made a packet in the same line. When Dreverhaven drew up the balance of his speculations, he did not seem to have advanced a step. Also the money-lending produced no profit; it had to pass through so many hands in order not to compromise him and risk losing his office, that the administration together with the bad debts ate up the profit. Nevertheless, many people and the whole of Stroomkoning's office knew of his money-lending activities.

When Dreverhaven drew up the balance of his last year, losses came to mind that made his heart bleed, but he had the soul of a speculator; he could not stop gambling. He was, at one and the same time, extremely avaricious and extremely reckless. It cost him an effort to undress. Whenever he could, he kept on his hat and his overcoat, as he had the spirit of a miser who feels that if he takes his clothes off he is robbing himself. There were times when he drank heavily and ran after women. But he never went on the spree in Rotterdam; for that he went to Brussels, where he would drive round with a taxi full of women; vulgar, caddish, repulsive. He was generous towards the women; he would get through a heap of money and then kick up a terrific row over a few extra pence for the cloak-room in a café-chantant.

He was bailiff for the police-court. Twice a week he stripped off his outer garments, and what he would not do before God he did here; he bared his head, for here reigned the Law. And in an indistinct, growling voice he called the roll in the small court-room for civil affairs, crowded with those summoned, and where the rascally 'proxies'[1] had hurriedly occupied the best seats. He stood behind his own desk, the orange ribbon with the silver badge bearing the coat-of-arms of the Kingdom around his neck like some high order; the names of the various parties came in a slip-shod boom from his mouth, and many of the inexperienced thought he must be at least the Public Prosecutor.

He always got there earlier than necessary, arriving an hour before the session. Then he stood in his overcoat at the top of the steps, looking down on the stream of people who, with various objectives, were slowly mounting them. He directed the people to the various waiting-rooms.

'What are you? Probate?'

'No, sir, I've received a summonings.'

'You must say summons, and you must say you have been summoned. That door!'

Men of all colours, twisting their caps in hands tattooed blue with anchors, with the smell of tar and of the sea

[1] Shady individuals, representing interests in police-court cases, sometimes self-appointed.

clinging to their clothing, often with the encrusted swellings of syphilis on their lips, came climbing up. These were the men for the shipping enquiries and were always accompanied by a solicitor's or a notary's clerk with the papers, and with an interpreter. Dreverhaven did not look at them; the clerks knew the way.

The 'proxies' stood in groups, swinging mangy brief-cases from which, at the session, they would dig out their memoranda, often grubby papers, full of the grossest spelling mistakes – kitchen-maid's stuff – and teeming with bewildering quibbles. Towards Dreverhaven they were deferentially confidential.

Sometimes someone would come and whisper intimately in his ear.

'That door!' he would bark.

For the atmosphere of the law-courts sometimes worked on newcomers like a laxative.

One of the judges came along, his gown fluttering all around him. Everyone made way, and behind him his court-clerk fluttered in precisely the same way. The judge tapped the bailiff on the shoulder.

'Are there many extra-judicial cases this morning before the session, Mr Dreverhaven?'

The latter turned about.

'Yes, sir, three ship's declarations, and there are already six for Probate. But first of all, Notary Noorwits wants to speak to you about a deed of separation. I let him into the court.'

At half past nine began the work which had to be heard *in camera*, the shipping declarations and so forth. And when that was finished the bell rang shrilly. Dreverhaven threw wide open the doors of the court-room and his voice reverberated through the whole staircase:

'The court is open.'

The rascally 'proxies' were already in the best seats, where they formed a leprous background to the distribution of justice. Behind them was packed an extremely shabby, fusty, and evil-smelling bunch of people, who had come to hear judgements against them for the payment of debts, compensation for damages, eviction from homes.

There was indeed one man amongst them who came seeking his own rights. Very rarely, though, did one hear anyone challenge the judge with an 'I stand by my rights'. On the other hand, at every session, the judge heard from the mouths of those summoned : 'It's not lack of goodwill, sir, but inability.' For with debtors no formula is more popular than this, and yet each one thinks he has discovered it afresh.

Twice a week Dreverhaven was thus on duty for the whole morning sometimes for part of the afternoon. What had to be done on other days fell to the lot of his colleagues. The rest of the time he spent in his office or he walked about the town, his inside pockets filled with long envelopes, serving summons, seizing goods, arresting for debt. Often he was followed by his two witnesses, his dry clerk, Hamerslag, and the unpleasant creature, Den Hieperboree. Whoever met him in the street on duty did not forget him easily, as he came along with all his coats open – whatever the weather – and two rows of official envelopes, in battle-order, sticking out of his formidable chest; and the picture became one of absolute terror when in his wake they saw the giant rolling along, with his spineless neck, his huge wobbling head, and his mouth which at the sight of his prey could open, open, open. Like a crane with a steel cable and a hanging grab – thus he might appear to a fantasy strongly stimulated by fear. Dreverhaven had noticed this, and had given him a nickname; he never called him anything but Coal-grab.

This Coal-grab was phenomenal in clearing out families with small children. As he only had to roll his head over the small-fry and open his jaws and they would dash away from him; he then lurched slowly after them and drove them, shrieking, into the street. And the mothers he got in the same fashion. Many a woman, already in a state of nerves, rushed sobbing and screeching into safety outside, away from the dreadful Coal-grab.

But he had no real strength; he was all show; also he was particularly stupid and, by nature, gentle. The rough stuff was left to the tough Hamerslag. And should there be opposition – rare and invariably from the men – Dreverhaven came into action. He was so heavy and strong; he just picked them up by the collar and pushed them with a couple of kicks out of the house. And if they weren't terribly quick in saving their things, Hamerslag – a man with the muscles of a cart-horse – chucked everything into the street in armfuls, into the rain and mud.

And it was Dreverhaven's pride that he never needed help from the police in executing a sentence. Every door gave way at his ring, the hammer of his fist, his booming voice through window or letter-box. Once only had it been necessary, in a house full of communists, a house hastily turned into a fortress. With the help of two policemen he also captured that fort in which twelve rebels had entrenched themselves. And he was the first to step, axe in hand, over the ruins of the front-door and the shattered cross-beams.

The time was long past when he had had his office on one of the docks. He still retained his auction room on the Hooimarkt; he still lived in the same house in the Schietbaanlaan where Joba had left him. But his office had been moved over ten years ago to the Lange Baanstraat, in the heart of the very poorest part of the old town. There he felt at home.

In later years he was mastered by a weariness of life, as far as one can say he had a master. But here he showed a certain greatness. For weariness of life manifests itself in weak natures by melancholy. In strong ones, by indifference. As with him.

The older he became, the more reckless. He invited attacks on his own person and restrained them by his indifference. Here he sat in the very heart of poverty, he, the executioner of the poor. He knew that they would never dare to attack him from the front. But a knife in his back, that was something he considered possible, yet without taking any precautions. He *felt it* coming. He did not know whether he desired it or not, but in any event, it left him completely indifferent.

The older he became, the more restless. He only took a cab from utter necessity. He walked to the police-court, the Hooimarkt, his house, his office, walked all over North Rotterdam and South Rotterdam. The shoe-shops earned more from him than the clothiers. Sometimes in the evening, he felt the need to go to his auction room. It lay behind a row of houses, a hall with a glass cupola and a rostrum for the auctioneer. He would switch on a couple of lights and wander aimlessly past the shimmer of vastly assorted articles, mostly cheap and trashy, which stood neatly arranged, with aisles between them.

At home he only ate and slept; in the evenings he was generally in his office. He kept no regular hours; if he were there, he would always see anyone. Sometimes they rang him up, but whether anybody came or not he was always there. At times he fell asleep, but only half asleep; like a beast of prey, he never lost contact with his surroundings.

The house was quite unique for Rotterdam, which was the reason it had appealed to him. In him it had found its first real proprietor, a worthy occupier. Except for the floor where he had his office, he had let it all off, below and above, up to the attics. It swarmed with tenants, all deadly poor, some of them fantastic and some shy of the daylight. But it had been built for *him*; it formed a block of brick around him; without him it had no soul. The neighbourhood spoke of Mr Dreverhaven's house just as tourists talk of the pyramid of Cheops.

That evening he was sitting at his desk, coat and hat on. He had, in his mind, been striking a balance of his undertakings and it did not come out right. He had had a lot of money. He had taken knocks, but the question was :

had he still got money or was he really poor? He didn't
know. His affairs were all mixed up. The one good thing
he still had was his versatility. But the number of writs had,
in recent years, considerably diminished. To be sure, he still
had his coal auctions from which he earned a good deal.
But lately everything had been going wrong. He could, of
course, suddenly find himself on top again, but times were
bad. Every year he had a row with the tax authorities.
Looked at fair and square, he hadn't a penny; if he valued
his assets correctly he was a minus quantity. He had only
his sources of income still, uncertain, irregular. That little
shop, *Au petit Gaspillage* – a name he had picked up in
Brussels though here it had no magnetic value – he would
now get rid of. The losses hurt his miser's heart, but they
did not prevent him sleeping, behind his desk, filling the
broad desk-chair, both eyes closed and his mind's eye open.

There had been a short ring at the bell; he had heard
it, keeping his eyes closed. A light step approached through
the rooms : that knife ! he thought. The noise ceased; it
was so quiet that he could hear the breathing of another.
He kept his eyes closed. Then he opened them and looked,
without surprise, into the eyes of his son.

His bearing did not change.

'And?' he asked.

The first word between father and son. A word without
meaning, very ordinary. And yet also *not* an ordinary word;
a word that defined a relationship in its finest nuances, that
was heavily loaded with history, that was uttered in the
voice of a Caesar.

Katadreuffe and Dreverhaven

It was early one morning towards the end of August.

Katadreuffe had been working for an hour in his room. He went downstairs and found the letter-box full of mail. As always, he laid the mail on Miss Te George's small table for she opened all letters, keeping her own correspondence, the rest being distributed later by Rentenstein. It was still holiday time; some of the gentlemen were on leave, but Stroomkoning was already back, also she and De Gankelaar.

As usual, he glanced through the addresses. There was sometimes something for the concierge, Graanoogst, and also often the corrected work from the courses he was taking, and fresh exercises. This time there was only one letter for him, from the district court.

He felt a sudden premonition; he could almost guess what it contained before he opened it. And yet, on reading it, he was completely dumbfounded.

They were applying for his bankruptcy. He was summoned to appear in court on the following Wednesday morning, the People's Credit Company through Dr Schuwagt having applied for his bankruptcy. That left him five days.

He dragged himself upstairs, his face ashen-grey, to De Gankelaar's room. There he concentrated his whole atten-

tion on the text of the bankruptcy law. He could already
find his way about well enough to know where to look.

And he found a clause which read : If after annulment,
a new application for bankruptcy be made, the applicant
is obliged to prove that sufficient means are available to
cover the costs of the bankruptcy.

He read the clause three times, and by then the meaning
had sunk in. He had, with inexplicable, absurd shortsighted-
ness never given further thought to his debts. He had
reasoned like any ignoramus would do : bankruptcy cancelled, then the debts were washed out. Now he realized it
was otherwise; that the debts remained until he had paid
to the last penny. And what made him mad was that he
ought to have known this, that it was only logical that a
debtor could not get rid of his debts by just going bankrupt, that there was only one way to be free of debts : to
pay them.

Ashen-grey, though completely calm and lucid, he re-
viewed the situation. He remembered the words of De
Gankelaar when he was his trustee : you can't pursue a
bankruptcy on fifteen guilders. That had been his position
then. Now he had a regular income, eighty-five guilders
a month. A bankruptcy court could pursue that. The matter
had now become serious. The everlasting shame ! How had
he been able to remain so indifferent about it? His daily
contact with the law now made clear to him what a
bankruptcy meant, for his studies, for his name, for his
future.

He stuck the letter in his pocket. He did not go to break-
fast, but he was already in sufficient self-control for no one
to notice anything when he entered the office. He sat on
tenterhooks, awaiting De Gankelaar's arrival, as he *had* to
tell someone, and it would have to be De Gankelaar. But
that morning the latter happened to be late – no doubt he
had gone rowing or swimming – and did not come until
around eleven; it was still the off-season.

Katadreuffe could not find an opportunity to speak to

him at once, but about noon he was able to show him the letter. De Gankelaar took it seriously.

'That's confoundedly stupid, not having given it a thought. I must admit I had forgotten all about it. Bring me the file; I can't remember it all.'

Katadreuffe quickly left the office. A blush had risen to his forehead; the small file was in his own room. He had hoped it would remain buried there for ever. Now he must bring the cursed papers out into the open again.

De Gankelaar looked through the file. His look remained grave.

'Not a penny paid off yet? . . . No? . . . That's a pity, that's a pity . . . The People's Credit Company, three hundred guilders plus so much commission and now naturally an extra year's interest at ten per cent in addition, not forgetting the costs. Then your landlord, I see, two months' rent; thirty guilders borrowed from a certain Jan Maan . . . Why, man, you've so many debts, I must say I fear the worst . . . Schuwagt's a difficult man to deal with; that blackguard should have been sent about his business long ago, but he's too smart for them. At least once a month he's had up before the Dean, but he's too slick for the whole Supervisory Board. In fact, the lowest of the low. But that doesn't help you. They won't accept payment by instalments – that ruffian will want his pound of flesh. And now you're in another position; there can't be any talk of annulment for lack of means. They'll just pick up your salary or at least part of it.'

'I realize that, sir,' Katadreuffe said.

'Yes,' De Gankelaar hesitated, 'we might perhaps between ourselves here . . .'

'No, sir, there can be no question of that; I won't have that. Thank you, all the same, but I won't borrow, not from you, not from anybody. But I thank you.'

Unwittingly, he had spoken like his mother when, in the maternity ward, she had refused the help of others. His answer pleased De Gankelaar. Although inclined to be

cautious in his dealings with his fellows – a good-natured
young man, ready to help, but with an eye on the pennies
– he had just now been ready to lend his typist the necessary
money and was glad, after all, that this had been refused.
He did not suspect that Katadreuffe, apart from his pride
which made him refuse any present, needed, by his refusal,
to castigate himself for his lack of comprehension. He went
on :

'Then it's a hopeless case. Even if Schuwagt would personally be willing to come to some arrangement – though
that's out of the question – Dreverhaven certainly wouldn't.'

'Dreverhaven?' Katadreuffe asked. 'What's he got to do
with it?'

De Gankelaar leant over with a look of surprise.

'Dreverhaven? Don't you know that the People's Credit
Company is Dreverhaven? Don't *you* know it when the
whole office knows it? . . . Good God, boy, half the town
knows it.'

Katadreuffe had borrowed money from his father. The
father was now busy making his son a bankrupt, for the
second time.

'Will you excuse me, sir. May I go?'

He had left the room before the answer came. No doubt
a tummy upset, thought De Gankelaar, feeling a slight dis-
appointment, a little contempt for his protégé. But the latter
was soon back. He had gulped down a glass of water, taken
two puffs at a cigarette – he who seldom smoked – and
come calmly back to De Gankelaar, pencil and note-book
in hand. He pocketed the letter from the court, which still
lay on De Gankelaar's desk. He said :

'I shall have to see how I can deal with it.'

The lawyer liked that, too.

'I shan't fail to do what I can to keep you here.'

'Thank you. I only hope you will be my trustee when it
gets so far.'

And now he smiled, that rare attractive smile of his. De
Gankelaar also smiled, but he answered cautiously :

'I doubt that. The chance isn't great. And it would seem to me better not.'

But Katadreuffe already had a plan; he would go that evening to his father. He first had to find out where the street was on the map. This town-plan is its X-ray, and Katadreuffe found a sick spot between the Goudse Singel and the Kipstraat where it swarmed with alleys and cul-de-sacs. Dreverhaven's office was there.

That summer evening, he entered the Lange Baanstraat where it debouches on the Goudse Singel. The old street smelt of poverty. In the middle of the street, being led by a rope, was a cart-horse, one of those powerful products of the Ardennes; small head, belly like a barrel, tufts of hair round its huge hooves. He had done his day's work and, in the twilight striking sparks from the cobbles, he danced along very slowly behind his companion.

Then Katadreuffe saw his father's property. It stood at the corner of the Lange Baanstraat and Brede Straat. A house standing out like a barracks, a century old. The side wall, eight windows long, rose up over the Lange Baanstraat; in the front were five windows, and high up round the whole block of dark-brown brick was a massive cornice, supported on short joists; above that a double roof. Under the eighth window, the furthest from the corner, was the only entrance to the upper floors, a half-open door with a winding staircase behind it. By the door was a board : A. B. Dreverhaven, bailiff. The board was covered with scratches and streaks, but the large black letters on the white-painted wood were clearly legible. Dozens had vented their wrath on this board.

Katadreuffe did not go in at once. He stood at the corner and regarded the house from the front. It was not only canted on one side but leant forward, a considerable threat overhanging Brede Straat and Lange Baanstraat; its shadow on the pavement must be sinister. Just then a double door was opened and the horse from the Ardennes was led into its stall.

Katadreuffe stood surrounded by poverty. It was like old times in the court, but worse because he was no longer used to it. And indeed, this poverty enclosed in a district of tall buildings gave a still more dismal impression. At his back lay the small street, Vogelenzang, zig-zagging towards an invisible end; to the right the Korte Baanstraat, and further back a pitch-black paupers' alley with the dismal name of Waterhondsteeg. The house was densely populated. It was dark now; he could see lights everywhere and, curiously, many different kinds of light. In that house everything was used. In some rooms electric light shone, in others livid-looking gaslight; and he also saw swinging lamps with the friendly, out-of-date paraffin glow. The side-door in the Lange Baanstraat was the only one leading to the living quarters; the door stood half-open, the poorest of the poor passing in and out all the time.

Then Katadreuffe reflected how he was standing here just as many had had to stand who wanted to wheedle something out of the bailiff, and who hesitated on account of this building. And he turned back and went in through the door. The winding stair was of stone, worn by millions of feet. A small landing and the stairs went on like the steps in a church tower; one could not see the end. But on the landing was a door and beside it the same board as outside : A. B. Dreverhaven, bailiff. A heavy door of old wood, painted white; no bell, no door-handle, only a keyhole. But at a push the door yielded, and at the same time a bell, far off, rang for a second. He found himself now in a tall apartment, plastered white, with a floor of bare boards, a ceiling composed of small white beams, from which hung one solitary electric light bulb, high up, out of reach of the visitor. The room contained nothing else. But at the other end was a door like the first, without handle, with just a small window. This he also pushed open, and behind it was a second room which differed from the first only in the racks containing files, lining the walls. And here, too, was a single, paltry bulb, and a door on the other side leading to a third room, a door with a fair-sized pane of glass. In the centre, behind it, at a desk, his father.

The house seemed very quiet. The thickness of the old walls and floors damped the noise of the other inhabitants. Street noises scarcely penetrated the eight windows, five in front and three at the side, covered with double curtains, heavy and drab. But it was not this that struck him; the office itself was so quiet. He sensed at once this enormous difference from the bustle of his own office, although it was only later that he became conscious of the fact. His whole attention was fixed on the man sitting there. He had often seen him and never properly taken him in. He recognized the hat and the jacket better than the features. It was now as though he were looking through a magnifying glass, for amongst the shadows of the tall room the man sat in a fierce light. In one corner stood a cylindrical stove, as large as in a railway station waiting-room, never black-leaded, red with rust; here and there some vague pieces of office furniture, files, cash-books, a copying-press, a typewriter; but dominating it all the large flat-topped desk – once a fine piece – and the head and shoulders of the man in the fierce light. As sometimes in a dark corner of a museum a single light is thrown on a picture, as a jewel shines from under a shaded lamp in a shop-window, so his father's head and shoulders were lit up against the shadowy background of the room. For a green-shaded light shone straight down on him. He sat there as if inviting an attack on his person. Knife or bullet from some debtor driven to desperation could not fail to miss this target.

The son stood silently watching the older man. He saw the unwieldy head sunk on the chest. His hat-brim shaded his eyes, but they were closed and no steely shafts of light came shooting from them out of the darkness. The hanging cheeks were a grey stubble, as if he had not shaved for a day or two, a silvery growth over the lower part of his face; the sensual upper lip was covered in the same way with stubble, not a moustache. The hairy hands were folded over his stomach; the man might be asleep. He might equally be deep in prayer, or engaged in some devilish blasphemy.

The eyes opened, like stilettos.

'And?' asked the voice.

In the hypersensitiveness of his nervous state, Katadreuffe understood the word immediately. It bridged the hiatus in a conversation that had already been going on for a long time. This was no greeting to a stranger, to a son never yet spoken to. The most natural thing in the world, a conjunction which meant : here we are together still. One word, three letters – that was all.

Bewildered by this unexpected word – here, now, out of this mouth – the absurdity of it took the young man by surprise, threw him for a moment off balance. But he suddenly realized that the older man knew him, even before the voice continued :

'Jacob Willem, have you come to pay?'

He had thought that if he applied in person to his father all would be well. His one idea was that a father does not, after all, make his son a bankrupt. And now, all at once, he saw the opposite. Ridiculous, crazy, like an idiot, like a baby, he had imagined this man would allow himself to weaken. Every word was wasted here. For the father he was nothing but a debtor.

'What have you come here for? To pay? Wipe the slate clean? Principal, interest, and costs. "She" hasn't sent you, you don't need to tell me; that I understand damned well; that's nothing for "her".'

'She', 'her'. He also spoke thus of his mother. And it at once formed a bond; he felt, in spite of all, that man was his father; he couldn't reason it out, but perceived the blood-relationship in the voice. This man would always be his father; in his thoughts and words he would never be any other than his father; he had always been his father. Then all the anger in his blood welled up from the depths of his being. For the awe, the fear even, of a father has its limits. In extreme cases, the child either loves or hates.

'Pay? Pay?' he stuttered, livid.

His legs trembled; though he supported his hands on the top of the desk, his wrists trembled visibly, and his voice was no longer under control.

'Pay? . . . What you are doing to me is a crying shame, lending me money on sharper's terms, then making me bankrupt and then, just as I am starting to work for my future, again bankrupt . . . How, in God's name, is it possible for a father to treat his son like that! . . . They warned me about you. De Gankelaar said I'd be crazy to come, I wouldn't get anywhere. But De Gankelaar doesn't know you're my father . . . but you're a brute, even if you're a hundred times my father, or worse, just because you are.'

'Now listen,' said the older man impatiently, 'there's no question of father and son. If I had the President of the High Court in my clutches, his house, too, would go under the hammer. What do you imagine? That I'll make an exception for you? You're a debtor. If you don't pay you're no use to me.'

As if he were alone, he started to write a memorandum, with slow, heavy, gigantic writing, in pitch-black ink. That drove the other to utter frenzy.

'Brute, bully! You're nothing but a cad!' yelled Kata-dreuffe.

Then he went on shouting the first thing that came to his mind; about his mother, his bastardy, always coming back to his bankruptcy. Dreverhaven paid no attention.

'Can't you hear, you? Can't you hear?' he cried, his voice rising to a shriek.

Did the old man think he had gone too far? That he was going to attack him? He was rummaging in a drawer, his hands out of sight. There was a clink of steel; then he looked up and spoke, keeping his one hand hidden.

'Anyone else I would long ago have taken by the collar. As you are my son I don't want to do that, at least not yet. There is still one way to get clear of me. I will assess your debt with interest and costs at five hundred guilders;

that is about what it really amounts to. But now listen carefully. You called me a sharper. Well, I'll be one. You don't get a penny out of me unless you will sign an acknowledgement for eight hundred guilders, and the interest is twelve per cent, you understand? Twelve per cent. And you'll have to pay off four hundred guilders a year, you understand? Four hundred guilders a year.'

Then Katadreuffe grew calm and clear-headed. He could see himself as through a crystal; he was crystal-gazing at his own future.

'Oh!' he said truculently, 'so *that*'s what you have in mind. A clever move, I must say. Lend me more money so as to be able to strangle me better later. But I don't want your philanthropy; I've experienced enough of it, more than enough.'

The older man, as though he had not heard a word of contradiction, said :

'And of course you will have to give me a lien on your salary . . . And if you don't like my proposal, here you are !'

And, across the desk, he pushed towards the boy a large open clasp-knife. His eyes now suddenly shone with curiosity.

Katadreuffe mechanically picked it up; then suddenly realized what he was doing and, in a blind frenzy, thrust it with all his strength into the top of the desk.

'There ! You're a cad ! A cad !'

And like a madman he stormed out of the house.

With magisterial calm his father pulled the knife out of the wood. He could stand up to a stab; he was undamaged.

The Second Time

It was a long time before Katadreuffe could sleep. He regretted, not his words, but his gesture with the knife and, moreover, he was afraid of himself. He was by nature temperamental and impatient, though his mother's hard hand had early taught him self-control. He remembered how he had once kicked the boy from the court in the belly, without a thought, like lightning. It had been in self-defence, but it was base, intensely base. His mother had seen it and had not said anything, but all the same, she had thought of the consequences and had had to leave the court. But it had been cowardly; it had worried him for years.

And now this knife. A little madder, the stroke a yard further forward, and he would be on trial as a parricide. Provoked, true enough, but a murderer none the less. And he regretted it.

He was also ashamed of himself, as he found he had behaved ridiculously. Of a sudden, he understood the difference between anger and fury – anger impresses, fury compromises one.

But now at least he knew how he stood with his father. He would for ever keep out of his way. Borrow more money from him – let him bleed him? He'd be damned if he would. Rather go bankrupt, pay off the debt to the last penny, with all the extortionate interest and costs, and then be free for ever from the blood-sucker.

Tomorrow would come a fresh day, and with a great effort of will he forced himself to go to sleep.

But the following morning found him feeling very low, right from the moment he woke. Would he be able to keep his job? If Stroomkoning put him on the street he was lost beyond redemption. If not, then with difficulty he could recover, and only his studies would suffer until he had paid it all off.

De Gankelaar advised him to discuss it with the chief. He was a man of moods and at the moment not so interested; he couldn't go on protecting the boy for ever. But what he would not admit was that he did not like asking favours of Stroomkoning, not for himself nor for another. Recently there had been some friction between them. He had flatly refused to take on a case for which he saw no chance. You could only quibble and wangle, and that was against his nature. He was one to pronounce wild theories in badinage, but in his actions he was straightforward. Above all, he was correct in his behaviour – his father a *jonkheer,* his mother not an aristocrat, but of good English family – he came of a milieu where one behaved correctly. Actually, he had expected more from Stroomkoning's office. It was a good enough office, but not in the top class. There were some fine clients of whom you weren't ashamed, but also others, not so good. Stroomkoning was so keen on his practice that he found it hard to turn anyone away. From his early days he had hung on to a number of second-raters; that was where the colleagues came in . . . No, he would ask no favours; this time the boy would have to manage for himself.

As the day progressed Katadreuffe found his nerves getting more and more on edge. He hung around to see when his chief would be free, but he could not get hold of him. He did not dare go into the conference-room; he had still never been there.

At the same time, no one must notice anything wrong with him.

To make matters worse Mrs Stroomkoning came in the car to fetch her husband. It was around six o'clock when he heard the emphatic toot of the klaxon whilst she waited outside in the car. When Stroomkoning came rumbling along the marble corridor, he plucked up his courage and, at the front-door, asked if he could speak to him for a moment. Stroomkoning noticed that the young man's face was drawn and grey with misery. His first thought was: he's been pinching my money. He only remembered Katadreuffe vaguely; he had never spoken a word to him, but this was De Gankelaar's protégé and De Gankelaar was full of praise for him, he knew. And now probably embezzlement. Well, he'd see.

'Come along with me,' he said.

He opened the door and called to his wife:

'Iris, just a moment . . . Or, wait – better come in.'

And he thought: a second witness if there's going to be a confession.

In the large conference-room he switched on the light again; artificial light was always necessary here. To put the boy at his ease, he indicated a chair and sat down himself. Mrs Stroomkoning sat to one side, a little behind Katadreuffe; he could sometimes even hear the rustle of her dress; he did not see her but felt she was looking at him. The colour returned to his face.

'What exactly is your name?'

'Katadreuffe, sir.'

He explained that he was going to be made bankrupt, for the second time, for the same debt. He mentioned Dr Schuwagt, but not his relationship to Dreverhaven. He hoped that he would not be dismissed. From his salary he could certainly pay off the old debt and then resume his studies.

'What studies?' asked Stroomkoning.

'I want to work for my matriculation, sir.'

Stroomkoning looked at him. He remembered now. De Gankelaar had told him how the boy had been teaching himself from an old encyclopedia with part of the alphabet missing.

'Oh . . . matriculation . . . no doubt later on to become my competitor?'

He gave his leonine, jovial laugh.

'That I don't know yet, sir,' said Katadreuffe cautiously.

Stroomkoning grew serious. He was a good fellow at heart. And like De Gankelaar he thought: that boy ought to be given a chance. But his thoughts went further. He, himself, had been of working-class origin; his father had been a mere water-clerk, and yet his parents had scraped and saved to enable the gifted child to study and become a man of note. Two small portraits of his parents adorned the fine marble mantelpiece in the conference-room. It is true they were very much put in the shade by two large portraits of his father and mother-in-law, as Iris's family was worthy of display.

'How much are you earning?' he asked.

'Eighty-five guilders, sir.'

'Mr de Gankelaar is very satisfied with you; he has often told me so . . . You can stay, of course. My office won't go up in the air because I've got a bankrupt clerk, and I appreciate your having told me in advance . . . Now we'll make this agreement: when your bankruptcy has been declared and the trustee has fixed the amount of your salary to be withheld, we'll then raise your salary to a hundred guilders – the trustee needn't know that – and then you'll be a little more mobile. Agreed?'

He got up without waiting for an answer. Katadreuffe was immediately on his feet. He had not been able to find any words, as Mrs Stroomkoning could see from his face.

'What an unusual name you have,' she said. 'I have never heard it before.'

She smiled at him, a lady from another world, charmingly dressed; never before had he been spoken to by such a beautiful person. She was a head shorter than her husband; the fair hair under her hat lay so lightly that it seemed to float.

He suddenly felt himself strong; it was nearly on his lips to say : that is my mother's name. But he kept the words to himself.

In the car, Stroomkoning said :

'I thought at first the fellow was going to tell me he had pinched a thousand or so from the cash and didn't know where to turn. Fortunately it's nothing so serious.'

That evening, Katadreuffe sat working as though nothing hung over his head. He intended to collect as much knowledge as he could before the bankruptcy made further study impossible for the time being.

But on the following evening he was unable to keep this up. The image of his coming disgrace forced itself upon him. His mood was very subdued, but his anger had left him.

In this state of mind he went to call on 'her'. Jan Maan was sitting in the room, reading a pamphlet; now she was all alone he often came to sit with her in the evenings.

'Another cup of tea, Jan?'

'No, mother.'

The bell rang. He opened the door and Katadreuffe came in.

There was nothing special to remark about him; he so often had a quiet spell. Jan Maan just went on reading.

'On Wednesday I'm for the high jump,' said Katadreuffe.

He had learnt the expression from Rentenstein, who so often spoke of the high jump. He would say : 'First the pennies and then the high jump,' meaning, first the deposit and then the law-suit. Or 'He'll be for the high jump today or tomorrow.'

Katadreuffe continued :

'It's still the old debt from that rotten Hague. They've applied again for my bankruptcy. I thought at first that I'd finished with it, but it seems the opposite. Now I'm earn-

ing money my bankruptcy can't be annulled through lack
of means.'

He glanced at her. She seemed to be taking it calmly
enough, but she asked:

'Will they confiscate all your salary?'

'De Gankelaar hopes not. But that I'm for the high jump
is clear. I could of course borrow, but that's merely stopping up one hole to make another; I won't do that.'

Jan Maan had been listening with only half his attention. Now that he no longer had a girl he had gone right
over to the Communist Party Holland, but he could see
from Katadreuffe's face that serious matters were under discussion. He got up.

'Stay here, Jan,' said Katadreuffe, 'I've got no secrets.'

Jan Maan answered:

'I've got something I want to do.'

He went off. Katadreuffe actually felt freer without his
friend, for he wanted to say something to his mother alone.
Jan Maan knew he was a bastard, and he didn't mind a
bit; but Jan Maan did not know who his father was. With
the innate modesty of a working-class boy, he had never
asked him; that type is seldom inquisitive about others'
family affairs. But Katadreuffe wanted to tell her more:
'Do you know what I've fallen into? That People's Credit
Company who lent me the three hundred guilders – that's
Father. God defend us when your father makes you a
bankrupt, and twice at that.'

She did not give an immediate reply. He began to grow
irritable. Keeping silent would have been easier, after all.
Then she said:

'In a matter of law it doesn't matter whether it's your
father or another. A debt's a debt.'

So that was his consolation. Oughtn't he to have known
it beforehand? She was always like that. A debt's a debt.
Of course. Debt of a son to his father gives the father the
right to wreck his son's future. That's all he came here for,
to hear that.

In the meantime his mother was thinking of her savings book. But, no, no; she wouldn't touch that; the boy must work out his own salvation.

He got up, his tea untasted, and said :

'I'm sorry, but for the time being I can't give you the fifteen guilders any more.'

'All right,' was her answer.

On the Wednesday morning, he went to the Noordsingel. De Gankelaar had advised him against it; it was unnecessary, you could be declared bankrupt by default. Yes, he knew that from the last time, but he was so grimly angry with himself that he did not want to be spared any part of the punishment. He stood before the bankruptcy court. He acknowledged the debt; he admitted that he had two other debts. Dr Schuwagt was standing behind him, a little to one side. He had taken good stock of him. He had expected a face upon which meanness was deeply stamped, but Dr Schuwagt was a very ordinary man in a gown, with a tuft of hair between fair and grey. He had a lot to learn still. A lawyer for disreputable business did not have to have an unfavourable aspect. The president of the court said to the lawyer :

'The previous time the bankruptcy was annulled. Are there, this time, sufficient means?'

But Katadreuffe, who wanted to spare himself nothing, gave the answer :

'Yes, Your Honour, I am now employed. I earn eighty-five guilders a month.'

The president again turned to Dr Schuwagt.

'Can't a settlement be made?'

'My client insists on immediate payment, *meneer de president*.'

'Do you raise objection to the application for bankruptcy?'

'No, Your Honour, not at all.'

'You can go. That is all.'

He waited for another hour in the building. Then judge-

ment was made. A certain Dr Wever was his trustee. De
Gankelaar said that afternoon :

'Wever? You're lucky. I know him. We'll be able to fix
things all right with him.'

Actually, he scarcely knew him, but had said it to cheer
up the bankrupt, as now he was really sorry he had not
pressed Katadreuffe harder to borrow from him. He was
impulsive. Now, all of a sudden, he was sorry.

Katadreuffe had at once told Rentenstein that he was
bankrupt, but also that the chief had been told and had
raised no objection to his remaining.

Dr Wever came the following morning. He was a stiff
little man, who looked one straight in the face, though he
did not stare. He could see right through anything, even
through granite. De Gankelaar had asked him to go up to
his room first, which he did. He sat silently listening whilst
the other told him something about Katadreuffe. His face
remained completely passive. De Gankelaar's nature and
his were hardly ones to harmonize; they felt that mutually,
already at this first interview.

Why is the man making such a fuss about a clerk, thought
Wever. Bankrupt is bankrupt.

With concealed disapproval he looked at his confrère and,
now it was summer, the freckles round his nose. He judged
him to be some sort of superior play-boy.

You're just a plodding mule, a time-server – I shan't get
far with you, thought De Gankelaar. Still, he offered him
a cigarette. The other refused with a polite little smile,
which completely altered his face, displaying the tiniest
teeth.

Together with Katadreuffe they went to the latter's room.
It was necessary to switch on the light. De Gankelaar, here
for the first time, looking around him, felt his pity for Katadreuffe increase, the boy who spent his spare time in this
dreary room working on exam papers. And how far still
from his goal! Would he ever attain it? He feared for
him now.

In the meantime, Wever was also taking a look round. De Gankelaar forestalled Katadreuffe.

'This all belongs to the concierge or to my typist's mother.'

'Except,' corrected Katadreuffe, 'the radio and the divan-bed. I have them on hire-purchase.'

The trustee examined the contracts; they appeared in order; that was not yet his property.

'But,' said Katadreuffe, 'the books you can see are mine.'

'Have you any contract with your mother?' asked Wever.

'No,' said Katadreuffe.

De Gankelaar did not like the way things were going. This fellow was capable of putting it all down to be sold. He said:

'Look, Wever, let your valuer make a note of all the stuff. I would like to have another word with you. Come along to my room.'

There they talked. He had the greatest difficulty in keeping Wever off the mother's furniture, although there was little enough of it. The latter just said, bankrupt is bankrupt, and should he find something lying on the bankrupt's floor someone would have to prove whose it was.

Finally, De Gankelaar was able to get the trustee off this subject with an argument which, to his surprise, worked. He said: 'And look here, above all you mustn't forget what a rotten impression it will create if *you* include things which *I* omitted to enter down on the other occasion because I had no reason not to believe the boy or his mother. The court will now think I failed in my duty. In that way you'll end by compromising me.'

Then, at last, Wever showed some fraternal feeling. The sum involved, to be sure, was negligible; he just happened to be the one who would not abandon a principle.

As regards the books, however, he was immovable. Now the bankruptcy was going through they fell under the heading of property and would have to be sold. De Gankelaar had an inspiration; here was something he could do for the bankrupt.

'They were previously taxed at fifteen guilders. I'll offer you twenty per cent more. I'll buy them from you for eighteen guilders. Agreed?'

Wever considered the matter. De Gankelaar misunderstood the trend of his thoughts.

'Do you want to see the valuation? I have the file here.'

It was not necessary. Wever wrote a receipt and received eighteen guilders.

Then came the most important thing, the salary deduction. At first, Wever did not want to leave the bankrupt with more than forty guilders out of the eighty-five. After a lot of persuasion De Gankelaar got him up to fifty-five guilders, but then, on this point he also became intransigent. And he added with emphasis :

'On condition that the judge agrees.'

Katadreuffe would therefore have to live, for the time being, on less than when he had started.

By the time they had finished, De Gankelaar was dead-tired with all the pleading he had put in for his protégé; his manner of dealing with things was so entirely different. He said, on parting :

'You've got an incredibly hard head, you.'

Wever smiled, once again showing his tiny teeth.

'Others have said that, but I regard it as a compliment.'

Later on, De Gankelaar sighed to Katadreuffe :

'Yes, lad, there are trustees and trustees.'

Business and Love

The first days of his bankruptcy were for Katadreuffe extremely distressing, much more on account of his character than for any external reasons. Actually, nobody made any allusion to it; Rentenstein, alone, showed something in his bearing.

Rentenstein was not pleased with the way things were going; he began to sense a rival in Katadreuffe. It was pretty steep that the bankrupt youth had been able to hang on to his job here; it was a bit too steep. Stroomkoning no longer controlled his office; he was letting them make a fool of him. A good story and he was won over; he had, in fact, let them talk him round to a salary increase. And yet there was nothing so special about Katadreuffe; he'd like to see him draw up an ordinary police-court summons. What did the others see in him? But his obvious ambition was becoming a danger. Added to that, Rentenstein had, of late, begun to suffer from a guilty conscience.

That afternoon, when Katadreuffe returned from the court, he first of all told Rentenstein in private that he was bankrupt. Later on, he seized a moment when there was no one in the waiting-room. Then, again, he said to all in general :

'I'm bankrupt.'

All those who were not on holiday happened then to be

in the general office. He said it out loud; a silence fell, the typewriters stopped. Miss Sibculo was still away, and also the two Burgeiks. It sounded almost ridiculously challenging, this 'I'm bankrupt.' But nobody laughed and no one said a word except Miss Van den Born :

'I'd like them to try that on me !'

It was just the remark for her, the greatest stupidity imaginable. Yet there was a certain solidarity about it.

Miss Te George turned towards him for a moment; the lad, Pietje, looked very serious; Kees Adam clearly could not find any suitable reaction and scratched his nose in embarrassment. Katadreuffe had the feeling that they had all been prepared for what was coming, that someone must have informed them of the pending bankruptcy.

When, after a day or so, the staff were all back, Miss Siboculo found in what had happened the occasion to rekindle her love for Katadreuffe. She would look languishingly after him as he went up the stairs, or as she, herself, with pencil and pad, minced out of the door towards one of the lawyers.

The brothers Burgeik showed the most passive stolidity. They always went on holiday together – nothing else was possible – why, no mortal understood. They returned from the fields with fresh distrust of the town. They looked at one another and then together at Katadreuffe. That was all; their faces appeared to be carved from rock. But they both thought exactly the same thing : going bankrupt was an ugly matter, very ugly; you have to have the town for that, such things don't occur in the country. Their faces remained stony, and also their look.

Only Rentenstein put on a supercilious irritating air when, at the end of the month, he paid him his fifty-five guilders. When, the following month, Katadreuffe should have received his increased salary, he forestalled any comment by the head clerk.

'I don't want more than fifty-five guilders. From now on will you please send Dr Wever forty-five guilders a month.'

As, thinking it over, he felt the salary increase should also come under the bankruptcy, and had advised Dr Wever of it.

His manner had been cold but straightforward; in such matters he was absolutely his mother. Dr Wever had answered dryly on the telephone :

'You will pay it off all the sooner.'

From this same sense of honesty he also refused the concierge's proposal to reduce the price of board and lodging. Twelve guilders a week was not a penny too much for the good food, everything cooked in butter. With his mother, in his early years, he had sometimes not had it so good; the best of the best sometimes meant margarine, particularly in the worst of the war years. He was a working-class boy; he recognized a man's due; no, twelve guilders was not a penny too much. But that he was also therewith punishing himself further was also a motive for refusing.

He only met the concierge's family at meals. It had been agreed that he should eat with them. Later on, Mrs Graanoogst suggested she should serve him in his room, but he would not have that. He was quiet and uncommunicative, and he studied; all that impressed her. He was very neat in his dress; his underclothes must always be immaculate; quiet colours, never showy; that also made an impression. Perhaps she saw in him a future gentleman. But to eat alone he refused.

She was a quiet woman, herself. She must have gone grey early as her child was still young. She was a colourless person, with glasses. She could cook well; like his mother she had the knack of preparing meals to a man's taste from simple means. In the morning she brought round coffee or chocolate for the whole staff, and again at half-past twelve; in the afternoon tea was served twice. Her chocolate was her speciality, served in large, blue cups, with a thick light-brown foam on it and bubbles showing all the colours of the rainbow. What was remarkable were her long dresses, down to her toes, completely out of fashion. Possibly they hid some deformity, but nothing was noticeable from her walk.

At meal-times, Graanoogst displayed a wonderful appetite. His wife was, in the first place, his cook. He inquisitively lifted the lids of the dishes, his nose starting to twitch in anticipation. The food was always to his liking. He was younger than she, still brown-haired, with a large bald patch on the top which, during the meal, began to blush. He was generally good-humoured, though his dark, shallow eyes had the look of melancholy that is sometimes so touching in people who are unaware of their melancholy.

Together they kept the large house clean, but the husband had also other activities. They could not exist from the low wages in spite of free accommodation, heat and light. He acted as messenger and was always on the move. They had a daily girl, Lieske. In the evening he did the heavy cleaning work himself.

The girl, Lieske, ate in the kitchen, and served the four of them at table.

'She's well developed,' Graanoogst would remark.

But he was only assessing her as he would a tender joint of meat, and his wife knew it. Katadreuffe felt a secret dislike for her. Her face was marred by the strangest eyes, cloudy, almost a film over them, yet by no means blind. It always worried him when a girl looked at him; he had already experienced that with Miss Sibculo. Now, with this Lieske, he was bothered by the quiet observation from the foolish eyes in which lay a troubled question. After a bit, he did not look at her any more.

The concierge's little daughter, on the other hand, he found nice. He did not know her real name; she was called Pop. The child was far from refined but very fresh-looking; she would later grow into a buxom wench. It was only a pity that the white teeth were irregular.

To a better-formed and more exacting taste the child would not have appeared so nice. But Katadreuffe had little judgement as regards children. The child understood too well her comparative charm, which he did not see. He found the little smiles and eye-play at the table amusing. The father often quickly undid whatever the mother tried to instil as regards training and manners. He did not realize it. Katadreuffe could smile at her wiles, tantrums and fits of impatience; they brought back memories of his own childhood. The girl had wonderfully long, thick eyelashes. She could languidly make eyes like any hussy; he did not see it. Sometimes, just after the meal, he would play with the child, but had to get quickly back to his work.

He had once more got over his depression and was working again. He could not now get down to real study – his bankruptcy would last at least a year – but he could at any rate do something. The courses from the People's University were supplied free; his correspondence courses had been taken over by Jan Maan.

Jan Maan was suddenly animated by a great desire to learn, his interests in this direction being by chance identical with those of his friend. He passed on all exercises and answers to Katadreuffe, saying that he had studied them. Katadreuffe did not believe a word of it, but accepted this help. Perhaps, in the end, some of it would stick to Jan Maan, so he left it at that. He merely thought : just wait until I've finished my studies, then I'll cope with you. In the meantime, he was able to extend the basis of his general education. But he wanted more to do; the work was insufficient for him and he hankered after real study; Greek, Latin, mathematics. He had to know six languages; with the four modern ones he could at least do something for himself, and also something in history. Yet his progress was too slow, a mere mouthful a week. Sometimes his bankruptcy made him suddenly despair. A year of dawdling – it would never end. He went back to the old lessons, but he knew most of that inside out; his memory was so good; nothing of importance escaped it. His German was going reasonably, at least the reading. Then, for a few pence, he bought some trashy literature in the market, French and

English; he borrowed dictionaries from one of the lawyers and then struggled through the novelettes. He had now at least something on which to concentrate his mind.

His bankruptcy had affected him more than he suspected. One winter's night he was seized by a panicky fear when he found himself standing in the large corridor downstairs, in complete darkness, in his pyjamas. The stone-cold marble under his feet had finally awakened him. It happened again a few times that winter, and he shuddered when he thought how often perhaps he had done it and then gone back to bed.

But his strong will would not allow him to spend much time on brooding or self-pity. When the bankruptcy was over then that would stop, too. And the bankruptcy, he realized, would have been easily supportable but for the high goal he had set himself. There were many who had less than he. But he wanted to get on, *in spite of* the bankruptcy.

Something good came out of the affair of which he was unaware. It had made him more human; his eyes had an almost different light in them than formerly. His mother noticed it.

It was on a certain evening in spring. He had just eaten and was going to his room when the bell rang. The little girl, Pop, ran down the stairs and opened the door. He heard a voice below and something clanking, but he paid no attention.

A little later he went into the general office. He wanted to type out a memorandum for De Gankelaar. The work was urgent and De Gankelaar had a difficult handwriting. He was met by the noise of a typewriter. Miss Te George was already sitting at her table, with the lamp lit.

He said good evening and took his place. He sat at the other side of the office, looking at her back. Rentenstein was nominally head of the office; there were otherwise no ranks. Yet Katadreuffe felt that this girl was his superior. Day after day she was in Stroomkoning's room, and sat taking notes at every meeting. French, English, German, she was equally fluent in them all. She must also have a good salary, not much less than Rentenstein, as he was only her boss in name. He never gave her anything; her work came straight from Stroomkoning.

They had never spoken except to pass the time of day. Maybe he still desired to take her place, to sit with the important business men, but the desire was vaguer than formerly; his aspirations were directed elsewhere; he hoped to do more than that.

For a long time they typed away under their respective lamps, with many a pause in the sound of typing. He saw her bent over, concentrating on what she was reading; her work appeared to be difficult. Then she went into the back room, returning with a file, typed a few words, turned round, and said of a sudden :

'You shouldn't work *too* hard.'

He looked up; the ice was broken.

'How do you mean?'

'You aren't looking too well.'

They naturally did not use the familiar form of speech. Between the adult male and female members of the staff the polite form was always used, except by Rentenstein. Rentenstein had introduced that, not on principle, but by way of contrast; it sounded as though he was using the familiar form with everybody, even when using the polite form. But he only used the latter with her. She was someone possessing a quiet dignity, who never spoke about the office, although she knew the most important things, the things connected with the main cash account; she alone.

'You work too hard . . . It's a good thing to study but you should recognize some moderation.'

He did not know what to answer. He felt he was blushing. At last he said, in a subdued tone :

'I don't work anything like enough, just because of that wretched bankruptcy.'

For a moment, she seemed slightly embarrassed. He asked :

'How do you know I'm studying?'

'We all know that here. You want to take your matriculation, don't you?'

They typed on, and then resumed their conversation, both by fits and starts. She asked him what he was doing. She, herself, had a contract in English to translate, an affair which Stroomkoning – she said Mr Stroomkoning – was handling together with C. C. & C., a gentleman's agreement. She did not explain further. He wondered what that expression could mean; she had used it without any sign of showing off, though she must realize that he did not understand it.

'Tremendous – that you can do all that without a dictionary.'

'Oh! I need one every now and then.'

She asked him whether he was satisfied with his room. He asked her whether she would like to see it. She answered :

'Presently.'

Her work was finished, his not, when they went upstairs. Miss Te George found the room dreadfully gloomy, but she did not show it. It was chilly, large and bare. A piece of cloth had been hung in front of the cupboard-bed, more than horrible. He followed her look and said :

'Not my choice, Graanoogst's.'

She sat on the divan-bed, he opposite her. She had watched him for a long time, from that very first day, with the enigmatical woman's gift of gauging a man completely; in a fraction of a second the man is analysed down to his bones before he, himself, has realized he is being looked at.

He had also taken her in on that first day, well and accurately, when they had passed one another on the stairs, she coming out of the conference-room; but he had looked at her as a man does, taken in her appearance from head to foot, no more, no less. And then he had put it all out of his thoughts, driven by a vague, odd uneasiness.

This uneasiness he felt anew; he was being drawn towards something obscure, though at the same time unmistakably pleasant.

There was a knock at the door; Mrs Graanoogst brought him his cup of tea. He gave it to her and the concierge's wife went and brought him another. He wondered whether this would give rise to gossip, but he didn't mind. Yet he was faintly afraid of something else – he did not know what. As if he might be losing his way, it seemed to him.

'Would you like a cigarette?' she asked. 'I like to smoke two or three in the evening.'

Her cigarettes were much better than his had ever been, and at present he lacked the money for even the worst kind.

Their talk was not fluent and yet was unrestrained. Through the smoke, he looked at her now and then. She was a tall girl, about six years his senior, rather too slim, her legs on the thin side, her feet remarkably small and neat. She dressed with taste. Her face struck one at once as unusual, and one soon saw that it was charming, with a smooth, high forehead and broad cheek-bones which fell sharply to a little round chin. Two thin lines from her nostrils to the corners of her mouth aged her a little; it was as though she had some secret sorrow. The mouth was slightly arched, showing her white teeth, the upper incisors strong and square.

At once Katadreuffe thought : I'm just like the zoologists, I'm looking first at her teeth.

'Why are you laughing?' she asked.

He would not say. Her hair was auburn; the look in her eyes, hesitating between grey and blue, was gentle. Her neck appeared to him rather weakly modelled, particularly in contrast to the fine, large head. Her hands, slender and thin, he found full of character. He examined her very thoroughly, and she of course noticed it.

She asked about his family, and he told her about his mother and Jan Maan. The office was not mentioned. She

lived with her parents right in the south. Did he know the
Green Belt? He did not. It was in that district – nice to
live in, sunny, quiet, but a long way off. She always came
on her bicycle. There was sometimes a strong wind, particularly on the Maas bridge and the bridge over the Kon-
ingshaven. She loved the wind, the more the better.

He was surprised at this seemingly rather frail girl's like-
ing for gales. The clanking he had heard came to mind.

'I suppose you have your bicycle with you now?'

Then he noticed her shiver slightly.

'Are you cold?'

'No,' she lied, as she had grown chilly in this drab room
with the poor light.

He did not wish to appear too poverty-stricken with no
heating and said :

'In the winter I have a paraffin stove in here.'

Then he let her out, fetched her bicycle from under
the stairs, and saw her ride away in the balmy evening. On
the Boompjes it was quiet at this hour. The spot of light
from her lamp glided peacefully further and further away.
He could see that light better than he could picture her.

Then he stood in the corridor, pensive, motionless, far
from satisfied with himself.

A Dull Period

This was the only intimate conversation between these two. They gave no sign of its having taken place, not even to one another. Indeed, nothing had happened. But for Lorna Te George the first weeks were very difficult. Every now and then her thoughts would wander back to that one moment in the room when he had smiled. It made his features so exceptionally engaging, just because one saw nothing but seriousness there. The memory went right through her with a bitter-sweetness. She must not think too much about it. It would be the greatest stupidity; she was at least six years older, and the boy thought of nothing but his future. It was fortunate he did not know how captivating his smile was; he would be making conquests by the dozen. No, *unfortunate*, as if he had known his charm his laugh would have been insufferable, like the merest false note in the most beautiful music – then at least he would have made no impression on her.

In the meantime she went on with her work, revealing nothing. They were not sentimental times; the languishing female was a thing of the past. The human race creates its periods; the individual does whatever the times demand of him. And so this girl, but in spite of all standardization, she remained a creature apart. She was a person to attract attention; one was not immediately sure through what qualities or what continued to hold the attention; she just emanated charm. To Rentenstein she was far too unapproachable for him to allow himself to joke with her as with Miss Sibculo. The jokes were innocent enough, but she would not have permitted that, even.

Stroomkoning's biggest clients all knew her, and their eyes were often on her. She sat on the lawyer's left at a small table, pushed up against the green cloth of the large conference table, a little behind him. She missed nothing of the conversation; if something funny was said she laughed with them, but otherwise sat correctly and modestly, though not stiff or prim. Many wondered that she wore no ring; it was unthinkable that such a girl had never been kissed; this created an atmosphere of mystery about her that was a better protection than the insignia of an engagement. Once one of them made a more personal allusion, but she did not react, and Stroomkoning was secretly pleased. She was for him absolutely indispensable, always knew where to find the papers, yet all the same he was never too familiar with her. He addressed all the girls with 'Miss' followed by their surnames, when he could remember them. The only people in his office that really existed for him were she and Carlion, not even Rentenstein.

He had a high admiration for Carlion. He was the specialist in inland water transport, but he was much more than that. Stroomkoning knew his law and jurisdiction, but Carlion knew them better. He would refer to judgements of the High Court of decades back; he knew when this august body changed its attitude; he could almost by heart have written the whole history of Dutch jurisdiction. But he was no all-round lawyer. In spite of his admiration for this walking encyclopedia, Stroomkoning felt that that was all he was. Carlion could work up a case excellently, but he could never have created a practice; he did not possess the gift of tying down a client, gaining his confidence; he was too speculative and dry. Stroomkoning, himself, was by far the best all-round lawyer of them all, but he was also by far the oldest and, in addition, his was a personality to bring in business.

Carlion, in his dry way, had expressed his condolence to Katadreuffe over the bankruptcy. He was sitting working at his desk. Without looking up he merely said :

'You're bankrupt aren't you?'

Still without looking up he thrust a hand across the desk, a sinewy hand with a fairly strong grip.

But Piaat had not reacted at all. He was very restless, very like a butterfly. He had to make a note of everything so as not to forget it – unless it had to do with the practice – and he had omitted to make a note that he ought to show Katadreuffe some sympathy. He was always deep in the feverish atmosphere of criminal cases, dreary work for most, but he liked it. He was very quick-witted and had a host of funny stories on tap; in court he could always find something applicable to the situation. His belief in the blessings of laughter was unshakable. The judges liked to listen to him, a smile appearing on their faces together with the appearance of his *baret*[1] in court. And he was so popular that one laughed out of politeness even when the joke was insipid. They respected him even then, when to another they would have displayed an icy coldness.

He was so full of jokes that he had no time to think of Katadreuffe. At lunch, at the lawyers' exchange, he chatted about his own cases and brought out his jokes afresh. Then he was in his element. On one occasion – Katadreuffe could hear it from the next room – he told about a complicated embezzlement, with examination of books and experts : 'Just listen, it was priceless. There, this morning, in court was a whole pile of cash-books. I took the top one and we all had our noses in it when one of the clodhopping experts knocked the whole pile on to the ground with his elbow, and I called out above the din : "Now you'll *have* to say the books aren't in order !" The whole court roared, the

[1] A square, flat cap, then worn by judges and counsel in Holland.

tribune was bent double, it brought the house down, that's a fact.'

It really had been said; it was already in the evening papers.

But his high spirits were partly a façade. He had a weak heart and pleading was actually fatal for him. He used to plead with his cap on, in the naïve idea that it made him a bit taller, but of late he sweated like a pig beneath it.

His worries were his heart and his short figure. With his big head, he was like a child, a myopic child in spectacles. De Gankelaar summed him up well when he said :

'You and your Christian name. You only write that Gideon Piaat in full to make you look taller than you are.'

'Now, now,' answered the little man, 'if my parents had christened me Theodore, I don't know so much !'

For Theodore was the name of the other. And Piaat laughed good-humouredly. Yet his heart worried him and he was gradually becoming more pierrot than clown.

The lawyers' exchange was held at half past twelve in the ochre-yellow room, an octagonal room with a skylight, the original four corners being hidden behind wall-cupboards. Through the skylight, on which wind and rain could make such play, the light came through uncoloured. From a distance it looked as though the daylight passed through ugly coloured glass, ochre-yellow, until one saw the skylight. The yellow came, however, from the walls themselves; a patternless wallpaper of one colour, strange and ugly, seemed to throw an unreal lustre on everything, on those present, on the food.

At a quarter past twelve the girl, Lieske, laid the table; at half past she brought the coffee and the chocolate. Rentenstein would then say to Miss Van den Born :

'Warn them that it's all getting cold.'

And the girl with the hoarse voice, through the house-telephone :

'Sir, your coffee's getting cold; madame, your chocolate's getting cold,' – as though they were holding things up.

It was a small matter but it always annoyed Katadreuffe. Such things weren't done in a good office; it happened because Rentenstein didn't know his place and so was unable to teach others theirs.

The lawyers' exchange could not always begin on time and was often not complete. Carlion and Piaat were frequently absent; the latter, in particular, travelled a lot, pleading from Groningen to Middelburg. De Gankelaar was a faithful attendant, also Miss Kalvelage. The door leading to the general office was usually open and also that into the corridor; when Piaat was present the exchange could be heard all over the building.

Often when Katadreuffe came down from his lunch he could hear a lot of what was being said. They did, in fact, discuss their cases until De Gankelaar, who was the first to get bored, gave a different turn to the conversation. Preferring to philosophize, he said :

'Don't always be so heavy-handed. All law-suits, as far as I'm concerned, can go to blazes. For me there is only one interesting phenomenon in the world, and that is Man. It's not the law-suit that's interesting but Man, because he has built up something so ingenious as law and jurisprudence.'

Miss Kalvelage said dryly :

'I don't find anything particularly interesting about any of us four sitting here.'

'There you're right, but you must regard Man as a species not as an individual.'

He was already riding his hobby-horse, about the facets of people, which were all different, and in so doing found himself more or less contradicting his previous assertion. Still, he once said something original.

'Man cannot be viewed as a whole and therefore we have to content ourselves with a few facets. If only we had the eyes of a fly which can look in all directions at once. Well then. For everyone Napoleon is a cocked-hat, a handsome Greek profile, a hand thrust into his coat, two legs clothed

in white on either side of a horse. But I assure you, some-
where in the world, there is an old, old school-book, such
a very small book, with a dedication written in a child's
handwriting : "Your loving little friend, Napoleon". It
exists in theory.'

No one was now listening. He laughed with a trace of
annoyance :

'Oh! You're all just lawyers. You don't know what a
human being is.'

And he lit a cigarette.

The only one who had listened to him, although affecting
not to, was Miss Kalvelage. She was a snappish little
creature, yet Katadreuffe liked her best of all after De
Gankelaar. She also had said nothing about the bankruptcy
and yet, in an indefinable kind of way, just through her
manner, he had understood that she had given it thought,
that she had at least not forgotten about it, like Piaat. And
this very silence, femininely delicate, had increased his liking for her. For the rest, there was little feminine about her,
certainly not in the limited, old-fashioned sense. She had
an office looking on to the street, right by the front-door.
The rooms on a level with the door belonged to another
tenant. As in many old Rotterdam houses, there was a
warehouse there, and as in all warehouses there were rats.
One day the summer before, a rat had scrambled up from
the warehouse and climbed through a hole in the wainscot-
ing, behind her chair, on to the linoleum, a great brown
rat. She heard it and there was a scream – but from the
rat. Quickly, quietly, sharply, and with perfect aim, she
had smashed its head with a ruler before it could spring.
She rang for Lieske. Lieske nearly fainted from horror.
Graanoogst cleaned things up, but she, herself, said not a
word about it; the story got around via the concierge. She
was a girl who always remained unruffled. Now and again
she commandeered him; he was so much better than the
Burgeiks, and all De Gankelaar did was to hold him up
with his babbling, as she knew well enough.

Katadreuffe felt himself almost humiliated the first time she asked him to take down something. The feeling disappeared at once, as this was no question of taking orders from a girl. This little creature had no sex. She certainly wasn't a girl, rather a kind of gnome. She quietly dictated two lengthy letters in a business-like way, stopping to think now and again, never altering anything. When he looked up he saw the variable, amber eyes, so large behind the round glasses, the thick, black hair, cropped short, already greying, surrounding the ageless death's head. He was almost attracted, not by anything feminine, but by something very out of the ordinary. And he almost had to hide a smile when, unconsciously, her voice was raised, sharp and cutting, not at him but in connection with her dictation. When she wanted to lash somebody on paper, then her voice lashed, rose and fell, rose again and fell again in accordance with her subject. She was a proper lawyer; in this small room she gave battle to an invisible, but to her so real, adversary. At the end, words and tone were calm; she had won.

When Katadreuffe returned from his first visit to her he felt, deep down, really very humble, and also to some extent defeated. I've so much still to learn, an enormous amount, he thought. He did not know how valuable it was that he realized this.

In his own eyes he was without work. He could not fill his evenings. The radio had been taken away, but he would not have been able to learn much more from that instrument; he had absorbed all that. He still went to the People's University, but it was too seldom. What he picked up there could be called stuffing or sauce; under no circumstances could it be described as meat.

He saw his father now and then in the office; they ignored one another as before. His anger had completely left him. He did not know whether he hated his father and, in spite of himself, he always felt a certain awe for him when they met. His father clearly aroused pugnacity in him.

He thought : you just wait, fellow, you'll not get me down; we'll confront one another again one of these days.

Nevertheless he was dissatisfied; his fits of depression drove him more often to his mother, and still more to Jan Maan. The latter had become inspired by the fundamentals of communism. The propagation of seditious theories had once earned him dismissal by his boss, but he was a capable fitter and had quickly got another job. Katadreuffe noticed that his friend was no longer so gentle and amiable in manner; perhaps, as he grew older his disposition had changed, just as some animals left too much to themselves can become dangerous. Towards Katadreuffe and his mother, however, Jan Maan did not change in the least; even Lenin could not drive a wedge between the friends. Katadreuffe was, himself, too loyal for that; also at this time he again began to have some respect for the other's principles. They went more often to red Caledonia on the docks; once Jan Maan made a speech there, doing it really very well. Katadreuffe clapped him. A little later the police came; they had gone too far, distributing seditious handbills outside. The meeting was closed, the clearing of the hall took place without incident. Katadreuffe stared challengingly straight in the face of a policeman; he would have died rather than drop his eyes; nor did the policeman drop his.

By the end of the new summer his bankruptcy had been worked off. The three creditors each received a hundred per cent. Katadreuffe was glad that Jan Maan had now got back the small sum he had lent him. Wever called for him and went over the account with him; there was money left over, nearly a hundred guilders. Wever looked hard at him, right through him, as through granite.

'If you will sign the receipt all's in order.'

'He'll see through it,' De Gankelaar had told Wever on the telephone. 'You're a good fellow but you'll see; he'll understand it and refuse categorically; he's much too proud.'

Katadreuffe did *not* understand it. It was impossible;

there couldn't be a hundred guilders over. At the most, he might get something back from his last month's salary. He said:

'You must have made a mistake. There's a difference of some seventy-five guilders. That's too much. I can't possibly accept it. Your calculation is wrong.'

Little Wever looked straight at him across the desk.

'I've made no mistake. There is no mistake. Here, sign, and take the money.'

Then Katadreuffe grasped it. It was his own fee, the trustee's fee, seventy-five guilders, which Wever wanted to make him a present of. Katadreuffe had noticed the figure on the distribution list. He turned a deep red and, scarcely aware of what he was doing, he stood up. He picked up some of the money, leaving exactly seventy-five guilders lying there.

'No,' he said.

He did not add:

'Thank you.'

Wever smiled, showing his tiny teeth.

'Bankrupt is bankrupt, but study is study.'

'No.'

Then Wever lost his patience.

'Don't be so stupid. Those notes mean more to you than to me. It's your money; you've earned it.'

But Katadreuffe did not possess the magnanimity which can accept a present in due season. It seemed like charity to him; he was being treated like a beggar. He was almost seething with rage.

'No, Mr Wever, I simply won't consider it. No, no, no.'

His self-control was at an end; he sensed it and hurriedly left.

Katadreuffe did not mention the incident, and De Gankelaar had gradually come to stand a little in awe of his protégé's intransigence, so did not like to question him, himself. He learned about it from Wever, and then felt really nervous that Katadreuffe would vent his wrath a second time on him. Hadn't he bought back his books from Wever? But Katadreuffe had not noticed this item on the list. De Gankelaar wisely kept his mouth shut.

At the end of that month a new face appeared for a short time in the office. Young Countryside came over from London, the youngest partner of Cadwallader, Countryside & Countryside. He was not in reality so youthful, and an uglier man it would be hard to imagine. But he was not commonly ugly; it was a polished ugliness; a man, almost middle-aged, who would no doubt be attractive to many women. He just wanted to come and have a look at his friends in that office on the Continent. His father used to do it. With his casual English air of distinction, it was second nature to him to treat everybody very politely.

'How are you?' he asked each of the staff, giving them his hand.

'How are you?' he asked Miss Te George, shaking her hand too long for Katadreuffe's taste.

'How are you?' he asked Katadreuffe.

'Yes, thank you,' came the answer, which Katadreuffe himself felt was far from right.

The only member of the staff who could converse properly with him was Miss Te George. Katadreuffe stood watching them a little way off, obviously angry and jealous behind the back of the Britisher. It was a little triumph which she enjoyed and held on to as long as possible. Their relationship did not progress; nothing can ever come of it, she sometimes thought with bitterness. This was some small consolation.

And Countryside had realized at once that she only could talk to him. They chatted a while and even laughed a little, until Stroomkoning arrived. By means of this conversation Miss Te George rose in everybody's estimation, for though it is clever to be able to speak a foreign language, to be able to laugh and joke in it is a real feat. She felt the admiration, and smiled as she went back to her typewriter.

Young Countryside carried the traces of a dissipated life

in the lines and creases of his face. He had a weary manner about him, and his voice sounded deep and tired. There was black hair on his hands almost up to the knuckles, but it was neither unappetizing nor vulgar. Even in this excessive hairiness he remained a man of breeding. His teeth were no longer good, being attacked by decay; whenever he laughed, all round his mouth the gold gleamed. His cigarettes had a sweetish, clinging aroma; he had been hardly five minutes with Stroomkoning before the 'real Dutch gin' had to appear on the table.

Stroomkoning never kept alcoholic drinks in his office, so Pietje was sent out for a stone bottle of the oldest and best, a piece of earthenware with a black seal, encrusted with cobwebs.

He stayed at Stroomkoning's villa on the Bergse lakes. Mrs Stroomkoning was an ardent admirer; they rowed and swam together. But Countryside came to the office a lot, to the conference-room or to De Gankelaar, and he strolled about in the mud on the Boompjes with a pink carnation in his button-hole. He liked the busy traffic in the street, close to the office. It was so everlastingly quiet near his own office, in Gray's Inn, by the end of Chancery Lane; sedate but dull and always gloomy.

Countryside and De Gankelaar also got on well together. He soon had enough of the others, but De Gankelaar spoke English fluently; it was actually his native language, that of his mother. Though not in fluency, he beat Stroomkoning in pronunciation. In De Gankelaar's office, they both sat with their feet on the desk, only able to see the soles of one another's shoes. What little air there was, was quickly blue with pipe and cigarette smoke, and the Dutch gin was soon called on to do its duty.

Katadreuffe once saw the three of them walking in front of him, Stroomkoning, enormous in the middle, De Gankelaar active and sportsmanlike. Countryside in a silver-grey suit, rolling along like a grey ape, and yet in no way ridiculous. Then a question flashed through his head : if I were a lawyer, which of them would I want to be like?

His answer came promptly : none of the three — myself.

After a month, young Countryside left, with a few clogs full of straw in his suitcase as souvenir of the Low Countries. Katadreuffe was, already long since, plunged back in his work.

Katadreuffe and Dreverhaven

Then a riot broke out, inexplicable for Rotterdam. There is an important difference between the inhabitants of the two largest towns; the Rotterdammer is quieter, more balanced than the Amsterdammer. By far and away the most popular paper is the independent *Rotterdams Nieuwsblad*; almost every family reads it – it is known just as the *Nieuwsblad* – the political papers trailing behind. The Rotterdammer, as well as being quiet, is loyal. He swears by the *Nieuwsblad*; he swears by the Savings Bank. When he talks of the Savings Bank he does not mean the Post Office Savings Bank. It is the private one on the Botersloot; the other comes second. Mrs Katadreuffe read the *Nieuwsblad* and had a deposit in the Savings Bank.

In inexplicable fashion, some of the people allowed themselves to be stirred by a communist wind, over some political event abroad. The grey district where Dreverhaven reigned rose in revolt. They were just busy improving a good stretch of the road surface of the Goudse Singel. Cobbles and blocks of asphalt lay ready to hand. They built up childish barricades in the alleys. In the evening there was shooting, and Mrs Katadreuffe could hear the detonations in the distance when it was quiet around her.

Jan Maan sat at her table. He had never sat so awkwardly, with his elbows pushed right forward over the table, his hands in his hair, half-reading; but she saw how he had clenched his teeth, how his cheek-muscles stood out, and how his fingers played nervously with his fair hair. In her heart she felt sorry for him; she was so fond of him, but she was determined. She did not mind him talking revolution, but it must not come to deeds, and she pulled at the reins.

There was a short but eloquent conversation.

'Jan!'

'Yes, mother.'

Unwillingly the head was raised and he looked into two eyes glowing like a distant blast-furnace.

'*If* you have a heart.'

The head sunk down.

'Well?'

There was a short silence; then came unwillingly :

'No, mother.'

A moment later he went off to his room, whistling angrily to show his independence. She merely nodded quietly to herself; there was no more danger with that lad.

In the meantime, the riots had not been quelled but had moved over towards the north, in the vicinity of the slaughter-house. She, herself, had formerly lived there, though not in the very poorest part. There was now an absolute uproar in the poorest district, in a cluster of very narrow little streets. A detachment of troops came to the assistance of the police. The whole quarter was cordoned off, and those of good will who had gone off to work in the morning could not get back to their homes. Mrs Katadreuffe now heard shooting from the other side.

In one of the little streets, Dreverhaven had to evict a family. It was at the heart of the riot, the Rubroekstraat. In a day or two order would also be restored there, the police having taken extremely vigorous measures. Dreverhaven could have waited, but he was not the man for that. He went off there that afternoon, together with Hamerslag and Coal-grab, a raw afternoon with a cutting wind. In the distance the rattle of musketry could already be heard.

They reached the danger zone. At every street-corner soldiers were posted on the roofs, raking the cross-points with machine-guns. As soon as a hand from inside approached too near to a closed window, as soon as a curtain moved in a house, the bullets flew.

Dreverhaven came up to the police cordon. They did not want to let him through, but he said :

'In the name of the Law !' and showed on his chest the orange ribbon with the silver badge bearing the arms of the Kingdom.

They let him and his satellites pass.

A little later, on the actual battle-field, he met a patrol led by a lieutenant.

'In the name of the Law !' he said, repeating his gesture.

The lieutenant merely answered :

'On your own responsibility.'

Again he was allowed to pass. Then he was walking in the most desolate part of the town, the streets strewn with broken tiles, bullet holes in the windows everywhere, the woodwork scored by ricocheting bullets. The three of them walked on. Coal-grab was oblivious to the threat of death, slouching beside the clerk under the fire which revived every now and then. On the wharfs he had so often heard the hammering of rivets in the hull of a ship, the drumming of pneumatic drills; this was exactly the same. Hamerslag displayed another character, the dry comedian. All he said was :

'Hell, what a damn cold wind.'

Stopping in the middle of the street, he blew his nose laboriously, and it sounded like a hunting-horn.

Dreverhaven saw that the firing was turning now and then in their direction, but something powerful emanated from this big man, calmly marching with ribbon and badge spread on his chest, all coats open and filled with the wind like a frigate in the open sea. Here was no trouble-maker. That man had a large cigar sticking up from the corner of his mouth, which he was puffing at vigorously. At the same time he was cover for the two following in his wake.

Then, in the Rubroekstraat, he stood in front of the house. He did not trouble to ring; with one kick of his heavy foot he dislodged the door so that it banged against the wall; the plaster poured down and the house shook. There were cries of alarm. The woman stood in the room with a whole troop of children. None of them had eaten for over twenty-four hours. For two days they had been searching for the man, one of the worst of the rioters, who had escaped to a friendly house. The bailiff was sorry about this; he would have loved to encounter the fellow; as it was, it was all over in the twinkling of an eye. Coal-grab was already driving the children before him into the murderous street, whither they streamed. But the youngest, a little boy of about two, had caught hold of his trouser-leg around the knee, laughing fearlessly and friendlily up at Coal-grab with the vague smile of a very small child who doesn't know why he's pleased. Small and futile beneath the big, slobbering mouth, his mother pulled him away.

In the meantime, two soldiers had been consulting Hamerslag. One in front, one behind, the wailing woman with her brood in the middle; so the party moved off between two bayonets with a fluttering handkerchief on each, high in the air. In a trice the meagre possessions were dumped in the street; the wind had full play on the few rags of curtains.

That evening, Dreverhaven sat reflecting on the most beautiful eviction of his life. He thought of the laughing child which had seized Coal-grab's trousers in that fetching way; such a little rascal. But he, himself, did not laugh. He was thinking: it was well worth the trouble, not for the money, for the daring of it. He no longer knew, or scarcely knew, whether he had wanted a stray bullet to lay him low. In any event such a desire had been only hazy; for that his indifference was too ingrained. But of one thing he was completely sure, and it was sufficient to know that. He would never, never fall ill. That was pre-ordained;

a life's end with pain, with a gradual dissolution of his strength, that he would be spared. However it might be, from exterior violence or a devastating force from within, he would slump down suddenly, unexpectedly, and the ground would rumble where he fell.

He looked around the great, cavernous room, barbarously bare, and began to think of his son. The son's office vibrated with life, the father's was quiet as the grave. It was not the quiet of repose; it was, like that afternoon in the rioting quarter, the breathless quiet of fear. As his years mounted he had gradually spread terror around him. His own clients rarely sought him out; he was too frightening, too brutal; they preferred to deal with him by telephone. A few attributes kept him going, and had he not possessed these, his practice would long ago have run to seed.

And in the unheated room, in his chair behind the desk, coat and hat on, he surveyed his life as if it were a landscape. It was getting more and more to appear like a landscape. The strong eyes of his memory could make out the finest details on the horizon; later as his memory dimmed, the clouds would drive over and eliminate whole stretches of it. No, no, then he wouldn't exist any more.

He drank a lot lately. He had bursts of it, like going with women. He could as easily do it as leave it alone; he had but one addiction, money. Drink had, however, tasted particularly good of late. He took an earthenware bottle and a glass from his desk; the first glass he drank at a draught, the second in two, and the third he left standing before him.

Then he rummaged in a drawer and started to write a memorandum or two, in his concise, formidable style and his black writing. He kept no copies of these notes; he had not used his copying-press for years. He did not forget what he had written, and it would not have worried him if he had forgotten. He never signed his letters, only his writs. That was the kind of writing he did best.

In the year such and such in this or that month I, Arend

Barend Dreverhaven, bailiff of the Rotterdam police court, declare and give notice . . .

Or better still :

. . . I, Arend Barend Dreverhaven, summons . . .

Still better :

. . . serve a subpoena . . .

Best of all :

. . . I order to pay immediately to me, bailiff . . . etc.

But it was not these writs (you earned something with them, that was all) but the execution of them that was his life and delight; seizure of goods, their public sale, evictions, breaking locks, overcoming obstacles in the houses, grasping debtors by the collar in order to take them to prison as hostages, all this in the name of the Law, in the King's name, in the name of the all-highest God, Money.

The telephone rang. He picked up the receiver. It was Dr Schuwagt. He used him as his solicitor for his dirty business, that connected with the money-lending bank. He was indeed bailiff for Stroomkoning's office, but the latter was not his solicitor. He knew well enough that Stroomkoning would refuse to act for business which always had a scruffy side to it, so he made do with that crawling lawyer, Dr Schuwagt, at the same time hating the fellow for his cringing servility. Schuwagt was the most miserable specimen of the whole Rotterdam bar, though that does not go far enough as the bar was in general respected, but he was by far the worst, and was despised by all. Dreverhaven who could use him, who had to use him, did not scruple to treat him like a bit of dirt. He brayed his answer into the receiver, banged it down, drank his last glass, and fell asleep at once. But the cigar remained burning in the corner of his mouth, and his mind's eyes stayed wide open.

It was thus he heard the light, nervous but definite step which he knew, like the beast of prey recognizes its own whelp from a distance. First one eye opened, then the other; his son stood in front of the desk. He stood at ease and calmly stated :

'Father, I've come to borrow money from you.'

'What for, Jacob Willem?'

'I can't get through my matriculation without private lessons. The modern language classes are all right, but history, mathematics and, above all, the classical languages – there are courses for them.'

Dreverhaven had long since shut his eyes again, but Katadreuffe knew the old man now; he supposed he was considering the matter. It was as though he had somehow always known him, even if they avoided one another like strangers.

Dreverhaven was not considering the matter; he was thinking : what a nerve the boy has – it shows good blood. Seeking out the lion in his den. Of the strange, slim boy with his mother's features – he had always thought : he's my child. He had felt the boy part of his own flesh when Stroomkoning engaged him, he felt it immediately : that boy will go his father's way; he wants a law practice; he will live from the law, but he also wants to aim higher than myself. And now the fellow was taking a step of which he knew the consequences in advance, now that he came to borrow money, he felt a bond with him in the most secret and precious thing he possessed, his blood. But blood poses many an enigmatic problem; he felt antagonistic, and said ironically :

'So my dear sir appears to have second thoughts. Does he want to borrow from the bloodsucker?'

'Yes,' said Katadreuffe.

He thought for a moment and continued :

'Yes, I defy you. Give me the opportunity and I'll stand up to you all right.'

Dreverhaven shut his eyes again. That showed blood; that boy had character. And he asked in a toneless voice, as though he were talking in his sleep :

'How much?'

Katadreuffe had reckoned that he could manage with two thousand guilders.

Dreverhaven looked at him again. The ash from his cigar fell on his chest, making its way between the many greasy streaks on his clothes. Katadreuffe, over-sensitive anew, feared he was going to draw a blank. Dreverhaven said :

'Remember that if I lend you money today, tomorrow I can break your neck.'

'Yes, I know.'

'Read this.'

And he pushed a printed form towards him.

'I only lend money on these conditions, and if you sign that you are at the same time committing yourself to the gallows.'

'I know.'

He really meant : I'm not frightened of you.

Dreverhaven's eyes were again shut.

'Then tomorrow morning at the bank – eleven o'clock.'

The following day the money was paid out to him and not on excessive terms. The interest was eight per cent. The only danger lay in the possibility of immediate fore-closure at any time. He also had to give the bank a lien on his salary, as security.

He had planned to take the examination in two years' time, reckoning from the coming summer. He had found a young Doctor in Classics who, for seven hundred and fifty guilders a year, was ready to cram him as far as Greek and Latin were concerned. For that he was to have a two-hour lesson on three evenings a week. That worked out at three guilders an hour, and he did not find it too dear when he considered how intensively he would have to work during these lesson hours, his time during the day being taken up with other work.

Katadreuffe had learnt to be provident. He paid his teacher a full year in advance. The latter found this un-usual and did not at first want to accept, but Katadreuffe insisted with the greatest determination. For he thought : if the bank goes for me in the meantime, this year at least is paid in advance, and I shall be able to continue my lessons for a whole year and nobody can stop me.

He took to it remarkably quickly and made great progress; the languages presented no special difficulties to him. The foundations of his general knowledge as well as the grasp of a mind above the normal scholastic maturity helped him on. It was a good year that followed; the languages appealed to him just as his gift for them appealed to the teacher.

Already months ago Katadreuffe had resumed payments to his mother. Promptly every month, without a word, he laid fifteen guilders on her table-cloth. He even found some recreation of which he greatly felt the need. Jan Maan took him along again to red Caledonia, where recently such fine Russian films were being shown to the communist cell. Guests could be invited, and so they went there. 'She' also sometimes wanted to see something and joined them, walking between them.

A bare, chilly room, smelling of poverty, but very quiet; women even brought their babies along with their dummies and milk-bottles. They saw 'Der Weg ins Leben' by Ekk, and Wertov's 'Three Songs of Lenin'.

Jan Maan was in ecstasies. He joined in the general applause at the end of every film, and even Katadreuffe felt himself swept along with them, but he restrained himself. He would never become a communist, and when it was all over it was Dutch reality which, with a cool hand, kept him on the path of moderation.

The least affected was 'she'. Yes, yes, it was very nice, and now and then really beautiful; that she had to admit. But then you heard from behind the screen some man or woman's voice giving a sermon in Russian. She did not understand a word and yet grasped it all. It was all about communistic ideals, but she just had to laugh at that gushing voice which didn't fit in anywhere, as the film merely continued turning. She said, scarcely realizing how accurately she summed up the situation :

'The Russians are just great children.'

That had deeply offended Jan Maan. Children, children? Not exactly. And he expressly brought up the bloodiest deeds of the communist movement. Had she forgotten the execution of the whole Tsar's family in the Urals, the Hungarian Soviet under Bela Kun and Szamuely. Did she know anything about the Russian prisons? If not, he would give her something to read at home, about those in Moscow, Lubyanka 2 and Lubyanka 13, for example. When you heard about them you shuddered – not the literature for her to take to bed – just wait.

She answered shortly :

'You mustn't let children play with dangerous things.'

Jan Maan gave it up in despair. Katadreuffe began to think again of his studies; he'd soon be back at work again.

They also saw 'Bed and Sofa' by Room – and it was curious how Katadreuffe found this film offensive, his chasteness being at times exaggerated – but she found it nice, just nice; she liked that film best; she had a broad enough outlook.

One mild Sunday afternoon in the winter, she was sitting with Jan Maan on the 'Hill' in the Park. She always liked sitting there; the moving water had a soothing effect on her.

Then a completely square lump of human flesh came rolling along and sat down next to her. It was the *bokschipper*, Harm Knol Hein. She had never met him since the letter. He gave his hand to her and also to Jan Maan.

'You haven't changed at all,' she said.

'Now you, ma'am, you've changed a lot,' he said naïvely. 'And yet I knew you at once.'

He sat there, broad, heavy and bursting with health, a chunk of Rotterdam at its best.

'Are you married now?' he asked.

He looked towards Jan Maan. He couldn't be from any marriage; he was too old for a child and yet too young for a husband, but perhaps a child before marriage.

'No,' she said, 'and this is my lodger. But are *you* married?'

He spat out his quid. He dried his lips on the back of his hand and looked meditatively at the water.

'No, not exactly that,' he said. 'I'm so to say living with a woman.'

He sighed and looked again at Jan Maan. Then he continued:

'Now they are talking about marriage. Could be, could be, but there's nothing in it.'

And, truly feminine, she felt from these words that he was still fond of her, that she only had to raise a finger and he would follow. She did not for a moment think of doing so; she still could not understand and, as years ago, she asked herself what he could see in such an old corpse, particularly as now she was so much older and so much more of a corpse.

In the meantime, in the rough and naïve way of a man of the river, he told his story. Around three years ago he went with a few friends to a pub where you could see serving at the bar a fat woman, a real whopper, the talk of all South Rotterdam. She came from the east, in fact, bursting with health, no chicken any more, between forty and fifty, and still only pouring out drinks. And he'd got caught up with that woman – three years of torture – with the devil of a temper. And she all the time fatter and fatter. He kept her on the quay as if she'd climb up to the cabin the whole crane would capsize – no, he couldn't start that. And she wanted to marry but to the deuce with that. Now he'd brought along a friend, a shipmate, just as tall and broad as he was. He came a lot to the house and he was hoping . . .

He said:

'The rest you'll understand, ma'am, good-day to you.'

And he went off with the slow, rolling gait of a heavy Rotterdam waterman. But he had asked for her address, and a few weeks later he called, just like that, and, uninvited, drew up a chair under his powerful hams.

'You can come as often as you like,' she said, 'as long as you don't smoke. The doctor won't allow it here.'

'Doesn't matter to me,' he said, 'I chew mostly. If you look at it straight, smoking's just silly.'

He neatly cut off a slice of jet-black tobacco, and placed it with care between jaw and cheek.

And so he came every now and then. She was quite fond of this simple fellow. He was like a stretch of brackish water, a living bit of the docks. She would never marry him, but had she been young and chaste, she wasn't quite sure. Limited, yet not stupid, just slow, but so open-hearted, so substantial.

Once she took him with them to Caledonia, with Jan Maan on the other side. It just chanced they were going out when he arrived. Well then, he'd like to have a look at the puppet-show for once. But it was not a success, in fact rather annoying, yet she could not be cross about it although Jan Maan was. He reacted wrongly to everything. When there was nothing to laugh at he roared with laughter, naïvely and deafeningly amidst the protests and hisses of those sitting in the dark. Also, during a deathly silence with lots of blood flowing on the screen, he said twice :

'Gor lumme !'

The Way to Leiden

During the first year, Katadreuffe's path to Leiden was strewn with roses. It was now obvious that he had an excellent head for languages. His young teacher was enthusiastic. There were so many who tried it, but nearly all gave up; the difficulties appeared insuperable, right from the beginning. The teacher had not actually had this experience, but it was confirmed from all sides. How seldom did a working-class boy seem to be suited to study. A good brain was generally hereditary; the children of the upper classes came into the world better equipped; their heads were rounder, their foreheads higher; narrow, sloping skulls were the exception with them.

But this one was coming along well. He was a rare phenomenon who, with his qualities at his age, would go far.

Katadreuffe managed the modern languages by himself. All he would have to do would be to translate a bit of prose into Dutch. He bought books. He was now in a position to acquire better literature, and at an auction he got hold of a parcel of thirty French, German and English books for a few guilders. These lots never contained the latest publications, but what did that matter? There were often some very good books among them. Now and again he would translate a piece taken at random; he improved all the time and soon had less need of the dictionaries. However, he was well aware that this was only a first step; later he would have to learn to write reasonably well, speak fluently, and easily understand the most slovenly or rapid speech. Without that, he could not become a good lawyer and without that he was a long way behind Miss Te George, even. He must surpass her, but he no longer had the ambition to take her place; that had been a mere brain-wave like taking Rentenstein's. It would mean promotion if he could sit with Stroomkoning, but he no longer for a moment wanted to fill that place permanently; it would suffice if he could do so occasionally. His ambition no longer lay in her place but alongside it.

With Rentenstein it was a different matter since he still harboured the same dislike for the fellow, justifying his feeling in the fact that the man simply did not do his duty. Actually, he did precious little, for as Stroomkoning grew more important the police-court work dwindled and the smaller clients gave way to big business. And Rentenstein, on the whole, organized nothing; things were run more laxly than before. Only Stroomkoning's own files and everything touching his business were kept in excellent order by Miss Te George, Rentenstein having nothing to do with them. There was, in fact, no single reason why Katadreuffe should not try to supplant Rentenstein. The organization would be much better under his leadership. There was also nothing magical about the police-court work. Sometimes, in the evening, he looked through the files – mostly minor cases in which logic proved more useful than knowledge of law. A little study of the laws governing work contracts and the regulations covering rents and leases would carry him a long way.

Naturally, should he take Rentenstein's place as head of the office and solicitor's chief clerk, it would mean real promotion, which he would accept readily if offered to him. But again only as something provisional, never losing sight of the fact that it would only be a temporary post. After all, this would also help him towards his goal. In the meantime, he had no intention of undermining Rentenstein's position, however much he might dislike him, however much he was convinced of his own greater excellence. It offended against certain principles of fair play; it was not how a working-class boy should behave towards a colleague; for he possessed that feeling of solidarity one so often finds in subordinates of the same chief.

Katadreuffe studied some mathematics, though not much. He had only one lesson a week at this. The subjects seemed of less importance; he would pick up most of it in his second year. It was the same with history.

Young Miss Van den Born had turned out to be an extraordinarily rapid typist. Between telephone calls she rattled off her copies on the typewriter, all the time posing as a boy, a man, and her thoughts apparently miles away. That brought about a slight change in the office arrangements. The Burgeiks were given less copying work and more dictation. Because of this, Katadreuffe would also have had less to do, had not other and better work been found for him, though still work of minor importance.

It was again De Gankelaar who helped him here. De Gankelaar, himself, had not given him anything like enough work. With summer approaching, he again felt his enthusiasm for his protégé revive. It was when Katadreuffe told him that he had begun, all on his own, the *Carmina* of Horatius, though he couldn't make head or tail of it. De Gankelaar was so dumbfounded that he removed his legs from his desk, so enthusiastic that he shook him by the hand.

'Yes, but,' Katadreuffe said, 'I'm not getting anywhere with it.'

'Don't worry, old chap. That you dare tackle it at all after less than a year is incredible. Horatius – wonderful man – and his *Carmina* was my favourite poetry. I believe I would now sadly fail to remember much of it. Have you read that verse about the prostitute in the draughty alley?

I don't know now where it comes. It begins : *Parcius junctus quatiunt fenestras* . . . I've forgotten the rest. Don't you know it?'

Katadreuffe, who was very prudish, shook his head.

'Just an old tart in a Roman alley,' mused De Gankelaar. 'Bring me your book.'

Alone, he decided on impulse to give him a leg up. The boy was capable of anything. So De Gankelaar discovered Miss Van den Born as he had formerly discovered Katadreuffe, changed round the police-court work a little, and Katadreuffe was given his first police-court case to handle.

'All you have to do now,' said De Gankelaar, 'is to ask Rentenstein if you can take over a case. If you can't manage it come to me.'

But Katadreuffe could not ask; it would look too much as though he wanted to encroach on the head clerk. So De Gankelaar asked him, himself.

Rentenstein was taken aback but did not dare refuse. He was beginning to hate Katadreuffe, but secretly and impotently; Katadreuffe did not even notice it. Rentenstein had always been weak-willed, and of late had no more will left; his conscience was not clear; he feared discovery, and and his eyes became queer and furtive. It was all the fault of Dreverhaven and his cronies.

Katadreuffe's first case was one of those common absurdities, with which the police-court teems. A lady, with one false tooth on a denture, was used to placing this at night in a tumbler. On a certain morning the tooth had disappeared. The lady accused the servant of carelessly throwing it away; the servant denied it. An altercation followed, which ended in the termination of her services. The servant claimed damages for wrongful dismissal; the lady appeared at the office with the court papers. Rentenstein had drawn up a memorandum defending the lady's standpoint but, in Katadreuffe's opinion, laying too much emphasis on trivialities. There was a lot of talk about the tooth itself; according to the lady, a quite normal false tooth;

according to the servant, an unusual one with such a clamp on it that throwing it away with the water would not have been possible, as owing to its unusual size it would have stuck in the plug-hole.

Katadreuffe saw at once that this argument was of secondary importance, and could really be eliminated. The matter was a simple one : had the servant been dismissed or had she, as the lady asserted, taken herself off in a temper? In any case the girl would have to prove that she had been dismissed. Katadreuffe remembered a saying of De Gankelaar's : the facts don't count in a case, only proof of the facts count. He had immediately grasped this truth, and now it was ingrained in him. If the girl should be unable to produce witnesses of her dismissal, her case was lost.

Katadreuffe also began to take an interest in the clients themselves when dealing with their affairs. He was no longer the automaton taking down dictation and copying it out. With the exception of Stroomkoning's own work, which even Rentenstein knew nothing about, he was now *au fait* with a number of current cases. He was all the time learning to couple the faces with the files. Looking for the files in the steel boxes was Kees Adam's work, but the lad had scanty brains; he always had to look into the files, not recognizing a single one from its number. Katadreuffe, although there was absolutely no need for him to watch the clients in the waiting-room, could remember faces from months back, and could associate them with this or that case, sometimes with the appropriate file number.

He also learnt to differentiate between the clients. The higher their standing, the more business-like they were. The big business people were extremely matter-of-fact, the state-aided clients extremely verbose. There was no exception to this rule. Another rule for these two extreme types, reliable but carrying exceptions, was that the big business-men were easy to deal with, the state-aided difficult. The big men were easy over hundreds of thousands of guilders, the state-aided wrangled over a battered tea-pot from some common legacy. The state-aided clients also imagined they were done out of their right place on the waiting-list by the paying visitors, and that their solicitor received his salary, that is to say *their* salary, that is to say the salary *they* didn't pay, from the Government. The big business-men knew better.

There were, of course, a number of other categories in which clients could be placed. Thus Katadreuffe divided them into those who came once, those who came oftener, and those who never came at all but did everything on the telephone or by correspondence. The finest offices, De Gankelaar used to say, were those large offices where you never see a client in the waiting-room, unless by chance a state-aided one. And he said it with a certain regret; he was not employed in such a very fine office.

The category of those who came oftener was again sub-divided by Katadreuffe into those who appeared irregularly and those who appeared regularly. Of the latter there was, in Stroomkoning's office, one striking example, something which he imagined to be out of the ordinary, which, however, is not so rare. It was the divorce-lady he had seen at the time of his first visit whilst he, himself, was sitting in the waiting-room. He did not then know that she came about a divorce, though a practising lawyer would have guessed it from the tip of her nose.

She was the flashy apparition with the bleached hair, smart, but too heavily built to be every inch a lady, and she always went to sit on the one upholstered seat. If it was free she sailed towards it; if it was occupied, it was offered to her. She was the wife of a stevedore, Mrs Starels by name, and she was always imagining that her husband was unfaithful to her. She also had other grievances; that she was called an old trout and things like that. After six months' gay proceedings, the husband came to pay the bill, and they were reconciled. Before the year was out the lady appeared anew; her husband was deceiving her, et cetera. She showed a strong bent for quarrelling, but fortunately not with Stroomkoning; she remained true to his office, and the husband loyally footed the bill.

All the colleagues had, in turn, to deal with her. She would come and sit opposite them in all intimacy, look at them with dark, languishing stage eyes, and report the most dreadful particulars (obviously a pack of lies) which, none the less, embarrassed these gentlemen. Now Miss Kalvelage had been landed with her, and there she did not get on so well. As this girl felt no embarrassment, did not blush, but from time to time repeated :

'Let's keep to business, madam, let's keep to business.'

At the same time she rapped the desk with a ruler as though the stevedore's wife were a naughty child in class.

In the spring, Katadreuffe began to show signs of tiredness. His constitution had been weakened by the chickenpox, scarlet-fever and measles of his childhood. Even his teeth, though immaculate, were weak and the dentist thought this might be connected with having had his milk teeth knocked out, too early and too violently.

Katadreuffe's nature was the opposite of fearful, but he could at times be frightened of himself, frightened of the consequences, should control of his mind slip from him. He several times imagined that he had been sleep-walking again, but he had heard of a good means against this : a soaking wet cloth beside the bed, and the sleeper is awakened by contact of his feet with the damp and cold. He tried this out and, to his relief, it appeared that he had never left his bed. Even had he not woken up, his feet would have left traces behind them. But there was nothing; the wet cloths lay untouched in the morning, with all the little rucks he had deliberately made in them.

Yet he did not feel himself in good shape; he was not looking well, and dropping lessons during Easter week came as a relief. After that, he took things more gently, and decided to spend half an hour after the meal in Graanoogst's room with the child, Pop. She led a lonely existence at home. Her mother was very quiet, inclined to depression. He was unable to fathom the reasons for this; perhaps she was silently afflicted with a deformity in her leg, but he could never find out. Her father busied himself by fits and starts, but was unable to fix his thoughts for long on the child; they quickly wandered and he, bored, would push the child away. He had eaten well and went to smoke his pipe by the window, staring out of it with his dark eyes full of slight melancholy. The child loved the half-hour with Katadreuffe, although he seldom did what she wanted. She preferred to play, jig about, run around, but Katadreuffe always took a book and looked at the pictures with Pop. And the impulse to teach others was so strong in him – he had tried long enough with Jan Maan though in vain – that his eye was more open to what could be taught than the jokes, and he could draw a lesson from almost every picture. He understood absolutely nothing of a child's mind. Nevertheless, Pop was pleased with the half-hour; she did her best to spin it out. Although so young, she already displayed some womanly wiles. She made herself as charming as possible; she let her curls play over the book and, now and then, over his hands; attracting his attention with childish little coquetries; she made big eyes at him from under her long lashes, though her eyes remained bright blue, hard and childishly egotistical. And she was so calculating that she took great care her teeth, white but irregular, did not show too much. He noticed none of this, but she was unaware that he did not notice it. She was still too much of a child; she thought his earnest look was directed at her, whilst it was directed right through her at the broadening of her mind.

Katadreuffe was not competent to plumb the soul of a child and, as regards children on the whole, was completely ignorant. In other respects, he was very observant, also as regards women. And so he suffered a small vexation over the Graanoogsts' servant-girl, that Lieske who, according to the concierge was so well-developed, and who possessed the strange, filmy eyes. He had an instinctive aversion to the girl because she was always looking at him when she served at table. And no one noticed it but he; it was most embarrassing. Every day he sensed the same thing; without looking up he felt her eyes rest on him. After a time he began to feel pity and curiosity, and once he looked at her from the side when she could not see he was looking. For months he had not looked at her, which was really most uncouth, and now he had a shock. Well-covered, yes, but a wretched pallor, a face full of shadows, a black and white pallor, and visible through it a grief which this primitive girl probably scarcely understood, and which therefore the more deeply afflicted her. He had brought down his first victim, and though he did not realize it, he still felt a vague sense of guilt.

'I think she's got her eye on you,' said Mrs Graanoogst at table. 'Haven't you noticed anything?'

'No,' lied Katadreuffe. 'Thank goodness.'

And he at once felt ashamed of the clumsy, brusque reply. But Mrs Graanoogst found it quite normal.

'Of course, she's nothing for a gentleman, and a respectable gentleman doesn't start anything . . . I'd like to have got rid of her. Someone who after a year or so can't cook an ordinary stew will never learn to do it.'

And so Katadreuffe was left with the shameful knowledge that the silent, furtive glances of the servant-girl had not passed unobserved.

That year there was one change in the office: the elder Burgeik resigned. The only reason he gave was that he could not stay away from home any longer. And he was obviously too suspicious to give any further explanation, keeping all at a distance with his small, hard eyes; if the townsmen got to know no more they would not be able to take advantage of a countryman.

It was the better of the two who left, the elder, with the injured hand. His brother remained behind alone, and had now no cause to laugh; that silent, ludicrous laugh which indicated some huge, secret joke (though no one else understood what it was about) was heard no more. The survivor sat so pitifully at this table in the middle of the room, his square face with the short, black hair reflecting a woe beyond description, that one felt it coming : he would go the way of his brother.

In the meantime Miss Van den Born had taken the place of the elder brother. She sat opposite the younger Burgeik, and he certainly did not have much reason to laugh; the girl sat there so pertly and challengingly, something so strange for a countryman, so little of the girl about her, that he preferred not to look at her. He shut himself up in his natural reserve as in a safe.

Kees Adam was given the telephone, as his voice had now a sufficiently manly ring. He was tried out on the house-telephone. Stroomkoning, listening at the other end, was satisfied. For this was a matter for the chief to decide; the voice on the telephone was a vital office interest. Rentenstein would never have dared to act on his own in this.

And so, as in the normal course of things, a few of the staff achieved promotion, but not Pietje. This lad, who would not grow up, remained the errand boy for all and sundry.

A newcomer took Kees Adam's place, a tall boy who introduced himself as Ben. He had just left home and thought everyone would call him by his Christian name, as at home. At first, his exaggerated politeness was irritating; when he saw the lawyers leave their rooms he would always say 'good-bye, sir,' or 'good-bye, madame,' to Miss Kalvelage. It was very obvious that his mother had impressed on him the need for polite behaviour; well, they would soon knock the worst of that out of him.

That year, Katadreuffe received a very deep impression from an incident, unimportant in itself. A most urgent message had to be taken to Stroomkoning during the lunch hour. For years now, Stroomkoning had not been to the lawyers' exchange, and when he was in town he ate in a restaurant. Rentenstein was away at the police-court, at

least so it was said. Katadreuffe considered the message so
important that he took it himself to Stroomkoning.

It was a restaurant in the heart of the town, a very ex-
clusive one. Stroomkoning had his regular table there; often
he had clients or business friends with him. The stairs were
covered with a thick wine-red carpet, the restaurant being
on the first floor. The waiter let Katadreuffe in without
demur, thinking this simply but carefully dressed young
man was an acquaintance.

Katadreuffe presently saw his chief sitting in the distance,
alone, with his back towards him. But he wanted to take in
the whole restaurant; he was now for the first time in direct
contact with a higher world. For a few seconds he felt he
belonged to it; that gave him a feeling of exceptional calm;
he did not experience the slightest gaucheness or embarrassment.

It seemed just the thing for him.

There were several men sitting there, who all appeared
to be business-men. There was very little talk; most of them,
in fact, sat alone. They sat with a stolidity as only business-
men can sit, so solid and so self-contained that, with their
backs to him, they appeared like eating fortresses.

In a flash, Katadreuffe took it all in; the rapid eating,
but not guzzling; the quick gestures, but unhurried. The
only ones hurrying were the waiters, but that was their profession and they did it in a refined way. The restaurant
was entirely tuned-in to the business-man's requirements;
the portions were not too large, as the business-man is inclined to corpulence and has to take care of his weight – the
service was quick, as the business-man lives not only with
but also from speed – it was expensive, but the business-
man does not mind that so long as it is good – it was simple
(practically nothing but mineral water was being drunk),
as the business-man does not celebrate while he is working.

What however struck Katadreuffe most was the self-
containment of these people for half an hour – only a
quarter of one for the meal – the fortress aspect. And this

was in no way ridiculous; it had something rather grand about it.

Then he thought how he would like one day to sit here, sit like these people. It was a sequel to the vision he had had on that first day when he stood in front of the office, not yet accepted, still on the Boompjes, still on the cobbles. It was not five shining plates he had seen nailed to the door but *six*, and the sixth bore his name. He had never told anyone about this vision, not even Jan Maan. Now he saw it again, across the other vision; he saw his name as a lawyer connected with an important office; at the same time he saw himself sitting here, surrounded by the mighty walls of his resolve. The visions merged together, but the pictures remained sharp.

Then Katadreuffe approached Stroomkoning in the distance. He had only now seen him properly, just for a moment, in his place amongst the great ones of the town. The total impression was ineradicable.

Business, Love, Embezzlement

In Katadreuffe's second year, his path was not strewn exclusively with roses. Things began to seem less promising even before the beginning of the new office year; it had started already during holiday time or even earlier still.

It was not Miss Te George's fault, although she was the cause of a secret disquiet in his heart. He thought he had pretty effectively cured himself of her. But the contrary appeared to be the case. There were two episodes with her. The first bore an exclusively pleasant character; it was only thinking about it that brought up the old feeling of dissatisfaction.

After the one tête-à-tête in his room, they had exchanged nothing but greetings. It was an afternoon in late July, just before closing time. He met her on the stairs, as on that first occasion. She was coming out of the conference-room; Stroomkoning had not been there that day. Then Katadreuffe had an inspiration, and it was he who now sought contact. He asked :

'Could I have a look at that room? I've never been in there.'

She stood still on the stairs.

'Never?' she asked in surprise. 'You can't mean that.'

'Well, once I did have a short interview with Mr Stroomkoning here. But I have never really *seen* it.'

'And you living here!'

'Yes, but upstairs. I have no business here.'

She looked at him. The discovery of this abnormality in the boy, again made her feel rather sad at heart. He lived here and had never wanted to go into his boss's room. There was no doubt in her mind that he was speaking the truth, and furthermore, she now keenly felt his attitude was not one of diffidence, but of pride. He had no wish to slink in, uninvited, where he had no cause to go; there was nothing secretive about him. But she had a right to this room and if she invited him, that was another matter. It was sad; she was fond of him.

With a smile, she asked him in, and herself shut the door.

The lights were switched on again, as the room received only scanty daylight, the former back garden being built up with warehouses.

'It isn't nice for Mr Stroomkoning having to work all the time by artificial light,' she said. 'It can't be healthy, but there's nothing to be done about it.'

'Yes, but that chandelier' – and he pointed to it – 'that's a pity.'

The large electric light chandelier was hanging in the middle of the room under the richly painted centre-piece on the ceiling, the supporting rod sticking in the back of a Silenus.

He had an eye for such things. She looked up and, smiling, sighed.

'Yes, but that couldn't be helped, either.'

The door opened and Rentenstein appeared.

'Now, now,' he was about to begin.

But Miss Te George, tall, slender, lady-like, turned towards him and he disappeared without speaking.

'I don't think,' said Katadreuffe, 'that Rentenstein has been looking well lately.'

It was the first time that he had spoken about one of his colleagues, but then he was talking to *her*.

'Perhaps he's not feeling well,' she answered cautiously,

having noticed the same thing for some time now.

No more was said on the subject. He cast his eyes about the room. The dark furniture and upholstery were good, not ostentatious; warm but not luxurious. A room for the big clients; dark club-chairs, a large desk for Stroomkoning in a corner, a bright note being the large mirror over the fireplace and four portraits on the mantel-piece, two very large, two small; an old Dutch chest with blue vases, and also two large vases on each side of the portraits.

Above all, he took in the big conference table with the green cloth, the chairs arranged neatly around it, with a similar chair for Stroomkoning at the end, but near him a small, dark-brown table.

'That's where you sit,' he said.

Infallibly, he knew it at once, and they both laughed. There it was again, his smile.

But he was already serious once more and looked at the portraits and along the walls. What he found nicest was a framed map of the port, like in the lawyer's rooms; but this was an old map of the whole town of centuries ago; a small town with little old docks, still in use. The colours were so beautiful; the houses terra-cotta, the streets pale yellow, the background pumice-stone grey, the water forget-me-not blue, and over it all the brownish discoloration of more than two centuries.

'That's lovely, that's fine; I'd love to have that,' he said with childish enthusiasm, whilst she stood behind him, looking at him.

Yet he was not otherwise childish, but a man who had only one aim and that aim was not a woman.

That evening he again had the feeling that he had committed a sin against himself. This relationship was a mistake and yet he had taken the first step. But these two young people were destined by turns to attract one another.

She had the whole of July for her holiday, whilst Rentenstein would go in August; only these two had a whole month, the others only two weeks. Katadreuffe had never

asked for leave. He lived here and a holiday would be folly
for him as he never left the town. As long as he stayed in
this house, his legs would carry him every day to the general
office. Thus no holiday. Only on Saturday afternoon or
Sunday did he accompany Jan Maan to the Waalhaven
or the Hook.

In this way, shortly after the last meeting with Miss Te
George, Katadreuffe had another one, though this was less
innocent and the recollection of it led to some bitterness.

One Saturday morning, he and Jan Maan went off to the
Hook. It was warm, the distance considerable, with a lot
of traffic, though now Katadreuffe at least had his own
bicycle.

They wandered between the numerous tents on the
beach; a little further on Jan Maan was going to bathe,
but not Katadreuffe. He had left his bathing things at home,
not being such a lover of sea-water as his friend. Jan Maan
saluted several acquaintances, whom Katadreuffe did not
think much of, a lot of hoodlums, certain comrades from
the Party.

Suddenly he heard his name called :

'Mr Katadreuffe, Mr Katadreuffe.'

Twice. The high, clear voice. Miss Te George was standing in front of a small tent, a perky little orange, white
and blue flag at the top. Katadreuffe was at first only too
pleased at the surprise meeting. She was dressed all in
white, looking more alive and fresher than ever. A bathing-
costume fluttered in the wind on a line from her tent.

'Have you bathed already?'

'Yes,' she said.

She gave him her hand; it was the first time they had
shaken hands. Her hand was so cool from the sea; it felt
delightful. He introduced his friend, Jan Maan, and his
friend also received the slender, cool hand.

Then Katadreuffe's cheerfulness was considerably damped
as from behind her, on hands and knees, a fellow came
creeping out of the small tent; someone he did not know

who, when he stood up, appeared reasonably young, and who was now introduced by some name to which Katadreuffe was quite indifferent. It might have been Van Rijn, or Van Dommelen – it left him cold. It was, in fact, Van Rijn.

Katadreuffe was so obviously jealous that he felt ashamed, but he could not help it. Why the deuce did she have to come to the beach, day after day probably, bathing with Van Rijn. *He*, too, had been in the sea, as his damp hair was combed back. That would sound fine later : Mrs Van Rijn, née Te George. What *was* her Christian name? He didn't know.

Already the answer came.

'A cigarette, Lorna? . . . Will you have one too?' asked the man politely, offering his cigarette-case.

Jan Maan alone took one, and Katadreuffe was inwardly angry with his friend as well. Now they couldn't leave immediately; you couldn't do that with your host's freshly lit cigarette in your mouth.

Host. That fellow said *jij*,[1] and her name was Lorna. She had never mentioned a Mr Van Rijn; as far as he knew she had never been brought or fetched by a Mr Van Rijn. Now she suddenly presented him with the facts. And he surreptitiously glanced at her hand.

She saw it; his jealousy was as obvious as that of a small child. She followed his glance at the fingers of her left hand, quietly spread out in the warm sand. She looked at him, a little sadly, a little archly, but he was much too angry to return her look. He got up as soon as it was possible. Jan Maan had to follow him, and after a step or two could contain himself no longer.

'What a charming girl . . . How do you know her? . . . Is she from the office? . . . A real lady . . .'

But Katadreuffe simply could not stand his frivolous friend, the communist skirt-chaser, speaking in such a way

[1] Thou – familiar form of address. (Pronounced **yeigh** as in height.)

about someone like Miss Te George. He kept silent. He did not answer. Jan Maan went on unconcernedly, indefatigably.

'As for you, I thought it seemed dreadfully queer the way you sat there. You didn't say a word.'

'I've got a headache,' said Katadreuffe. 'I'm not feeling well. If you want to stay you must stay by yourself. I'm going home.'

He was not fibbing; he looked ill; he had a dreadful pain above his eyes. That whole Sunday he felt wretched, not from the pain but because things had gone so far with him. And it could not be, it could not be. Even if that Van Rijn, or whatever he was called, meant nothing to her, it could not be, because of himself.

He was glad she would be away for a few weeks. And in August, when she came back, everything between them was quite normal, as of old.

In the second half of that same month, Stroomkoning suddenly appeared in the office. He had broken off his holiday in Scotland, missing thereby a trip to Staffa and Iona, and his visit to C. C. & C. His wife would have to carry on with the rest of the plan with the children. Rentenstein was having his month's holiday when Katadreuffe naturally, but unofficially, took his place and distributed the mail. Stroomkoning called him to one side, having at last remembered his name :

'None of the clients must know I'm back in the office, Katadreuffe. Tell all the rest of the staff.'

None of the clients expected Stroomkoning to be back already. He was thus able to remain alone, shutting himself up in the conference-room with an accountant and all the office books. The reason was a note from the tax inspector. Only once had his books been examined by an official accountant. That was nothing out of the ordinary; it happened in all offices. But irregularities had shown up. The inspector wrote that there was suspicion of embezzlement, in which one or perhaps more of his staff was involved.

This note had been forwarded to Stroomkoning and was the cause of his hurried return.

He sat the whole morning in his room with his private accountant; from time to time fresh papers were brought to him; the accountant came into the office to ask for all kinds of folders containing cash receipts.

At half past twelve they went off. Stroomkoning did something he had never done before; he locked the conference-room. Within an hour they were both back.

A depression hung over the office, though this did not appear to affect the two lawyers who had returned from their holidays, Miss Kalvelage and Carlion. But both were so resistant to emotion that they behaved as though nothing out of the way was on hand, and that struck Katadreuffe as the best line to take. But they knew that something was going on. Stroomkoning was not to be disturbed by anybody, not even the colleagues; at lunch-time they shut the doors of the yellow room; now they were all together and no sound could be heard; they must be speaking very softly.

The depression settled over the general office; even Katadreuffe's face became darkly serious. There were two of them who understood quite well all the secrecy : he and Miss Te George. Had they not recently exchanged words about Rentenstein's sick demeanour? But his terrible seriousness she found rather amusing; he was still so young, younger than she in every respect, except in his ambition. But to a nature like Katadreuffe's stealing from your chief was pure imbecility.

At four o'clock he was called in. The big table in the middle was strewn with papers. The chief looked up, his moustache bristling, the light-green eyes looking darker. He said seriously, but not angrily :

'I won't hide it from you any longer, Katadreuffe; there's money missing. At the moment there is a shortage of two thousand. Rentenstein has been systematically taking it. How long it's been going on I don't know yet, but what we do know is sufficient to have him under lock and key for a bit. I shall have to get advice, but in any case he won't be putting his nose inside the office again. He'll be fired at once; tell Miss Te George I want her. And you can now go and tell the others.'

The next day Rentenstein sent his wife. On the Boompjes she had already begun to snivel, and in the conference-room she went on sobbing, worse and worse. She was a slovenly, withered, faded little thing, with yellow hair, no hat, dressed in something that looked more like a grubby bathing-wrap than anything else. Web-like stockings and extremely smart shoes with bright red, very high heels were scarcely in harmony with the rest of her.

But the greatest surprise was that Rentenstein actually had a wife; no one had known anything about it. The little woman sat there, sobbing uncontrollably. Katadreuffe finally indicated the yellow room to her, as the clients in the waiting-room were already getting restive.

Stroomkoning allowed her in sooner than he had intended, just in order to be rid of her irritating whimpering.

Sitting in front of him, she held back her tears, and began talking quickly. Dreverhaven was the real cause of it all. He had led her husband on to drinking and gambling.

Stroomkoning had an uncomfortable feeling when he heard Dreverhaven mentioned in this connection. Not that he would have considered it impossible for his bailiff to lead another into bad ways, on the contrary. But he had done a lot of business with Dreverhaven, although recently less than formerly, and these things always created a bond.

There was no need to interrogate the woman; it all came out on its own. Dreverhaven knew so many proxies, her husband went so often to the police-court; it had become quite a clique. There was betting and, she believed, they gambled on the Stock Exchange, and he was always losing money; that was how it had happened. Then, in the evenings, they drank terribly – they always went to the same pub – and sometimes they had been to her house, Mr Dreverhaven and the proxies. Then she had to drink with

them and sing songs, and dance with all the proxies, sometimes two together, in the new fashion where one lady
dances with two men, until she was all in. And Mr Dreverhaven sat there in a corner like a big country yokel with his
hat and coat on; and when he had drunk the whole lot
under the table he went away, and seemed just as sober as
when he came.

Stroomkoning nodded. He knew well enough that there
was some relationship between Dreverhaven and his head
clerk; he had seen them whispering together. Undoubtedly
Dreverhaven then gave him tips which went wrong, just
as he had often done with him. And all that drinking; so
that was how the weakling had come to ignore the difference between mine and thine.

And Rentenstein, naturally, had acted half stupidly, half
cunningly. He had increased the cost of the writs, which
was cunning – you didn't look so closely at them – as was
also the case with the petty cash expenses, Graanoogst's
weekly book for example, that didn't attract your attention.
But it hadn't been enough for him, and he went on to do
stupid things, like booking bills that didn't exist, entries
under 'to Meyer', or any other arbitrary name, sometimes
merely an initial and no more. From carelessness, stupidity,
or despair, his malversations became clearer and clearer;
one look at the cash-book brought them to light.

And Stroomkoning felt that he, himself, was not entirely
free from blame, as he had let things slide, even though he
had had the suspicion that all was not quite as it should
be. For a long time now he had had the feeling that he
was being robbed. And so it was; not by Katadreuffe, but
by Rentenstein. But he was never able to decide on an investigation; he could bark at his opponents, his clients if
necessary, but not his own staff. Well, that's just how he
was : too easy-going in the office, and so lacking control.
Such occurrences were then inevitable.

Taken altogether, he was glad things apparently weren't
any worse; two, three, four thousand, it couldn't be more.

He had feared an amount of at least five figures. Thank God, also, that he kept two separate accounts.

'Now listen, Mrs Rentenstein,' Stroomkoning gruffly interrupted her, 'first of all, I didn't know that your husband was married, but we'll leave that, although it doesn't go in his favour – I don't mean his marriage but that he kept quiet about it (here had had to suppress a fit of laughter, but the little woman did not notice anything). But he cannot reckon on any consideration – my letter stands. And he can be very pleased if I don't prosecute him, if I take the deficit for my own account, that is to say if I act as if there were no deficit, if I ignore it in my tax declaration and ask them to leave it at that. There is then a reasonable chance that Rentenstein will not be prosecuted. I will go so far as to have a word with the Public Prosecutor, if it seems necessary, but that is all I'm willing to do. Now you can go.'

He was, at bottom, a good and generous man; he had never had a member of his staff on the carpet; he could not stand rows in the office. But *this* particularly soft treatment sprang, to a considerable extent, from his decision to keep Dreverhaven out of it. Not that he had anything at all to do with the embezzlement, but that drinking, gambling, probably womanizing, must in no case leak out in connection with Dreverhaven, the man who had made him, just as he in his turn had been made by him, Stroomkoning.

She was certainly a repulsive little woman, vulgar, a proper slattern, with her mop of coarse, straight hair, grubby bathing-wrap and fashionable shoes, howling and snivelling, attracting the attention of the whole office, filling half the Boompjes with her misery. And yet she was a woman with primitive scruples, for she had defended her husband as well as she could, without mentioning her unhappy married life. Also this blubbering must have represented a sort of gratitude; the whole world must be witness to her relief.

'And just remember,' Rentenstein had said to her as she started out on her mission, 'if you don't see to it that I at least keep out of the clutches of the law, then I'll begin on you from the top, and I'll break every bone in your scraggy body.'

But to get Stroomkoning to condone the offence was, as she experienced, not difficult, and Rentenstein had anticipated this.

The Way to Lieden

Stroomkoning called for Katadreuffe.

'You're the obvious successor to that thief. I know you're not the oldest member of the male staff, certainly not in years of service, but you're the only suitable one. I can't make the one remaining twin . . .'

'Burgeik,' Katadreuffe said.

'That's it, Burgeik, I can't make him head of the office, you can see that. Moreover, all the partners are satisfied with your work; I personally don't know much about you, and that will probably remain so, as I didn't have much contact with Rentenstein. Also it's not necessary, and I haven't time for it. If I attend to my own affairs and distribute the rest among my colleagues my day is full enough. I'll leave everything as it is, not bother about details, and rely on you. I have absolute confidence in you. I'm convinced that you, altogether apart from any question of honesty, will make a better head clerk than he did.'

Katadreuffe remained silent, as Stroomkoning had not yet finished. The latter looked straight ahead and stroked his moustache, reflecting.

'There are one or two difficulties. Whether you are any good at organization or not I don't know, but with that serious face of yours you look as though you ought to be. I'm not frightened of that; most serious-minded people are systematic. But you've had no bailiff's exam, you know next to nothing of the police-court practice, and that's more important. But it's not insuperable. If you strike a difficult case, go to one of the lawyers for advice. There remains the question of your salary. You're of course not fully qualified. Rentenstein had thirty-five hundred guilders. To begin with I'll give you twenty-five hundred. Agreed?'

'Mr Stroomkoning,' said Katadreuffe, for the first time using his name, 'I find your offer very handsome. I'll speak honestly : I had more or less expected it, but I would rather not take it on in exactly the way you propose. May I make one or two changes?'

'And they are?'

'To start with, you don't make me officially your head clerk.'

'You don't want to cause any jealousy?'

'Exactly. Further I would rather not attend the police-court.'

'Oh! You're afraid of contamination.'

'I was warned about it.'

'By whom?'

'Mr de Gankelaar.'

'That's just like him,' Stroomkoning mumbled, 'but he's right. There you get all sorts of scum. Anything more?'

'Yes, I don't want more salary than I can earn.'

'Earn?'

'Yes, in my own eyes. If to start with you gave me fifteen hundred guilders . . .'

It took a long time for Stroomkoning to bring him up to two thousand. Stroomkoning was generous towards his staff; to be sure, he earned money like water and had lately had some lucrative cases. He liked to pay well, and a chief clerk at fifteen hundred guilders seemed in his eyes absurd for an office like his.

But he was also once a working-class boy, who had risen. He seldom tried to hide his origins, at the most in things like the too small portraits of his parents. There would no doubt come a time when he would become proud of his father, the little water-clerk, and then the portraits would grow larger. In the boy he felt a vague reflection of himself. He also studied, though under greater difficulties, as he had to do so at the same time as earn his living, and was so much older than he had been. He sensed something of the enormous difficulties, also of the latent intellect, which did not yet emit illumination, which merely absorbed, but which perhaps one day would surpass his own. He found him such a first-class fellow that the dispute over the salary disappointed him. Katadreuffe could not diddle himself, he could not accept presents. In the last few years he had grown so exaggeratedly conscientious that he grudged giving anybody the pleasure of making him a present. In him, absolute honesty was combined with a great deal of narrow-mindedness. Stroomkoning had the utmost difficulty in getting him up to two thousand.

He said smilingly :

'According to your reckoning you're no good yet. And yet you want to be a lawyer.'

Katadreuffe answered in all seriousness, without even considering how kindly the other meant it :

'I believe I can become a reasonably good lawyer.'

And Stroomkoning felt that their opinions about law practice were not exactly identical.

He went on, still smiling :

'Well, in any case I now have the feeling that I ought to be thanking *you* for being allowed to raise your salary a bit.'

Katadreuffe showed tact in his new job. He did not move over to Rentenstein's chair, but stayed at his table. He continued to take down dictation, though not so much as formerly; he did the police-court work and, on a few rare occasions, asked the advice of De Gankelaar or Miss Kalvelage. In the evening when they had all gone he worked at the books, and then sat at Rentenstein's desk. After he had mastered the principles of simple book-keeping, he found this work boring but he did it with his usual meticulousness. He was now busier than before, but yet that did not interfere with his studies in the least. The one thing that helped him enormously was the confidence that he would pass his matriculation easily. It was only the mathematical subjects which he found difficult, but he would be able to put up a reasonable show even in these. He was now getting lessons from three teachers, and had also begun on history. And his large increase in salary enabled him to pay off more of his debt to the bank than was required. He thought now of moving his quarters, but in the end considered it wiser to postpone carrying out this plan until after his examination.

He did not realize that he was living entirely on his nerves, that he, even with his qualities, could stretch the bow too tight, and did so all the time. For the material for his studies was becoming more and more difficult, more extensive, and his fierce concentration during this second year of study undermined his health considerably. Yet he found time for his mother, for the films, for Jan Maan, but he was not aware that from these recreations he did not derive any fresh energy, that they were no real recreation for him. He was all the time in continuous danger and right outside normal reality, yet did his work, in the office as well as his studies, excellently. He also slept well, but however absurd it may seem, it was his nerves which made him sleep, and he did not derive any real vigour from his sleep.

One symptom should have indicated to him how critical was his condition, but he did not see it. That was his relationship with Miss Te George. They now behaved completely normally with each other; she, alone, had guessed his feelings, and he knew that he had given himself away that day at the Hook. It was, however, not this knowledge which worried Katadreuffe. Also her presence did not disturb his equanimity. He sat in his old place, a little to one side behind her, far away, looking at her back, but he seldom looked up. She was completely banished from his thoughts, and he was able to concentrate on his work. Then suddenly came the vexing memory of that one incident on the beach. It did not happen often but when it did, it was intolerable. He saw the fellow, that Van Rijn, on his hands and knees, crawl out of the tent, get up and stand before him, a fairly presentable, reasonably acceptable young man. Once or twice that stinging headache returned and, once during office hours, he felt sick and dizzy and had to go to bed with an aspirin.

Although Katadreuffe, in his new position, did not place himself on a pedestal, he seized the opportunity to re-organize the office. Kees Adam was not allowed to copy Miss Van den Born and call through the telephone :

'Sir, your coffee's getting cold.'

He said respectfully :

'Sir, your coffee is ready.'

He had received permission from Stroomkoning to have the waiting-room and the general office done up. Stroom-koning who made such a fetish of the first impression via the telephone, saw that the first impressions of his waiting-room and general office were no less important.

Katadreuffe cleared out the ugly furniture from the waiting-room. The shabby old red, upholstered seat had always irked him. He went for what was most modern : white curtains, steel chairs, a powerful light in the middle, the bulbs shaded by a plate of clouded glass, hanging from white cords. He did away with the old-fashioned cushions from the window-seats; he got a large round table for the middle, on which the literature was arranged every morn-ing in an orderly fashion, not in the untidy heap from which the clients formerly pulled out something at random, whatever condition it might be in. The conference-room was to get a lighter wallpaper the following summer. The general office was already made much brighter. Mrs Starels, the divorce-lady, missed her favourite seat with a disap-pointed 'hey !', and planted her heavy bulk of Rotterdam specific gravity in a fragile steel chair without any back legs, which stood up to it wonderfully.

He had a similar light fixed in the general office. Otherwise there was nothing much necessary there except to introduce a little more system. And he had the hideous, ochre wallpaper in the room with a skylight replaced with a quiet brown, so that during the lawyers' exchange the colleagues' hands no longer looked as if they had jaundice. Now that he was responsible for the staff, he went thoroughly into their individual capabilities. His dislike of Miss Van den Born turned into speechless astonishment. Her wonderful speed in mechanical work was amazing. Dictation, reading back, typing, all went at a remarkable rate. Suddenly she had left Miss Sibculo miles behind. When, sitting in the middle opposite Burgeik junior, visible to everyone, she really got going, even the attention of the clients in the next room was attracted by her *élan*. Her machine no longer tapped, no longer rattled, it rained a cloud-burst of letters, the keys flashed like rays of light; striking special signs, throwing back the carriage for a new line zigzagged through it all like flashes of lightning. In any speed competition she would have easily won first prize. How modest by comparison was the sound of Miss Sibculo's typewriter : how still more modest was that of Burgeik who, to emphasize the contrast, sat opposite her.

But she was not thinking of competitions; she wasn't thinking of anything. Katadreuffe was fascinated by her talent. What this child would not be able to achieve if she wished. He chatted with her occasionally after office hours; he was always possessed with the idea of helping another to climb higher, just as he wanted to do. He enquired about her plans. The girl with the peculiar boy's hair with its little parting, the wide nostrils, whether laughing or sneezing, sat high-spirited, proud, unapproachable, in her incredible jumper and skirt, arms crossed, the hands which were so fleet under her arm-pits, an impossible attitude for listening. She said nothing except yes and no as shortly as possible, her answers being quite irrelevant. Katadreuffe was sorry to see the girl so completely wrapped up in herself and that he could not really get anywhere with her. The excellent qualities would always be overshadowed by the absurd bearing, the repellent conceit, the forbidding tone of the hoarse voice – a voice and tone partly natural, but to a certain extent, deliberately cultivated. She was worth keeping just for her formidable rate of work, and, in spite of all there was against her, he could not completely suppress a feeling of admiration for her neat and faultless work.

Kees Adam, too, would not go very far, not even so far as she; but he was no complicated character; his rise would simply be checked through lack of natural aptitude. His was a type to be found in every office, the adolescent who cannot find any lasting employment, whose parents could think of nothing better than to get him just any job in an office, who generally after a short time goes an entirely different way, becoming a barber, or a waiter, or entering his father's business. Kees Adam was destined for the latter. He liked rough games and his love was the motor-cycle; whether it was in action or not was all the same to him. His father, the garage-owner, had recently started making twin-saddles for joy-riders. This seemed to show promise, and he intended to take his son into the business.

With young Ben there was nothing to be done; he was the worst of all Rentenstein's legacies. But Pietje, who would not grow up, had lately been ill, so Ben could always do his work, and he was in any case stronger and older.

At the end of the month Katadreuffe, himself, went to take Pietje his wages. He was a person who liked children without understanding anything about them. Just as with Graanoogst's Pop, he also had a weakness for this Pietje. However, with Pietje, it was due rather to a certain sympathy for the underdog which he had picked up from Jan Maan in past years.

The child's name was Grieve, according to the name on

the door. He was lying in an alcove, sick. His amber eyes were still attractive, and he showed his ugly, brittle teeth when he smiled. He had a high colour and hot hands, and his voice had practically gone. Too young, he had had to run about too much in the office; also outside a lot in wind and rain, his shoes sometimes soaked with snow and mud.

The mother pointed significantly to both sides of her chest, and Katadreuffe understood from the gesture that the child was in the last stages of tuberculosis.

'I'll bring his money again next month,' he said on taking his departure.

But he wondered whether he would find the child still alive. It was really the fault of that cursed Rentenstein who had engaged a child, so young and sickly, rather than that of the parents who had let him take on the job.

'Now, I'm the boss,' Katadreuffe said to himself, 'such a thing will never happen again.'

Then he hardened his heart; he must not become sentimental, but get on with his work. But he had one more unpleasant experience that winter. This was the engagement of Miss Sibculo, and the little celebration arising from it, and what happened there in spite of it.

De Gankelaar had been right when he had reckoned Katadreuffe's good looks might be a danger to the tranquillity of the office. But he had thought : the fellow is not out to please; he is not thinking of himself in that way; it will work out all right. But it was in Katadreuffe's very reserve that the danger lay. And just as Lieske had become his victim, so to some extent was the case with Miss Sibculo. She was an insignificant girl, but love is a primitive instinct from which even a colourless character can suffer violently. Once she had been in love with Katadreuffe and then no longer so, but actually she had still gone on loving him, all the more when he became chief clerk, when he stood above her, with only Miss Te George as an equal. Now from the depths, she could look up and worship him.

She did not do this too openly. She was no coarse servant girl, lacking in good taste, but it had bothered Katadreuffe from the start, and he had exactly the same feeling of disquiet as with Lieske. He also found it humiliating that he should attract such nondescript girls, against any intention on his part. It hurt his pride; he was not conceited, but he was very proud.

This plump girl, Sibculo, with the dark, artificial curls, too short a neck, and engagingly swinging hips, had always vaguely and yet seriously worried him. Her work was not good, not bad : sufficient, passable, colourless. For a long time he had regarded her as a living example of mediocrity in every respect, as someone who did not deserve her position because a man would easily fill it better. Katadreuffe willingly admitted that, for certain office work, a woman can possess considerable ability, but should she not have this, the place should be given to a man. The fact that Miss Sibculo did not possess great ability annoyed him; he felt she was robbing another of his bread.

Now she was engaged. She had told them, asking for the morning off, and came to the office again in the afternoon. Katadreuffe was glad about the engagement; it removed part of his worries. That afternoon there was a basket of flowers by her table, to which all the staff had contributed, and the lawyers had already ordered a basket to be sent to her home.

But happy she was not. The engagement had come quite unexpectedly; there she stood with her sparkling ring without really knowing how it had been conjured on to her finger. The tears streamed. The gentlemen came downstairs to congratulate her; Miss Kalvelage came out of her small room and gave her her hand, all bone – she howled. Stroomkoning, between two telephone conversations, called her in; she went in and came out of the conference-room with a nice, little bonus in her small hand, weeping all the time. With red eyes, she stood by the flowers, by her table, helplessly twisting her ring, and would not calm down.

There is nothing to be said against a little crying on the part of a newly engaged girl, provided there are limits. Here they were greatly exceeded, and everyone was surprised at these highly exaggerated tears of happiness. But Katadreuffe noticed how, every now and then, she glanced stealthily at him, and when he went near her it seemed that she wept – just a little, calculated little – harder. He felt sorry for her.

For at this time, his character was developing new traits; he was gradually becoming more human, though he would always be the man with one aim, and an unshakable will. But what had formerly bothered him in some of the staff he now saw differently. He now and then commiserated with them; he sometimes secretly admired them.

When Miss Sibculo was called upstairs for her last dictation, the sentimental girl had been wiped off with powder and lipstick, and it was the everyday little typist who went out, tossing her curls as she swung into the corridor. And this did not harden Katadreuffe's heart; he remained pitying her. The thimbleful of brains had for a moment not known how to cope with a grief that was quite genuine. He had enough sense to realize what his own attitude must be; show nothing, no pity, not even interest – never. Then it would be the more quickly over, for however great her present grief might be, it would not last. He had outgrown his understanding of a child's mind, but he had keen insight as regards women, also men, and also himself.

The slight vexation of this discovery, the feeling of guilt without being guilty, had it not been for his strong will, might have upset his equilibrium. He was living more and more on his nerves. There were nights that winter when he hardly slept. He lay still on his divan-bed, in the pitch-black room, on his back, and had the feeling that his twitching nerves began a life of their own. Faint electric currents shot through him, causing the tips of his fingers and toes to tingle. A few times he had trouble from palpitations; on other nights he could neither feel nor hear his heart. He was again frightened of sleep-walking and spread wet cloths in front of his bed. In the middle of the winter the cloths sometimes froze to the floor, and then he was not sure the following morning whether he had left his bed or not.

It occurred to him that he was in danger of overworking, that he must arrange his studies differently and not stay up working at dead of night. At lunch-time he was entitled to an hour and a half, and he could surely use an hour of it for study. But he did not want to do this. After sitting for half an hour at Graanoogst's table, he returned immediately to the office.

The only recreation which he sometimes allowed himself from one to two was to listen to the lawyers' exchange in the room with the skylight, the door connecting it with the general office generally standing open. He found it difficult to follow the purely legal conversations, but they were rare, as De Gankelaar understood how quickly to give a turn to the conversation. He preferred to speak about Man, and recently about man, woman and marriage. He skirmished principally with Miss Kelvelage, just because that gnome hardly represented any sex, and he found something piquant in that. He sometimes completely forgot that he ought to handle her differently from Piaat and Carlion; he forgot it intentionally. This heedlessness was at times almost rude, but it nevertheless appeared to amuse her. Such conversations fascinated Katadreuffe, and he stopped his work to listen.

It always began with cases from the law practice. That bored De Gankelaar, and he would say:

'You're lawyers; you're warped. I am a human being, I want to marry. Let's talk about marriage. Have you ever realized how beautifully a woman complements a man's life? Just like the cattle, the field.'

'Oh! You're a shameless polygamist,' Miss Kalvelage interjected, but she was not serious.

After a moment they all laughed, De Gankelaar as unconstrainedly as the others.

'Your example is, moreover, hardly complimentary,' Piaat said.

'And the subject's threadbare,' Miss Kalvelage said.

De Gankelaar considered these last words, and shaking his head in negation, resumed :

'The man of today fortunately realizes that it's all been said already, and looks for merit only in some fresh form.'

Miss Kalvelage looked at her joyless, almost incorporeal little body.

'Now you're again insulting; as where must *I*, as a human being, now look for my merit?'

The eyes behind the round glasses looked at him with caustic mockery. It was not she who was embarrassed by the unfeminine harshness of her answer, but she embarrassed him. That was what she wanted to do; she liked him, but she was a very different type of person. He had recovered himself, and with a good deal of genuine seriousness he said :

'You needn't for a moment be afraid, Miss Kalvelage, that anyone will misjudge you. You are far too unique, you're a gnome.'

'Meagre comfort; however, Catherine the Second sounds more invidious than Catherine the Gnome.'

'Catherine,' he said with enthusiasm, 'let it be Catherine, just Catherine. The greatest honour that can fall to a man is to be known to the world only by his Christian name. That is the prerogative of kings, Miss Kalvelage, and of the great artists of the Renaissance; Michelangelo, Raphael, Rembrandt. But not Rubens, who quite rightly bears his surname; the man comes a long way behind. But *you* are entitled to that honour, absolutely.'

Piaat and Carlion were no longer listening, and had returned to their law cases. Miss Kalvelage looked exploratively at De Gankelaar, and at the same time right through him. These two felt a mutual affection for one another, in a cool and intellectual manner, and they were aware of it.

'You,' she said, 'are actually entirely European in your outlook. Your manner of thought, the clichés you use, your paradoxes are European. There seems to me something very limited about that.'

She was now serious, and he smiled again.

'That is a matter of belief over which discussion is difficult. But you are right if by European you mean Western European. In that sense I am European, for there is only one Europe, Western Europe. What can be called the world, has, for about five centuries, been Western Europe. That comes from the Nordic race. It is remarkable that a certain pigment of hair, skin and membrane can create such a superiority, but we are confronted with those facts.'

'Western Europe, I accept it, but as regards the rest you are absolutely wrong,' she said, almost violently. 'And, as a brunette, I'm glad to leave myself out of it; you too as a blond. But I'll torpedo your theory – in all seriousness – I just ask you to think of Katadreuffe.'

De Gankelaar then might have jeered in a friendly way that this answer, so typically feminine, was using the particular, on impulse, to divert from a general maxim, but his criticism was drowned in the pleasure caused by the mention of his protégé in this context.

'Yes, *he* is superior.'

Yet he could not entirely abandon his principles and added :

'The exception that proves the rule, at least, in my opinion. But he is superior.'

'No,' she said, 'he will be. He's still growing. In ten years' time he will have developed.'

Katadreuffe could not hear the last few words. They had started to speak softly, and the other two were talking at the same time.

Katadreuffe and Dreverhaven

A letter came for Katadreuffe from Dr Schuwagt.

The People's Credit Company had placed their demand in his hands. 'I request you, within three days, to pay your debt to my office, and in the event of your failing to do so, have instructions to apply for your bankruptcy.'

Katadreuffe did not accept the letter with resignation, yet with complete indifference. Had it come a year earlier it would have been a bad business, very bad. Not now. It was true that he could not possibly pay off the whole debt, although he had already paid more than he was obliged, but no one could now do anything to him. His matriculation started in a few weeks; he had been summoned to the Hague, he was taking his final lessons, and all his lessons had been paid for in advance. He was quite convinced he would pass; he would even do fairly well in mathematics, having caught up considerably in these subjects. And once he had passed it would not matter so much if he had to begin his academic studies a year later. In that year he would be clear of debt. It would not worry him if his father made use of the lien on his salary. The more he laid his hands on to what he was legally entitled, the quicker the debt would be liquidated, and Katadreuffe would manage through on what was left him from his salary. Then he would be finished once and for all with his father, as his earnings would be sufficient to enable him to study without any further loan. A year is soon past, he thought.

Looked at more closely, a year's delay was of course a pity. And he asked himself with bitterness why a *father* had to do this to his son.

In self-defence, he immediately drove away these thoughts, and regained his indifference. For he realized that at this time, with the exam on his hands, he must not allow any obstacle to deflect him from his goal.

Of course, if he really stood in danger of a new bankruptcy, then it was all up with him, as not only would Stroomkoning find it difficult to keep on a head clerk who was bankrupt – still more so a bankrupt colleague; but Katadreuffe would evade dismissal. He would take himself off first. That he would never allow to happen; for that he was much too proud, and he would rather his future were ruined than keep his job as a kind of charity. But there was no need to worry about it; he now knew sufficient about the law : bankruptcy was impossible. He only had this one debt. The old man was trying to frighten him, that was all.

And he began to think of his father whom he had not seen for a long time. Since Rentenstein's departure there was nothing more to whisper about and Dreverhaven had stayed away. They used to talk about it amongst themselves : why didn't Dreverhaven show up any more, why did the clerk, Hamerslag, bring all the bailiff's writs to the office? It was obvious; he had only been coming here for Rentenstein.

Katadreuffe asked himself whether his father was aware that he was demanding his money back at a very inconvenient time. He undoubtedly had a right to the money; out of a sort of bravado Katadreuffe had consigned himself to the gallows, as Dreverhaven had said. He had been warned that the debt could be called in at any moment, and yet he had signed in order to defy his father, at least partly so. For he had not quite known from whom else he could borrow the money. However be that as it may, calling in the debt was fully justified. Only the timing; just before his exam. And the way it was done : application for bankruptcy. That was just like the old man, yes, he must have smelt that he couldn't choose a worse time; from *his* standpoint, a better time.

But Katadreuffe was not afraid. His father would *not* get him down this time. And a few days later, with the same indifference, he received the letter from the court before which he was summoned to appear in connection with the application for his bankruptcy.

On their way to the Noordsingel, Katadreuffe discussed the case with Carlion. Although his mind was preoccupied with it, he remained calm. De Gankelaar was on his holidays, and Katadreuffe had shown the letter to Carlion. The lawyers knew that he had borrowed money, but it was a praiseworthy debt.

'I'll go with you,' said Carlion.

Katadreuffe did not consider this necessary.

'I'm going with you,' repeated Carlion. 'Between us two, that Schuwagt is a scoundrel. I really don't see what he can do to you but I'll come just to make sure. Now, think carefully : you have no other debt? Schuwagt can't spring a surprise?'

'No, that's absolutely impossible; I feel quite safe, at least as far as bankruptcy is concerned. Could the court find one debt sufficient to make me bankrupt?'

'Out of the question. That is the confirmed opinion of the High Court, and all the courts follow it. At least two debts, and also they have to be proved or the applicant doesn't stand a chance. So many applications which otherwise might be justified fall down on that point. Your case it quite different, though; you don't deserve to go bankrupt and you're not going bankrupt.'

'Then I don't understand why you want to come along.'

'Just precautionary,' growled Carlion.

On first sight, he did not make a very good impression. He was not brilliant and he had not got De Gankelaar's

charm. But this dry stick had shown he was interested and
ready to help, and Katadreuffe was grateful to him. Perhaps, after all, you could rely on him more than on De
Gankelaar. He was no creature of impulse but a man with
both feet on the ground.

An hour later, Katadreuffe stood in court, his own counsel with his gold spectacles and bald head behind him on
one side, and Dr Schuwagt, that very ordinary looking
man, hair still between blond and grey, on the other. Katadreuffe only looked at the judge. The latter made him think
of an elderly French marquis. He had a white moustache
and a neat square beard. He asked him whether he acknowledged the debt. Yes. And had he any further debts.
No.

'Is that correct?' The judge now turned to Dr Schuwagt.

The latter remained calmly behind his desk, his file open
before him.

'It is not correct, *President*. I would first of all like to
observe that the defendant has already been bankrupt – Mr
Wever was his trustee . . . I recognize that that bankruptcy
has been completely liquidated . . . But since then the defendant had incurred fresh debts – I must stress the plural
to the court – *debts*. For besides the one to my client the
defendant has another one to Mr de Gankelaar, in whose
office he works. A small debt, I admit, but still a debt . . .
eighteen guilders.'

Katadreuffe had, up till now, not moved; he felt so sure
of himself – the man could go on talking till Doomsday.
Now he turned round.

'That is not true.'

He had wanted to say: 'You are lying.' He controlled
himself, and added :

'You have been misinformed.'

Dr Schuwagt lost none of his calm.

'I beg your pardon, but my information comes from the
best source, namely, Mr Wever himself. This is how it is.
On the distribution list for the former bankruptcy, under

the assets, is the entry: "private sale of books: eighteen guilders." These eighteen guilders were paid by Mr de Gankelaar to Mr Wever in order to avoid public auction of the books. I am not aware of the reason for this, but can only say that the defendant was at that time in Mr de Gankelaar's office. But the defendant must still be in possession of the books, and in that way Mr de Gankelaar became a creditor of the former bankrupt to the amount of eighteen guilders, which, so far as I know, has not been paid off.'

'Hm,' said the judge, 'other explanations are conceivable. Don't let's get involved in that; the matter seems of little importance.'

'Excuse me, *President*, it is only necessary to prove two debts.'

The judge turned to Katadreuffe.

'What is the situation? Are the books yours or Mr de Gankelaar's?'

Katadreuffe had grasped it all. He turned deathly pale, but he did not consider lying.

'They are mine, *meneer de president*.'

'Do you owe a debt to Mr de Gankelaar?'

'Yes, I now hear I have a debt of eighteen guilders. I did not at first think of it, or rather, I have never known it; Mr de Gankelaar never told me. But now that he bought the books and left them with me, I owe him the money.'

Thereupon Dr Carlion came forward. He was not alarmed like Katadreuffe; it was part of his job not to be alarmed.

'*President*, I suggest that the matter is not worthy of consideration. I am wondering how my confrère could bring up such a trivial amount . . .'

'I beg your pardon,' said Dr Schuwagt.

Carlion continued unconcernedly:

'But apart from that, I can confidently declare here in the name of Mr de Gankelaar that the money was a gift. I also knew nothing about the incident. But Mr de Gankelaar and I are in the same office, as the court knows. I am sure that what I have said is completely in accordance with his wishes. I declare definitely that Mr de Gankelaar has no demand to make.'

'No,' said Katadreuffe, still white, turning round to Carlion, 'I don't want that. I owe the debt, certainly.'

For he could not accept a present, although his future was at stake, although a mere miserable eighteen guilders was involved.

The judge grinned :

'Hm, an unusual phenomenon. The creditor wants to cancel the debt and the debtor won't have it cancelled. I must say, the court is better acquainted with the opposite state of affairs.'

But Carlion had by no means finished. He explained about the origin of the debt : money for his studies, his client's plans, his progress, his office work, the punctual payment of interest and the already considerable writing-off. He was angry and wanted to fight for Katadreuffe – that Schuwagt was nothing but a money-grubbing twister – but he concealed his emotion, his face no redder than usual. He spoke rapidly, succinctly, with his exact speech, carefully pronouncing the ends of his words in his precise northern way. Schuwagt wanted to speak again, but the judge cut him short with :

'The court is fully informed. The gentlemen are requested to wait in the corridor. Judgement will be given immediately.'

Katadreuffe and Carlion walked up and down the corridor.

'You're an ass, Katadreuffe,' said Carlion.

'Yes, but Mr Carlion, I won't consider it for a moment . . . I just w-won't . . .'

He stuttered with agitation and nerves.

'Now, just shut up. That disgusting lump of misery, Schuwagt won't get you. But how carefully these cads at the bank must have followed you up. It's a pity Wever said

. . . although if asked as man to man he couldn't very well do anything else . . . and of course he didn't realize the consequences . . . Still, you've behaved like a fool, although there can be no question of bankruptcy . . . impossible . . . There's the bell.'

By the time Katadreuffe and Carlion returned to the office the court had dismissed the application for bankruptcy; the second debt had been insignificant and in addition problematical.

And whilst Schuwagt, with a bow, withdrew, the judge, the French marquis, kept Katadreuffe back and questioned him about his studies.

'There are two things they can do now. First they can force Stroomkoning to keep back so much of your salary,' said Carlion when they were alone again.

'That won't worry me, Mr Carlion. I just didn't want to go bankrupt.'

'They can also lodge an appeal.'

'They'll never win it.'

'I agree,' said Carlion, with a dry smile.

'As soon as Mr de Gankelaar is back I'll pay him.'

'You're an impossible devil, Katadreuffe. It's no good trying to do anything for you.'

That afternoon, Katadreuffe carried on with his work as usual. No one on the staff knew anything. He had, himself, found the letter, as he always cleared the mail from the box to be sorted by Miss Te George, who took out Stroomkoning's correspondence whilst he distributed the rest. The colleagues should be told of the case under promise of secrecy. Also Stroomkoning, of course, but no one on the office staff.

'To safeguard my authority,' he said to Carlion.

But he had felt ashamed with regard to Miss Te George and even Miss Sibculo. Now, fortunately, it was over. He just had a feeling of dog-tiredness in his back.

He was sitting in his room that evening. He could not at once get down to work. He felt that his control over his nerves threatened to give way, for he had for one moment been terribly afraid. He suddenly saw in front of him an abyss; he was not given to dizziness but he felt everything go round when he thought of it. He sat with his books in front of him but he did not read, he did not study. Everything was revolving; he convulsively grasped the edge of the table.

He was not elated about the outcome, though he was heartily glad of one thing – that this time his mother had known nothing about it. She was not one to lighten the load; on the contrary, she would have found words which would have annoyed him. And accept money from her, even if she had it, that he would never do. It was better as it was.

He again had that unsteady feeling; the tension must have tired him more than he suspected; those few minutes in court he would never forget. This was the reaction. No, there must be no reaction. Now it was more than ever necessary to keep his head clear and his thoughts free, as he *had* to pass his exam. At last, he decided not to do any work that evening, but rather to go out and get some fresh air.

It was early summer and still light outside. He walked up the Boompjes, deserted at this hour. Now and again a ship hooted in the distance. The majestic sound re-echoed over the huge docks, the most beautiful, the mightiest, most penetrating noise created by man, the commanding voice of the sea-going ships.

But he only paid small attention. He tried to appreciate the beauty of it. The docks were calling, and it sounded splendid, but his thoughts were already elsewhere. It was a calm, summer's evening; in the twilight the brightest stars began to appear. He tried to locate them, but his thoughts again wandered. He no longer had that drunken feeling, but he still felt light-headed; at times his mind was a blank and he did not know where he was going.

Then he saw a man approaching, lurching along the

pavement, thoroughly drunk, talking to himself and singing. There was a narrow alley on his right. In order to avoid the man, he instinctively turned into it. When he stopped he looked around him. He was in the Waterhondsteeg. Then he saw someone following him, not the drunkard. From the silhouette of concentrated strength he recognized his father. He was on the way to his father, and his father had followed him.

In the middle of the dark alley, he stopped; he would not give way to his father. The pursuer approached the nearby shadows; the father was shorter than the son, but so broad as to be almost too broad for the alley, damming it. From under the brim of his felt hat his eyes shone close to his son. In the gloom, the expression in them looked completely mad. Katadreuffe involuntarily started back, but Drevrehaven came on, pushing the boy in front of him out of the alley.

At the corner he seized him by the arm and stopped him. They were now in the corkscrew-like Vogelenzang, where there was some noise though they saw nobody. At their back gaped the hungry jaws of the Waterhondsteeg. They were standing on a small spooky spot of the otherwise sober town. In his supersensitive state, the potency of his surroundings oppressed Katadreuffe, the cross-roads contributing to this.

'What does this mean?' growled the older man.

'What do *you* mean by it?' snorted Katadreuffe in reply, of a sudden almost insane. 'This morning my bankruptcy was heard, that you know, hey? – You keep out of the line of fire and merely send that cad, Schuwagt, on the job. He had to clear up your dirty work, and your son can go hang. That would have been a huge joke. But, as you know, it didn't come off, hey? I was stronger than you today.'

In his mockery his voice did not ring true; it rose higher and higher, as he could hear to his own astonishment. He was in a state of cold, icy rage. Dreverhaven appeared to be listening, his head resting on his chest. But his hands were busy, there was a click and Dreverhaven, silently, mockingly, bowing, offered him the handle of a clasp-knife.

'Now pick up all the fruits of your victory,' he said. 'I'm defenceless.' But the son's rage had evaporated. He took the knife between two fingers as if it were filth.

'Bah!' he said, 'You and your childish tricks.'

At his feet he noticed a grating. He dropped the knife between the broad bars, where it fell with a plop in the mud, and disappeared. Now he was seized by the coat-collar.

'Childish?' his father snarled. 'Tricks? . . . Come along at once with me.'

He was normally stronger than his son; how much more so now.

'I'll come,' Katadreuffe said in a colourless voice, his teeth chattering strangely, 'as long as you don't treat me like a jail-bird.'

Dreverhaven took his arm. He guided his son, and it looked sometimes as though he were supporting him, as the son just then again had one of those turns where his senses left him.

He recovered himself as he climbed the spiral stone stairs after his father to the latter's office. Dreverhaven opened the doors with a handle which he took from his pocket, and which was notched in a peculiar fashion. During his absence, no one could unlock the doors; at each fresh door he pushed the handle further home. It is true there was nothing here to steal, but he had the soul of the miser who will hide or cover up even the most miserable objects.

They went through the bare room, then the one with the dusty files, Dreverhaven going first. Then they were there; the father at his desk, coat and hat on, brightly illuminated as if he were a jewel in a shrine; the son remained on the other side of the desk.

'And, Jacob Willem?' the father slowly asked.

Until a second ago the son had not known what he had

come here for. He only knew that in a semi-conscious state he had gone to find his father. But now he felt once more master of himself, cold and grimly angry. He knew at once what he must answer. He spoke half airily, but cuttingly:

'I have only come to ask you, father, to claim from Mr Stroomkoning what is due to you from my salary. Seizure of goods is something you understand very well. And, above all, don't forget to appeal against the judgement of the court; you have, perhaps, still a chance.'

But Dreverhaven had long since had his eyes closed; his hands lay comfortably folded over his stomach. They were badly kept and their backs covered with rough, grey hair. Katadreuffe looked at them. The claws of his father. He waited a little; the other did not move. The burning cigar stuck up from the corner of his mouth, but his lips, broad and coarse, the upper lip sensual, did not appear to be inhaling the smoke. A dollop of ash fell and remained lying in the fold of his sleeve at the elbow.

Katadreuffe left before rage should again take possession of him. He felt it rising, but he went, walking from the house as if in a dream. Outside he again had to collect his thoughts. There was still some light – it was one of those endless twilights – at the bottom of the street streaks of colour lay across the sky, all pastel shades. Then he turned to the direction he had come from. He saw the huge house-wall leaning over the Lange Baanstraat. His father's stronghold, a stronghold charged with horror.

That same evening he told his mother something of what had happened. They were both at home, she and Jan Maan. Katadreuffe had quite forgotten his determination to keep silent, but it oppressed him, he had to talk about it; Jan Maan being there did not bother him. On the contrary, his friend could hear it all. But he did not mention his recent visit; he only spoke about the abortive bankruptcy.

His mother made no reply, as was her way; only, her needlework stayed in her lap and, during the recital, her eyes were on him. Katadreuffe was then again inwardly angry. Did he come here just to be stared at? That woman reacted wrongly literally to everything. He wasn't made of stone; he had need now and then of an encouraging word, although in the end it was he, alone, who had to fight his way through. But nothing, nothing.

Jan Maan, at least, was different.

'I believe I ought to congratulate you, bourgeois,' he said, cross, serious and laughing all at the same time.

He was becoming more and more clearly a devotee of communism. He could no longer hear talk about money, for then he immediately saw the hated capitalist. Thus he was all three in one; angry because it was about money, serious because his friend had been in danger, and happy that the danger had been averted. Also, of late, he was saying 'bourgeois' almost as often as he said 'Jacob'. But they were not the men ever to have any real breach.

His mother picked up her handwork, and coughed a little. As Katadreuffe left he said :

'You're not looking too well, mother. You ought to go and see the doctor. Well, good-bye, both of you.'

Troubles

Katadreuffe dismissed these incidents from his mind. He was about to take his exam; he was in the midst of it. Nothing must be allowed to deflect him. If an appeal were made, if they made use of the lien on his salary, even then, he must not be influenced in the slightest. He actually expected either one or the other, or both, any day – but nothing happened. The silence was inclined to get on his nerves, but he controlled himself.

He went to the Hague; he came back, and returned again. In between, he was busy at the office. Everyone knew he was taking the exam but no one enquired about it; his face forbade any allusion to it. In his own opinion, it was going not exactly badly, but considerably less well than he had hoped. Sometimes he found he did not know the things he knew well enough, or remembered them too late. He made one or two dangerous mistakes. But gradually it seemed to go better, and by the viva voce he had completely regained his studied calm; his viva voce was very good, and he came out of it all tolerably well.

That afternoon he returned with the certificate in his pocket. He had not even read it through, just mechanically put his signature to it. He pulled it out – yes – there was his own handwriting, not a self-confident, business-like signature, but a weak, nervous scrawl : he tucked the certificate away again. He sat so pale and stiffly in the train that he attracted the attention of his fellow passengers. He was not pleased, not even inwardly; he was just dog-tired. The hard study, the persecution by his father, the difficult examination during the warmest days of a hot summer, his dreadful lack of sufficient sleep – his head was in a whirl. He intentionally did not include in the difficulties his feeling for Miss Te George; that he banned from his thoughts. Predominant over all was his feeling of dog-tiredness.

The office knew that he would learn the result today, and they were so convinced of his success that they had prepared a celebration in advance.

He came in with a set, almost gloomy face, and they feared the worst; but seeing the flowers he pulled himself together, his eye brightened – yes – he had passed, thank God.

And this celebration was quite another thing from that of Miss Sibculo's engagement. Several baskets of flowers, from the office staff, from the concierge, from the lawyers, and a very large floral arrangement from Mrs Stroomkoning.

It was quiet that afternoon, and around five o'clock they all came to congratulate him; even the single client in the waiting-room, Mrs Starels, shook him by the hand. She was just about to begin divorce proceedings for the seventh or eighth time, and she hoped that *he* would now be able to help her. She did not dare say that Miss Kalvelage's methods were far from her taste; she imagined that Katadreuffe was now a qualified lawyer.

But this did not complete the tribute, the best was still to come. At Miss Te George's request he went to his room, all the office following, and there he found a new German encyclopedia. Then he was indeed taken by surprise and almost overcome with emotion.

'That's *your* idea,' he said to her, and did not mind saying this in front of everyone.

She could not deny it. She had gone to his room once to see if there was anything he needed there; she had seen the

well-worn, incomplete encyclopedia, whilst Mr de Gankelaar had told her that he loved to read it, but never got
further than T. The rest he would understand. It was from
the same publishers, but the latest edition, in twenty
volumes.

This led up to what was almost a little speech. They all
stood around him in this gloomy, chilly, fusty room, with
the electric light burning whilst the summer sun shone.
But the twenty splendid books brightened it up, and Katadreuffe stroked them – the gesture of a book-lover. This was
Knowledge, *more* Knowledge, the best there is in the realm
of Popular Knowledge, for no one understands that like
the German.

'I thank you all most cordially,' he said. 'I can't say that
this was my greatest wish, because I never dared wish
it.'

Miss Te George took him to one side.

'I just want to tell you that the lion's share comes from
Mrs Stroomkoning, but everyone here has contributed, including Miss Kalvelage and the gentlemen and the whole
staff. *This* present is from us all.'

'I am most grateful,' he said in a firm voice, without a
trace of sentimentality. 'What is worth most is the thought,
and that was yours.'

He did not care for celebrations and parties, but he had
to do something in return, and that which comes spontaneously is generally the best. He talked with Mrs Graanoogst,
and with Mr Carlion.

Stroomkoning was abroad and Carlion took his place. He
agreed to closing the office now. They quickly got rid of
Mrs Starels. Port and sherry were brought in, with cakes,
sweets, advocaat. It was quite a party in the waiting-room.
The lawyers sat amongst the staff and the staff all felt completely at home. Every now and again something fresh was
brought in, including cigars and cigarettes. After some time
Carlion and Piaat's conversation followed the lines of the
lawyers' exchange, but Miss Kalvelage revealed a surpris-

ing side. Who would ever have thought that that death's head could smoke a cigarette? And she smoked a full-sized one, drooping from the corner of her mouth. With hands folded under her chin, her elbows on the large, round table, her arms bent over her glass of sherry, her head tilted to avoid the smoke of her cigarette, her attitude was that of a film-star in a smart bar.

What a pity De Gankelaar could not see her like this. But he had gone to a meeting of creditors in Amsterdam. Anyhow, those present were happy, fortuitously happy in the heart of the summer.

Katadreuffe's certificate had to be circulated. The lawyers were above all interested in the signatures, which aroused memories of their own matriculation.

At around seven o'clock they broke up, but the celebration was not yet over. Katadreuffe wanted another intimate party with the staff. They were asked to come back at eight or half past for a meal, something that had never happened before. Miss Sibculo was, without fail, to bring her fiancé with her. She thanked Katadreuffe, obviously touched.

And Mrs Graanoogst did wonders, although she had to borrow from neighbours the extra plates, cutlery, dishes and table-linen. Moreover, most of it came from the shops and the wine-merchant. But it had to be heated up, and she was kept busy laying the table, helped by her daughter, Pop.

At half past eight the company assembled, and they sat round the table in the modernized, severe, but cheerful waiting-room. Miss Te George and Miss Sibculo had put on flowered dresses. Miss Van den Born appeared, badly dressed as always, but it was considered good of her to come at all.

'A round table like this is nice,' said Katadreuffe. 'Then no one's sitting at the head.'

And here again his sense of social equality was speaking; he had never wanted to be the official head of the staff.

All the staff was there, including Burgeik and Kees Adam and Ben. And Graanoogst was also present. From the same feeling of comradeship Katadreuffe said :

'It's only a pity that Pietje isn't here.'

For Pietje had died that winter. The lad had not been actually replaced. They managed as best they could with Ben, but that blockhead was a trial to everyone.

They sat round the table at random; only, Katadreuffe expressly asked Mrs Graanoogst to sit on one side of him and Pop on the other. And he had stipulated that Pop should remain until the end. For he felt, at this party in the house where he lived, most closely bound to those with whom he lived.

There were two of them who said nothing. Burgeik, with his suspicious little eyes, sat watching that the townsmen did not try to put anything across the simple countryman; Ben just sat there eating. But Kees Adam was busy explaining in detail across the table to Graanoogst the working of a motor, two-stroke system and four-stroke. The girls talked to one another, one of them every now and then helping Mrs Graanoogst with the serving. Miss Van den Born once burst out laughing so hoarsely and loudly that no one, not even Kees Adam, could hear his own words.

Miss Sibculo, of course, sat next to her betrothed; she did not display a great deal of enthusiasm. And why on earth did we have to empty so many buckets over the engagement? For that young man seemed thoroughly presentable, a book-keeper in a small insurance firm, but he was capable of more than typing out policies and calculating premiums. You would have said : insurance office, dry as dust, a bit wet. But wrongly. During the pudding he was a complete Rotterdam Zoo; there was no animal you could think of which he couldn't imitate, including the peculiar noises of rhinoceros and elephant (at least so he assured them), and his audience was very ready to believe him. At the same time, he sounded klaxons, sirens howled, they heard a steam-engine, champagne corks popped, the wine

guggled and foamed, and, as a finale, a whole set of fire-
works where one had only to imagine the set-piece : 'Long
live Katadreuffe !'

The only one not in a happy mood was Katadreuffe himself, but one had never seen him particularly cheerful; he
was too serious-minded for that, yet he did not appear to
be more serious than usual. He did his best, but the strain
had perhaps somehow undermined him, and he lacked his
old resilience. He thought : Tomorrow I'll be all right
again; a good night's sleep and I'll wake up feeling rested,
in a holiday mood. But he could not throw off a sense of
unrest; there seemed to be something impending. But no
one must be allowed to notice it.

Before they got up from the table, he rose to his feet. He
felt a sudden need to say something. He spoke impromptu,
rapidly, simply – his first speech.

'Friends,' he said, 'I say friends, for that's what we are
all here, and Miss Sibculo's fiancé is our friend because
she belongs to us – well then, friends, I thank you all again
from my heart. You have made far too much of me, and no
one realizes that better than myself. For what am I now,
or rather what shall I be in the spring? Nothing more than
a student . . . But I want to add this. Almost everyone has
certain gifts . . .'

He paused for a moment, thinking of Miss Van den
Born, though he did not look at her. He felt Pop's saucer
eyes fastened on his face and – he did not know why – it
warmed him.

'Almost everyone has certain gifts which he must discover
and, having discovered them, must cultivate them. When
in September I am entered as a student at Leiden, then
I shall be a student just starting, and also, in the circumstances, a much older student than the majority. But that
doesn't worry me; a man can start late, the chief thing is
to start. A man sometimes discovers his gifts late. But the
soundest advice is : to make the best we can of our lives.
Let us begin by discovering ourselves. All I want to do is to

get on. Each one of us ought to want to do that, then he will . . .'

He again paused, and in a different tone :

'I only wanted to say *this*, also that I once more thank you, and may we continue to work together in harmony, and – to end up – I'm afraid – I didn't intend it – but I'm afraid this has turned into something rather like a sermon.'

Then he captivated them all, for his smile appeared, carrying them with him, irresistible; there suddenly sat a real man, one who by a slight alteration of his features could conquer the world, and did not know it.

Later on, coffee was served; also liqueurs. And – the girls in a group of their own – Miss Van den Born, in her hoarse voice, said unexpectedly :

'Good God, Miss Te George, are you a bit tight? Look how your hand is shaking !'

Miss Te George shook her head, and put down the trembling liqueur-glass.

Then Pop had to go to bed; all she wanted was Kata-dreuffe to carry her upstairs. He did so, and her mother went up with them.

When he came down again he was still out of breath; the child was already quite a weight. And he saw a white summer-coat in the corridor; Miss Te George was leaving. So strange, so hurtful, so upsetting, this silent departure without having said good-bye to him. He went down the wide staircase, calling softly and urgently :

'Miss Te George ! Miss Te George !'

Twice.

She turned round with a jerk, and they stood facing each other in the brightly lit marble corridor. They both stood in the same manner, hands spread out against the wall, of equal height, their eyes on a level, their faces sallow and drawn. He was still panting a little. And it was not the vision of the six brass plates; *this* was the greatest moment in his life. For he felt quite definitely, physically – there one moment and gone the next – a current pass between them; he felt it vibrating. But there was also a steel wall there; he was seeing her through the wall, lost to him; he only felt the contact of the current.

He felt it no longer. In silence, she had walked on and in silence he fetched her bicycle outside. And he did not watch her as she rode away; he quickly and quietly shut the door.

Upstairs there was the sound of the others' conversation, but he did not want to hear it. Through a crack in the door he caught a glimpse of Miss Van den Born from whose nostrils two columns of cigarette smoke shot out like the breath of a horse on a cold winter's day; he could not look at it. Graanoogst would understand his tiredness and make his excuses to the others. He went quietly up to his room.

He undressed but could not sleep. He got up again, turned on the light, listened at the door; all was now dead quiet. He walked about the room in his pyjamas. The window into the air-shaft stood open. Above and below was nothing but obscurity; the light from his lamp fell on the blind wall opposite, so close was it. He felt so wretched; he was almost sick from wretchedness.

But he must at last have gone back to bed, for he awoke there the following morning. He had not even overslept; the same dreadful tiredness pressed down on him as he walked about uncertainly.

Then he saw it, and he was suddenly quite clear-headed and no longer tired. On his pillow where his head had rested was blood; a track, a thread, a tiny snake had flowed out of his mouth. Yes, he knew it, with absolute certainty; out of his mouth. He clearly remembered it all now. In the night he had felt a tightness in his chest; he had sat up in bed; just a little tightness, a little cough, something insipid on his tongue. But before he had grasped what it was a leaden sleep like a block of concrete had knocked him out.

He did not forget to tell his landlady of a little mishap in the night, a slight nose-bleeding. He was downstairs punctually; Graanoogst had cleared up everything, but the flowers were still there and would remain good several days if watered. The telephone rang and he picked up the receiver instinctively; a strange voice said something about Miss Te George. She wasn't well and would not be coming to the office that day. This had not happened in years. And Miss Van den Born said meaningly :

'Well, she *was* slightly drunk; now she's got a headache.' But no one believed that of a girl like her.

In the lunch-hour he went to Doctor Merree, he who had once upon a time helped him into the world. He had his consulting-room on the Oostzeedijk, practising chiefly among the lesser well-to-do, with whom his waiting-room was always full. But he was ready to see people during the lunch-hour, when it was quiet, provided an appointment was made by telephone. Katadreuffe had rung him up from Stroomkoning's room, so that none of the staff could hear.

He was also Mrs Katadreuffe's doctor; as soon as her income permitted her to leave the panel doctor she had gone to Doctor Merree. She had remembered his name from the maternity ward. She liked him, and considered him the only capable doctor in the town, although she had in those days not followed his advice; but that was, after all, her own business.

Katadreuffe sat in front of him with his naked torso. The old doctor knocked and listened; he had to breathe and then not breathe. Katadreuffe looked at his hands, which were tanned from the summer, like his face; he always tanned quickly. But his body was white; he had, this year not taken any time off for afternoons on the beach at the Waalhaven and the Hook. Jan Maan had gone off there alone, and on the first day again come back burnt red, for his skin did not tan properly. And Katadreuffe thought with an ache of a laughing remark of Miss Te George, in the office, just to all in general; she also could not stand much of the strong sun; her complexion was not improved by it, and in that respect Mr Katadreuffe was someone to be jealous of.

'Antinoüs, not Apollo,' said the doctor, talking half to himself as he listened. He said it with that good-natured, soft-hearted cynicism of many elderly doctors. Katadreuffe understood and blushed. The doctor fastened a bandage around his arm, tightened it and looked at an indicator.

'I find you run down and nervy, boy,' he said. 'Your blood-pressure's too low, much too low, but I can't find anything else. You must have had a slight haemorrhage in the stomach. We'd better take a photo. If we hurry we'll still catch the X-ray man. My car's outside.'

The following morning a letter arrived by post for Stroomkoning. Above the address was written, 'Confidential'.

And Katadreuffe realized at once that she was not coming back; this was her farewell, her resignation. A large envelope, pale lilac, violet ink, a fine but large and well-formed woman's writing, the hand of a straightforward, distinguished character. He had known it all along; now for the first time he saw these qualities; alone at an early hour in the office he thoughtfully weighed the letter in his hand, On the back, not her name, but her address; Boogjes.

She had once said :

'Yes, on my bike from the Boogjes to the Boompjes and vice versa four times a day.'

He had never been there; it was right in the extreme south. And it was obvious that now he would never go there. He put the letter with the other private correspondence; Stroomkoning would be back in a few days. Then he opened the mail.

Two days later, he again visited Doctor Merree. He felt sure it would turn out all right; the first visit had already relieved his mind, although he was not particularly pleased about it.

The photo had shown nothing except that his lungs were not too strong. A couple of tubercular spots had dried up in an early stage and left scars. That did not amount to much, and showed sufficient resistance by the lung-tissues; many people had that. But he would have to take care, not overwork, and rest. And that spot of blood had undoubtedly come from the stomach.

Stroomkoning returned and shook Katadreuffe by the hand. But he was too full of other things, shocked and annoyed. He had opened Miss Te George's letter first of all, instinctivley.

'Now how the devil is that possible?' he asked.

He pushed the letter towards Katadreuffe, but Katadreuffe did not look at it.

'I understand what it is all right.'

'You understand it, and you haven't even seen the letter?'

'When Miss Te George gets someone to ring up saying she is ill and then the following day sends you a confidential letter, it is not so difficult to guess what she is writing.'

He said it calmly. Stroomkoning was too preoccupied to notice the strangeness of this answer; he again pushed the letter towards him.

'Read it.'

It sounded like a command. Katadreuffe read, whilst Stroomkoning paced up and down impatiently. She wrote :

Dear Mr Stroomkoning,
    I am more sorry than I can tell you that after so many years I must ask you to release me, but certain reasons that I can with difficulty explain force me to do so. Naturally, as regards my salary, I am fully prepared to accept the consequences of this step. I thank you for all the kindness I have received from you.
    With kind regards, also to Mrs Stroomkoning.
                        Yours sincerely,
                        Lorna Te George

Katadreuffe first read the letter right through. It was a self-confident woman's writing, but the style was far from feminine. It was the business-like, correct style of the lawyer; after years of service she was saturated with the office style.

Her signature in full. Lorna Te George. Then Katadreuffe re-read that one sentence, half out loud :

'Naturally, as regards my salary, I am fully prepared to accept the consequences of this step.'

'Does she mean, what she has already earned . . .?'

Stroomkoning stood still and interrupted him.

'Exactly, that's what she does mean. She renounces her salary. God damn it, I'll give her an extra quarter, an extra half year! I'll never strike anyone like that again. But I don't get it, by God. I don't get it.'

Fortunately he did not enquire whether the other understood it. He continued to pace up and down as he talked.

'*You* could fill her place all right, Katadreuffe, but I don't want that. Then I'll get another head clerk who'll rob me. And in a few years when your studies are finished you'll also be leaving me. No, that's putting the cart before the horse . . . But I'm not having it; we'll see – I can't have that. Just a note – kind regards . . . after ten years, or is it twelve? No, eight perhaps. Doesn't matter, I'll fetch her back. You'll see, Katadreuffe! tomorrow she'll be back in the office.'

His cat's whiskers bristled on all sides, the green eyes sparkled, the short lion's mane stood out in all directions; he had an inspiration; he got them to ring his house and whilst Katadreuffe withdrew, his wife came on the telephone.

The Path through Leiden

He was not one to let things slide; the following morning, he went with his wife to call on Miss Te George. He knew the street and number, though he did not know exactly where the street was. Past the viaduct over the railway, Mrs Stroomkoning stopped the car, and they looked at the town-plan together. Here an extensive new quarter began.

'It's over here, I think,' she said, pointing at the map. 'Let's see how we can best get there. Green Belt, Wilgenweerd, Enk, Leede, Krielerf; what pretty names they all have! Ah, here are the Boogjes.'

She began to drive more slowly; it grew quieter, sunnier, more countrified, the ditches broader, and yet it was still in the town.

'Delightful,' she said, 'I didn't know this existed.'

Slowly and carefully they drove under the foliage of the small but thickly covered trees. The house in the Boogjes stood in a curve, close to the Green Belt, a house standing on its own, the upper part built of wood, painted an attractive brown, with a sharply pointed roof. It expressed what they were both feeling : just the place for this girl to live in.

She opened the door herself, and in her calm reception he saw the irrevocability of her decision. It made him irritable and in the sitting-room he could not remain in his chair but paced about as if in his own room, with his hands either in his pockets or gesticulating.

'I don't understand it. I don't want to know any of your secrets, that's obvious. But so suddenly, after all these years . . . Can't we take a little more time over it?'

Miss Te George sat still between the two windows, her back to the light.

'I may be getting engaged . . .'

'Engaged, engaged? Now is *that* a reason? Whilst you're engaged you can stay on in the office. As far as I'm concerned you can have a ring on every finger . . .'

He realized that in his annoyance he was being rude and, with an embarrassed laugh, he corrected himself:

'Now, now, I beg your pardon. What I mean is I absolutely can't do without you . . . How hard you make it for me. Tell me now, in the name of all that's holy, who *can* take your place? I know it's difficult to take down my stuff – all those different speeds – first like an express train and then like a snail. *Who* can do it like you? You know all my business, *who* can know it like you, better than I know it myself?'

Miss Te George did not answer. Mrs Stroomkoning was sitting on the sofa, a small, fair elf. But beneath her elfin appearance she had muscles of steel, yet remained at the same time a woman. She had always felt a slight jealousy over the relationship of her husband with his secretary; this girl knew so much more about his work than she did; who was in continuous contact with him; more than she herself. She was jealous, like many business-men's wives. She was glad this girl was not going back. But that did not completely satisfy her; she must have her small revenge, fostered for years; the opportunity was too good to miss. She asked harmlessly:

'Isn't there something else, Miss Te George? Hasn't it got something to do with the office?'

She asked it spontaneously, remorselessly; for she was a woman. The two women had, in a fraction of a second, seen through one another, and they hated each other. The man noticed nothing.

'No, Mrs Stroomkoning,' said Lorna calmly, 'the office has absolutely nothing to do with it.'

If only at the same time she had not blushed a little. In spite of the shadow thrown by the curtains the other noticed it. With a woman's intuition she had guessed right and was satisfied. She got up, as did Stroomkoning. Whilst they were slowly driving away through the attractive quarter she said :

'Shall I tell you something? That Miss Te George is simply in love with your head clerk. That's why she's left; that's the sole reason.'

While speaking, she looked keenly at him out of the corner of her eye. He did not ask her how she hit on the idea; he rejected it out of hand.

'Impossible, absolutely impossible! Something's the matter with her, a child can see that. But she and Kata- dreuffe – out of the question.'

Why get so excited? She glanced at his profile; he was thinking. Then :

'Although, Iris, there may be something in what you say. She was up in his room one evening – as you know he lives with the Graanoogsts – but she went to his room. They had tea together there, quite normally, just as friends, nothing special, and yet now it makes one think . . . I don't remember who told me, Graanoogst, Rentenstein perhaps . . . But I remember the fact, quite definitely.'

He spoke without reserve, and she laughed. They had always been on terms of equality, and she said :

'You see? A woman's always right about these things. A woman senses a thing like that, and a man doesn't. That's the whole difference. I've suspected it for a long time; that boy is far too handsome.'

'Yes, yes, and now I've been the mug. As this morning, this very morning, I should have been able to guess it . . . Her letter of resignation, you know . . . now that boy knew what was in that letter before I gave it to him to read . . .'

'There you are – the proof of the pudding. Perhaps now you'll have the grace to say that I'm not entirely wrong?'

She had restored his good humour, and he laughed.

'All right, a woman *must* always be in the right . . . And please take more care – that lamp-post won't step out of your way. The way you're driving now, I could do better myself.'

Katadreuffe replaced Miss Te George so well that Stroomkoning gradually began to forget her. It was a slack time, midsummer; there were not any meetings and hardly any new business of importance. And Stroomkoning was generous enough not to hold it against Katadreuffe, for being the probable cause of her departure, and considerate enough not to ascertain this through questioning. Katadreuffe realized that Stroomkoning could not bring himself to find a suitable successor, although this was necessary. Eventually he said :

'If you have no objection I can look out for someone. I know the sort of person you need.'

'I was going to ask you to,' Stroomkoning answered. 'But don't take on anybody definitely, take them on probation for, say, two months. And although I don't need a beauty, after Lorna I couldn't put up with anyone positively ugly. It's perhaps stupid, but even in business a woman's a woman, at least for a man.'

He laughed; he spoke familiarly of Lorna, a thing he had never done before to Katadreuffe. It was almost a bond. Then he turned serious and looked searchingly at his head clerk.

'There's no hurry. It's the slack time. Tomorrow I'm off for a month's holiday. And you go away too, for at least a month. You look so run down after your exam; I *insist* on your staying away a month. When you come back, look out for someone for me. Let the office just carry on, it will be all right. You need some sea air, or the heather, or the mountains; in any case you must get away.'

The following day, he had gone and Katadreuffe, for the first time, took a holiday, leaving a day later. He now felt rest was an absolute necessity. He would, moreover, be free from the everlasting tiresome guessing about Miss Te George's sudden departure, for the general office continued to discuss it, and he had to join in in order not to raise suspicion. He did not take a month's holiday, only a fortnight. He did not go to mountains, heather, or sea; he remained quite near; he went to his mother.

She greeted him in her stern way, but his cubicle was always ready for him. She had the feeling that something was the matter with him; he looked so worn-out; she could not make out exactly what it was, certainly extreme strain, but not that alone; she guessed a girl was involved. But if he did not talk about it, she would not ask; that was not her fashion. She looked after him without fuss; he would get as good as with those people with whom he was so satisfied.

She let him sleep indefinitely. The first week he nearly slept the clock round. Once or twice she went to his room early and looked silently at her sleeping son. And then in her face could be seen a tenderness that she had never let him see; of which she was herself unconscious. Her child was clean, bright, tidy, fresh; the air in the room where he slept was pure; it was clean here. When he awoke, he did not immediately get up; he lay musing, and his thoughts turned to Lorna. Sometimes he woke very early, and then thought of her. She would be asleep now; he could see her sleeping as clearly as if he were a clairvoyant. It did him no good imagining this but the picture came in spite of himself, and he could not drive the charm of it away. He went into her room. She was sleeping on her side, turned away from him. He looked closely at her, and quite clearly, very sweet, he saw her profile. His imagination was quite pure, the imagination of a child. She seemed to make a movement as if she would turn round, and the vision vanished. Immediately afterwards he, himself, fell asleep again.

During the day, he no longer sat in his cubicle; he went to sit with 'her'.

After hesitating at first, he had taken part of his encyclopedia with him, letter U, which he was now reading. But his thoughts wandered so often, as she could see.

Jan Maan left very early in the morning, on his bicycle, for the factory. He took sandwiches with him, did his work there, and returned in the afternoon, slapping Katadreuffe on the shoulder with :

'Hullo, bourgeois.'

'Good day, comrade,' Katadreuffe would riposte.

After a week he felt stronger. I must stop this sentimentalizing; that dream's got to stop. I want to be the child of my parents, certainly of my mother, and she was never one to languish. It must stop; that brooding is absolutely worthless. Everything has really turned out for the best; I am certainly no man for marriage.

It did not stop at once, but lessened gradually. And he only had to think of his father for his old energy to revive. Now, for the first time, he had beaten the old man, and he intended to stay on top. The old man would be surprised at the rate he received his money back, plus the high interest. And if his father made use of the lien, well, even then he would make it, somewhat later, but he would still make it.

His talks with Jan Maan provided relaxation. He was now further than ever removed from communism, and Jan Maan was heavily involved. After meals, they argued in the sitting-room, as Jan Maan also preferred to sit with 'her'. He bragged that the Communist Party Holland was doing extraordinarily well. They were sure to get a seat in the Second Chamber. And there was a lot of unrest in industry; every day more and more people were going over to them – the socialists were losing visibly to the C.P.H.

'Exactly,' said Katadreuffe, 'that's just it. You aren't a proper party, you're just a barometer of the economic situation. Up and down, up and down, rain and storm in business, very fine for you, vice versa; so it goes on all the time.'

Jan Maan lost his temper. He screamed :

'And that from a damn fool who's not worth a picture of Red Square – Have I got to listen to a warped bourgeois insulting Lenin Ulyanov. Do you know what I'm going to call you in future? Bourgeois is too good for you. Capitalist I'll call you.'

'A little quieter, Jan,' admonished Mother.

'No, mother, this gentleman has got to have it for once. Up and down, up and down, he says. But it doesn't go down. And if it should go down – it won't – but if it should, then you capitalists will still have to respect us. We'll twist your noses so that you'll not forget. And if *I* have to go under, then I'll stink, Jacob; you'll be able to smell me – I'll stink all the capitalists out.'

In his anger, he became crudely polemical. Katadreuffe looked at him and his heart ached for his friend; not on account of his words – that was just wild talk but at his appearance. For Jan Maan was indisputably ageing, and he was only half way between thirty and forty. But he began to show the deep wrinkles of the factory-worker; the hardness was not in his soul, in spite of his words, but in his features. You could see it in thousands of factory-workers, as Katadreuffe knew; in the factory one could stay old for a long time, to be sure, but one did not stay young.

Katadreuffe looked at him. He had given up trying to arouse Jan Maan's interest in anything other than girls and the Party, in self-education. Of late the Party was what mattered most to Jan Maan. Katadreuffe wondered if that was much of an improvement. Queer people visited him in his room. Katadreuffe, out of curiosity, had once been present, but he would never be there again; these gentlemen offended his nose too strongly. Fortunately Jan Maan did not take them to 'her'.

'Aren't there any comrades coming this evening, Jan?' he asked.

He couldn't resist teasing him, but he received no answer.
'Come out with me then.'

They went out for a glass of beer. Katadreuffe always
paid now. There was no arguing with him as Jan Maan,
who had once taken out his purse, knew. It hadn't gone
down at all well, and he was careful in future. But he
understood the reason; Katadreuffe wanted in this way to
show his gratitude for being so good to 'her'. And he had
to put up with his friend paying everything back, including the subscriptions for the correspondence courses, down
to the last penny, and listen to curses whenever he hesitated to accept.

After a couple of glasses Jan Maan stopped sulking. He
became confidential. He was now having another terrific
row with his parents, and as always, he believed this was
the final breach. Well, he wasn't going to break his head
over it. It was always the old trouble about his going home,
whilst he wanted to remain free. He helped them at home
– so they weren't in a position to issue orders – and if he
wanted to stay with 'her', then he would stay with 'her'.

'One of these days you'll have to leave, Jan,' said Katadreuffe, 'and perhaps sooner than we think. I was speaking to her doctor recently. He finds she is going downhill;
then it stops, for a bit, but in the long run she is declining.
Thank goodness she knows it herself.'

'She never mentions it,' Jan Maan said.

'No, she's like that.'

'It may be that I'll have to leave her one day. But of
one thing I'm certain. It won't be to marry. I'm not one
for marriage; we are neither of us fellows ever to take a
wife, Jacob.'

And Katadreuffe was inwardly surprised that his friend
had fathomed him so deeply; he said :

'I believe you're right. And when "she" is no longer with
us we'll stick together – together, you understand? I shall
insist on it.'

While he was still with his mother, one evening, the

bokschipper, Harm Knol Hein, came to call. The men had gone to a Russian film at Caledonia and she was alone.

'Now I'm so to say free, ma'am,' he said from behind his cup of tea.

She understood that he had come to tell a story, and for more than that. She remained quietly listening; his childish lack of inhibition somehow touched her.

'And I'll tell you how it came about. That fat woman – you know – well, on the sly, I brought her into contact with that friend of mine, as I told you before. And was it a good idea or wasn't it? They just clicked like that. Well, the end of the story – just guess . . . yes, it's a blooming scandal when you think that woman is nearer fifty than forty . . . but yesterday she launched her first ship. And that friend's a real pal of mine – none better! And in the pub, over a drink, he says suddenly : "Knol" – my name's Harm and my surname's Hein but they call me Knol – "Knol," he says, "that child's a Christian, we must christen it, and we'll christen it like the ship-builders." Well, he then wanted to buy a bottle of pop and break the bottle on that boy's bottom . . . or no, I believe it's a girl . . .'

He paused, chewing his quid.

'Another cup of tea, Mr Hein?'

'Thanks, ma'am, that I won't refuse . . . But now just listen. That friend of mine is so to say a shipmate; it was only just an idea of his, and he was well under the weather . . . But I found that no way to talk, I must say, so I managed to get away as best I could . . .'

He looked at her with his small, friendly eyes, intent really on the sequel to the story, for so far it had been only a clumsy introduction.

'And now look here ma'am,' he said. 'That woman did her level best to tie me up, but she hadn't a chance. I have my wits about me.'

He pulled a worn wallet from an inside pocket, together with a work-book and a number of loose papers, large and small, grubby, dog-eared; no this wasn't it and that wasn't it . . . wait a minute . . . there it was . . . no, not that, but this, look now, that's it.

He unfolded a discoloured, dirty sheet of paper, greasy at the folds, but still intact; he handed it to her, and she read her own writing, twenty years old, the writing of her youth. It was the note in which, with a few words, she had turned down his offer. It was signed 'Mrs J. Katadreuffe'.

He watched her tensely. She was no experienced woman, but she understood him; she understood that by showing her the note she had then written him, he was repeating his offer. It was so simple, straightforward and naïve; it touched her deeply. But it could not be; she had been an old corpse then. And now? What *did* he see in her?

'I think just the same about it, Mr Hein,' she said, handing back the note.

She smiled; he saw the remarkable smile on the sickly features beneath the grey hair; above all he noticed the smiling eyes, where just a trace of moisture showed for a moment, though it was immediately controlled. It was the eyes which had got him in the past; they were still fine, with fire in them, wonderfully bright for an old woman; those eyes had retained their powers of attraction for him.

Carefully, cumbersomely, he folded the note in its old creases and put away his wallet. He sighed.

'All right. That's how it is.'

It was at least a consolation that he had not promised himself much from the conversation; also that he had got rid of the other one; also that she wasn't tied up. He would not stay and she did not press him, glad to be alone for a while before the boys returned.

After a fortnight to the day, Katadreuffe left, recovered and to some extent changed. For during this time he had made a decision: he would look for rooms. Remaining living in the office where Miss Te George had worked would, at lonely moments in the evening, bring his thoughts back to her too often, distract him too much in his studies. One week of dreaming, living on past memories, was already excessive; it was out of character. He told Graanoogst that it would be better for his studies if he went and, he was, in point of fact, telling no untruth. But he was sorry to leave them, particularly sorry to give up his half hour after dinner with Pop.

He had found a new secretary for Stroomkoning. The demands he was obliged to make were high, but then so was the salary offered. He had a reasonable number of applicants and succeeded in engaging a girl on probation for two months. She was already there when Stroomkoning returned from his holidays. She was a Miss Van Alm, not unattractive, with splendid teeth. And he had to smile for when he interviewed them, like a zoologist, the first thing he had looked at was their teeth. She wore glasses, but they suited her, and, if anything, gave her features a gentler look. She was no Miss Te George, but Stroomkoning approved of her and said she could stay.

Times were bad and they affected the office, but the chief, who found it difficult to dismiss staff or lower salaries, did not have to do either. The solution came of its own. Kees Adams went into his father's business, making twin-saddles for joy-riders; the younger Burgeik was called home; he had, after all, held on much longer than one would have expected, but now he went, still misunderstood and misunderstanding. The only one actually dismissed was Ben, but he was useless at anything but polite talk, and even that in the long run grew tiresome. His place was taken by an office-boy of Pietje Grieve's age, but much stronger; Katadreuffe saw to that.

The office staff, at the end of the year, consisted of Katadreuffe, Miss Van Alm, Miss Sibculo, Miss Van den Born, and the youngest addition. Miss Sibculo now answered the telephone; she had a soft, but cultured voice, and Stroomkoning felt this was not a bad thing for a change. It sounded well, a cultured woman's voice; the girls at the central exchange spoke similarly. But there were fewer phone calls now, and Miss Sibculo was able to take down letters as well. In that event, Miss Van den Born sat at the telephone. It was her old place, and she continued to speak just as hoarsely into the mouthpiece.

In the winter De Gankelaar left; he went off to the East Indies, to the Moluccas, as legal administrator of a spice firm. There had lately been some unpleasantness between him and Stroomkoning; he had never found the office quite up to his standards. Stroomkoning was not scrupulous enough for him. On the other side, this work-shy dandy's criticisms, in their presumption, irritated him.

In the spring, Gideon Piaat died suddenly. Neither of them were replaced; it was not necessary. Stroomkoning found two colleagues, Carlion and Miss Kalvelage, sufficient, and he kept a place open for Katadreuffe.

De Gankelaar's departure affected Katadreuffe the most. De Gankelaar was not industrious, but he had been his patron, a likeable and intelligent man; he had so much to be grateful to him for. De Gankelaar too, was sorry; he had attached himself to Katadreuffe, felt that a great future awaited him, and would like to have participated in his rise. But Katadreuffe's sorrow was much greater; he was saying good-bye to a protector; De Gankelaar was an aristocrat; a working-class boy would never reach his status; friendship on a footing of equality he would never be able to feel; he would always remain of a lower class. Also he failed to find in Katadreuffe the kind of intellect he required. For although he talked to him, *he* did the talking; the other was just a receptacle. The boy absorbed, indeed splendidly, like a new sponge, but no spark emanated from him so far.

He said good-bye to the real intellect in the office, and at their last interview they sat talking for more than an hour in Miss Kalvelage's room. He sat opposite her in the full light, the winter sun sparkling on the Maas, and she with her back to the light. With real affection she looked at the aristocratic young man, whose nose was always freckled (somewhat less now in the winter), with his broad white cuffs, the signet ring with the crest, the harmonious athletic figure, and the small doe's eyes in which she had often noticed a slight melancholy.

'The cultivation of spices, nutmegs, and cloves,' said De Gankelaar, 'appears to have urgent need of a new broom. To my honour, the choice has fallen on me. We'll soon set that little affair on its feet,' he said with careless bravado.

Miss Kalvelage laughed ironically.

'Now tell me truly, do you find it terribly bad to have to set something on its feet? Can't you begin by . . . standing on your own feet?'

He laughed back; she could never make him angry; at their last meeting they had to wrangle.

'You're always malicious. When are you going to start being really feminine, as I should like to see you?'

'When are you going to become a man of action? Maybe out there in the heat you'll grow and come back like a palm-tree.'

'Then I shall hope to spread my leaves like a tribute above your head, or shall we say around your dress? Academic palms, of course.'

'Hang it all, that's dreadfully trite. I *insist* on you taking that back. I don't want to have to remember you as a person of empty compliments.'

He stood up, suddenly serious.

'Miss Kalvelage, just remember me. As long as I've left some impression, whatever it may be – and I'm quite in earnest now – then I am satisfied. And I assure you, I shan't forget you, never. And when I come back I shall look for you here, or wherever you may be.'

They smiled as they said good-bye. But it was now not only De Gankelaar who felt melancholy.

And it was in the spring that the office lost the second colleague, through death.

Gideon Piaat's weak heart gave out. He could have lived somewhat longer if he had taken care of himself, but that he could not do. The atmosphere of the criminal court, not very agreeable to most lawyers, was his element. Stroom-koning himself, did not like it; he shared the opinion of most that the cachet lay in the civil practice, the criminal being really rather inferior. Piaat was of a different mould. He liked to visit his clients in the gloomy prison where the iron grills clanked so and the bunches of keys rattled. He could argue fiercely with the Public Prosecutor and the experts. When pleading his voice swelled, for he had a fine voice. The quick, orally conducted criminal case was what he liked; the written judgements in civil cases he found tame by comparison. A big criminal case was like a ship in the open sea – he had once used that metaphor, him-self. Great gusts swept through the court; everything heaved, the judges, the defending counsel, the public. Here one was suddenly presented with surprises, splendid, but horrible. Here was sensation, but it was the sensation of real life, not the false one of advertisements. The criminal case was alive, breathing; the civil, a corpse.

He had the small vanity of wanting always to be thought witty; if he did not carry the court with him he almost felt humiliated. But his witticisms were generally excellently conceived and to the point; the public chuckled, the judges who had to listen to so many monotonous cases, laughed. He had an excellent memory : he had already used this joke there, but not here, and it had not yet appeared in the papers; it would go like wildfire. And it did.

He was such a good defence counsel that he gradually built up a practice of his own; the criminal cases had not meant much to Stroomkoning; now they were important. And in order not to lose Piaat Stroomkoning made a con-tract with him for several years, on very good terms, just as he had done with Carlion. He thus tied him to him, and apart from his state-aided clients, Piaat did nothing but his criminal cases.

Thus he became a solitary figure in the office; he had hardly any contact with Katadreuffe. He had always very few letters, and Miss Sibculo typed his notes and

memoranda. And he displayed, inconspicuously, considerable delicacy. Whenever a case was one in which a girl
might be involved – were she betrothed – then he called for
a typewriter, himself.

His end was brought about through the strain of the
criminal court. He had foreseen it, but not spared himself;
more and more he had grown from clown into pierrot. His
landlady found him one morning sitting in a chair, dead.
A tumbler lay shattered at the foot of his table. He was
sprawled over the table, dressed, completely rigid. He must
have died late on the previous evening. It seemed as though
– and the impression was a very strong one – a final criminal
case was symbolized there in that room of death.

He was buried at Crooswijk. There were lots of flowers.
He had no family, with the exception of a brother in
Surinam, who sent a wreath. Quite a crowd of people stood
around the grave. Stroomkoning spoke simply and with
feeling; also a judge, the Public Prosecutor's assistant, and
the Dean.

During this year Katadreuffe worked with the regularity
of a clock at his qualifying exam. He was entered at Leiden,
but he could not join a college. The whole academic life
passed him by, including that of the students' unions. But
he did not miss it; his only object was success. With a letter
from Stroomkoning, he visited several professors. They
naturally were not pleased to see a student who did not
come under their authority, but exceptions were occasionally necessary. He spoke his piece well, and Stroomkoning's
letter did the rest.

Thus he was able to devote his free time to study without the fear that his absence from the academic life would
be held against him. He hoped to attain his Doctorate of
Laws within three years; it was the shortest time even for
a student with no other work to do; it was extremely short,
but then his plan was extremely definite. He had regained
his old strength of will; he would achieve the impossible.
An important aid – he could well see – was his practical

legal experience in the office. In contrast with most of the other students he did not approach the subjects for study without any preparation. For the same things that had helped him in his matriculation now also came in useful. He was building on a certain substratum of general knowledge, with gaps in it, a jumble, but still an aid. And again his age helped him, being much older than the rest. With his years, his mind was riper; he assimilated quickly. His study for the matriculation had been the more difficult. That study so many give up, and of those who reach the final barrier how few surmount it. But he had surmounted it, and without checks from the outside world he would, in the shortest time, obtain his degree; he was absolutely convinced of that.

There lay perhaps a danger in the debt which was still not paid off by a long way, as his studies were expensive. He paid the interest, however, and paid off a regular amount; and the enemy appeared to slumber; this was the key-point of the battle. But he remained wary; sometimes when he thought of his father, his nerves jarred, in revolt, for he must remain on top. Only once during that year of study did his father appear in the office. Stroomkoning had called for him urgently, and he went straight through to the conference-room. Katadreuffe did not see him come or go; only heard about it later. He did not meet him once that year.

His books of study, his borrowed lectures, proved insufficient; he had to take extra lessons. For three subjects he had tutoring in Rotterdam; for one of them he had to go to Delft. The travelling cost him an hour and a half of his evening, but it was limited to once a week.

Otherwise he hardly went out that whole year; only on a single Sunday afternoon he went for a stroll with 'her' and Jan Maan. Also it was seldom that she called on him. He had spent fourteen days with her, and she with him; that was amply sufficient, they would only end by irritating each other. The second week in her house had been already noticeably less pleasant; the first week, with the rest and all that sleep had acted and continued to act like a balm.

At the beginning of July he passed his qualifying examination. His nerves remained under control; he knew his subject; the examination went swiftly.

Dreverhaven

During the lunch hour Katadreuffe went to see Doctor Merree. He felt nothing wrong with him but wanted just to check his blood-pressure. It appeared to be in order. He then brought the conversation round to his mother; he had noticed she was not so well lately.

'You're quite right,' said the doctor, 'she's consumptive, as you know, Antinoüs, and she knows it, too.'

'Is there,' asked Katadreuffe, 'no danger of infection? A friend of mine lives there. And I, myself, go there now and then, naturally.'

The doctor shook his head.

'For adults any danger is practically excluded provided she takes a few precautions, and that she does, I know.'

The doctor gave a grin.

'I would only advise you not to kiss each other too much, but I don't think that will cause you any great hardship.'

He met Katadreuffe's blush with the wily smile of one who had already years ago seen through these two characters.

'She isn't old yet,' said the son. 'Can it go on for a long time like that?'

'That I can't foresee. Actually it is something of a wonder that she's as good as she is, she might have been bed-ridden long ago. But there is something in her constitution that

I don't understand, I don't mind admitting it. When
I helped you into the world, it was a queer case. It
all turned out differently from what I had expected. Such
a strong, healthy young body as hers should have been able
to stand up to the shock – for we had to use some skill to
pull you out, no time to lose – you know that? – but we
thought it would go like clockwork. And yet she never
really recovered from the operation. A case I shall never
forget. Already in the operating theatre you could see her
withdrawal. Of course she must have had something otherwise the birth would have been normal; it was a curious
case of contraction – she had a . . .'

And with the good-natured, gentle cynicism of a man
who has experienced so much that the corners are rubbed
off his finer feelings, he was about to describe in detail the
mother's case when Katadreuffe said :

'Good heavens, Doctor, please spare me that; I don't
want to know about it.'

The doctor continued :

'Just as you like. You started it, Antinoüs. I only wanted
to say that even that doesn't explain it all. But then, what
do we doctors know about anyone's resistance, anyone's
constitution? That is still a closed book.'

He gave him a hand, calling for the third time Katadreuffe by his nickname, for that was his own find; it
amused him; he was proud of it.

That autumn all was indeed not well with Mrs Katadreuffe. She was tired, she had a pain in her back. In the
afternoon she would go and lie on her bed when everyone had left, as no one must on any account know about
that. It sometimes happened that the neighbours living
above her knocked on her door. Then, light as a feather,
she got up, at once wide awake, neat and tidy; and when
she opened the door everyone thought she had been sitting
working.

Also for some years now her earnings had been less. She
still worked for the same shop, but it had changed hands

and the new owner was more frugal in her payments. Once she had found her work unsuitable and had turned it down. Mrs Katadreuffe, herself, had to recognize a falling off in the quality of her work, although she would never have admitted it; that would have been utter stupidity. But it *had* fallen off; her fantasy was exhausted.

Sometimes she thought that she would recuperate, in her work, in her health, in everything, if she could once again find that splendid green of those early days. These were of course ridiculous thoughts; she must not allow herself to brood over such nonsense. Yet she was sorry she had not preserved a hank or even a few strands of the wool, though naturally she could not expect to equal the work of those days. Also she could not remember the exact colour; quite possibly she had more than once passed by something of the kind without noticing it.

Things were, in fact, rather difficult, and without Jan Maan she did not know how she would have managed; yet Jan Maan was also earning less, and a grown man like that, who brought so much in, was entitled to a reasonable amount of pocket-money. And, in addition, he had to help his parents. She also feared that the revolutionary principles of her lodger would in the end put him on the street, as a boss naturally would not see the difference between words and deeds. He had been fired once or twice, and had been without work, sometimes for a week, sometimes only for a day. There was now labour enough available; employers wouldn't put up with someone who played the fool. One good thing was that he was such a good fitter, and there were not over many of his calibre. So he kept going and was always able to make a fresh start; he very seldom had to draw money from his union. But he was earning less.

It is true she had an account with the Savings Bank, but she would not touch that; that was for later. And then she had the allowance from her son; yes, she had him – no – she *didn't* have him.

That autumn evening – Jan Maan had gone to a meeting

– she was sitting alone, thinking how, taking everything together, the future did not look particularly bright. A vigorous pull at the bell. It was for her. She opened the outer door. Downstairs she could see a figure step in as though he were forcing his way in. She knew at once who it was.

The man found her silently sitting at her table, quite calm. He took a chair opposite to her, but said nothing. He had left the door of the room open. She went to shut it, and for an elderly woman she moved quickly and lightly. Then she resumed her seat.

'When's the wedding-day?' asked the voice.

That voice, so powerful, a voice that aroused the woman in her, *his* voice. Here spoke the master of the dynamic word.

'When are we going to marry . . . Joba?' repeated Dreverhaven, and for the first time in years she heard herself addressed by her Christian name. She had complete control of herself.

'Why do you go on persecuting him so?' she asked in return.

Dreverhaven sat there as though he were the head of the house, his stained, black coat open, his greasy felt-hat pressed down over his eyes. And his cigar. He showed no fight.

'When are we going to marry?'

He moved forward a little, laying his arms comfortably on the table.

Then it occurred to her: that was where the *bokschipper* had also sat, and he had proposed to her, in *his* manner, humbly, in a roundabout way, almost delicately. And it had been absurd – *nothing* – absolutely nothing. *Here* was the man who might ask her to marry him, the only one. And he asked her in *his* fashion, the only one.

She just shook her head; she was not in the slightest afraid; she asked :

'Why do you do all that to Jacob?'

And just as twenty-five years ago he had had to admit her superiority over the letters and the money, as he had had to give way to her, it was so now, for she did not answer him, but he, her. He answered her question, but he did it in *his* way. He again leant back; leaving one hand on the table, and the hand became a fist.

'By God,' he said, and his tone was strangely solemn, 'I'll strangle him, I'll strangle nine tenths of him, and the other tenth I'll leave him – and that little scrap I leave will make him great – he'll become great, by God, he will – great.'

She looked at him with a smile. She was not afraid; he had never been able to make her afraid. But now it was her turn to answer and she said :

'No Mr Dreverhaven, I shall never marry you, I'm not marrying anybody. But I don't mind you knowing there is no man I've ever liked more than you. So it was and so it remains.'

He had not moved and he said, acting as though he had not understood her words, as though he were just picking up his own thread :

'And, Joba, that one tenth, that small scrap – I may even take that from him.'

He stood up, and threatening her with his finger, he said :

'That boy of ours hasn't got there yet, mark my words, he's not there yet.'

And without saying good-bye he left her, standing in the middle of the room. But she was not afraid; she smiled. He *could* not frighten her, although she did not understand him. She certainly did not understand his last words. But he was like that, an enigma, and this enigmatical creature fascinated her just on account of the problem he presented. Not in his person, however strange, not in his relationship to her, but in his relationship of father to child. But she was not frightened of him, nor for the fate of her child.

Going over the short conversation in her mind, it struck her now how strangely question and answer brushed past one another, and yet no question had remained unanswered. It was just that one answer that was obscure, very obscure.

Then she opened the door and the window, as no one was allowed to smoke in her room; now she had not forbidden it.

Dreverhaven walked the many streets to his office. He did not walk quickly; he walked heavily, with the pace of the elderly but powerful man; he was capable of walking all night long. His gait was that of a man who is meeting opposition; he ploughed through the twilight darkness; he swam with a slow stroke against the autumn current.

The door of the large property in the Lange Baanstraat stood, as always, open; so many people passed in and out. On the badly lit spiral stone stairs, a couple of lovers made way for him. A man who saw him slowly climbing up, like a black puff of smoke rising through a hole in the floor, stood watching on the landing until he was past. Here came the landlord.

He passed through the dismal rooms to his office. He sat down at the desk, remaining there with his coats open, his hat all out of shape, a gutter-Caesar, and yet a Caesar.

He was not expecting anybody; he had only his thoughts to occupy him. He bent down, took a bottle of geneva from his desk, and poured out a drink. He stopped at one, and then leant back in his chair with his hands over his stomach, his cigar – the cannon – aiming up and across at an invisible target. And he spoke to himself out loud, as he was coming to do more and more recently when alone, a few words. His thoughts were with his son and with the latter's mother.

'All or nothing,' he said.

It was the conclusion of his thinking. For he had acknowledged his son, though he had not wanted to, because 'she' would not marry him. No middle way – all or nothing.

'She too : all or nothing,' he said.

And again he had reached a conclusion. She would never accept a gift from him; she could no more give way than he. She would have accepted everything from him had they been married. She would not marry him because she would not forgive herself for the child's bastardy, nor him. 'All' was impossible for her, therefore : nothing.

Whenever he drew up a balance of his affairs, he could see precious little profit remaining. He had scraped the money together and then chucked it all away. He possessed the soul of a miser, but he suffered from attacks of thriftlessness, a symptom of dissatisfaction. When he thought of what he could have been, above all, what he could have possessed, his heart bled; it burst open in his breast, it bled dry. For he had the soul of a miser. From the mountain of his years he wanted to look down on the panorama of his wealth, that promised land of the miser. He could very well see a landscape, immense, and of the greatest variety, but it was not rich, as he imagined a rich land; and above some of the country he could see rising clouds of a weakening memory; they were banking already on the horizon. Perhaps it is as well, he thought, that I don't know what lies hidden there.

And this result of his labours was bitterly disappointing. For he valued himself highly, and knew that he was entitled to do so. He had always been an exceptional figure, and yet a bailiff. He had wrought that office into something which, before him, had never existed, and neither would exist after him, and yet only a bailiff's office. He had always driven himself hard in running his office and his life, but this driving-force lay in his nature. Now the vistas unrolled themselves, far, wide, mostly sombre; his land-hunger had demanded enormous stretches, and they had borne precious little fruit.

He was not a man to repent; that was against his miserly spirit. Things had now gone so far that he did not know whether he would be able to keep his bank, the apple of his eye. For that bank had been his triumph over the untrustworthiness of a money-lender who, many years ago, had at the last moment gone back on his word. A rage, at first against the whole world, he had cooled by begetting a son. Later he had triumphed over his jealousy and bad luck and, with another's money – bought out long ago – he had founded his bank. And now the apple of his eye was no longer flourishing; the authorities were paying more attention; everyone knew it was his bank; the police had already once warned the public; that acted like a snowball. He had been called once or twice before the judge, but had denied with calm effrontery that he had anything to do with the bank, and only the cunning set-up of the business had, up to the present, prevented them being able to prove anything against him. But the times were against him, conditions were worsening, laws were stricter, the authorities were no longer asleep. That the bank could still carry on was only on account of his age, his popularity with the people, and the practical difficulty of abolishing something which has become established.

Then he returned to his first thoughts, about his son, whom he had not included in the formula : all or nothing. And although he did not say it out loud, he rounded off his thoughts with : it is also better for the boy that the last Dreverhaven should be a Katadreuffe.

Then, thinking of the mother who had always crossed him, that little grey carcass, he said out loud :

'By God, she's got guts.'

And he thought but did not say : but what eyes that carcass has, and her son too. For there was a grim admiration in his heart. And he went off to his auction-room on the Hooimarkt.

He was often there lately; he was gradually becoming more restless. Under the light of a single lamp he walked round, past the goods for sale, mostly poor stuff, junk in bad taste; he walked through the gangways and up the steps to the rostrum, from where the goods were auctioned – whilst the auctioneer shouted, he kept the record. From there he looked out over the pitiful rubbish, the jetsam of evicted families, the residues of legacies over which first the disappointed heirs had wrangled. His look gave nothing away, but already the restlessness in his legs hungered for further movement, and he walked back across his domain under the dull black glass cupola in the scanty light.

He sat less in his office in the evenings; he derived more pleasure moving about in the general bustle. On a Saturday evening he would walk up and down the extensive poor people's market on the Goudse Singel, several times. He did not get tired; he could not get tired. There, between the stalls on the pavement, he walked, but he did not saunter, did not look and examine like the others; he sailed along, in the full light of the hot gas-flares. The lighting of the stalls was quite a business in itself. Here they came with hand-carts, on which were crates packed full of lamps, whole galaxies of fierce green-white light, rolling out of the alleys. When the lamps were hanging in the tents, the result was a powerful, painful glare. Dreverhaven said nothing; he wanted to be seen; he pushed everyone aside. There is Mr Dreverhaven, the bailiff. Could he feel the knife? He was so curious that he would indeed like to feel it once. He walked on and on, sometimes an hour or longer. If it was late, then he watched them breaking up the market; the rubbishy goods were stowed away, the canvas taken down, the glow-worm catchers appeared and stripped the tents of these shining insects, riding off with their catch in the crates, some of them extinguished, others still fiercely sputtering and sparkling, all caged. Then came the noisy dismantling of planks, props and trestles, and finally – the people long since departed – the road-sweepers, with jets of water, hosed the great asphalt surface clean, together with the rubbish alongside the kerb. Sometimes Dreverhaven was walking there, with the water streaming under his feet.

He had had little trouble with his tenants. Underneath him were warehouses and a stable, above quite a number of tenements, but separated from him by an enormously thick, old floor; and he, himself, occupied the whole of the

first storey. He might occasionally hear them banging about
fighting, or shouting, but it was quickly over, for in this
house the landlord lived. But now he had above his office,
right over his head, a family with a harmonium, yet that
did not matter as they played it very softly. But with the
harmonium, evening after evening, three girls bawled so
penetratingly that it went right through flesh and bone, and
through the thick floor.

This aroused a spirit of opposition in him, stronger than
he had ever felt before. He would evict that family, but not
that alone. It would be the greatest eviction, the mightiest
deed of his life – his victory in the Rubroekstraat would be
child's play by comparison. The why and wherefore did
not worry him, nor the money; at the end of his life all he
wanted was power.

And he gave all the tenants a week's notice. No one left,
as no one was to any extent behind in his rent. It was
towards the end of November, and an early and bitterly
cold winter closed in on the poor. The whole thing was
too absurd, and opposing him for the first time, they drew
strength from one another.

Then he simply summoned all the tenants to the police-
court. And these limited brains all appeared in court, not
understanding what it was all about. For their landlord
was Mr Dreverhaven, and now their leases were cancelled
and they had been summoned by 'The Peace Building Company Limited'. They showed their rent books, on which
however the proprietor's name did not appear, only the
regularly stamped name, 'Hamerslag', for the clerk collected
the rents. But they could not deny that they had received
a week's notice, neither could they dispute that the limited
company owned the property. For the term, limited liability
company, did not mean anything to them, as they were
simple people and were ignorant of the tricks of denial
and the power there lay in them. What they understood
least of all was that a lawyer in bands and gown stated the
case for the proprietor. Dreverhaven, himself, stood behind

his desk, and merely called out the names in his booming, slurred way of speaking; but the lawyer did the talking and with each new case said :

'I declare that the proprietors persist in their demand, in accordance with the summons.'

It was Dr Schuwagt, his tuft of hair still between fair and grey. But no one understood his words.

The men and the women – one woman pregnant – departed in silence, but one of them seemed to have rumbled the game; he clenched his fist at Dreverhaven and called out with a curse :

'You wait, I'll get you all right.'

Dreverhaven just turned his stone-hard, round head with the short, grey hog's hair in the direction of the shouting man. The latter then hastily withdrew. It was all over; not a single valid objection was upheld; they were each in turn ordered to evacuate their rooms 'with all their family and belongings'.

Dr. Schuwagt left with a bow to the judge, Dreverhaven remaining to check off the names.

But the man who had shouted out, had indeed rumbled the game. For the Peace Building Company was none other than Dreverhaven. He had made a limited company of his property. A cynical desire for paradox had made him give to this housing of wrangling paupers the most peaceful name.

Even after the judgement no one departed; and now things became serious, and they started in on it. One stormy Saturday evening the bailiff executed what he might indeed call the greatest eviction of his life. He had not asked for any assistance from the police; he carried it out with Hamerslag and Den Hieperboree, nicknamed Coal-grab. It was almost a festival of misery and frenzy. In a strong wind, it was pouring, half hail, half frozen rain. Such a freak of nature had never been seen before. Icicles formed on the gutters of the roof, not firm ice but soft, breaking off in the wind. The streets were half white, half covered with puddles.

The cobbles were uneven and at the same time slippery, very treacherous to walk on.

Dreverhaven started with the family of the three bawling girls. Coal-grab with his whirlwind arms drove them from the room; Hamerslag, so sinewy and strong, carried the harmonium out on his back, both hands in front on a strap dangling from it. As he put it on the landing, he said :

'If you don't take it away from the staircase, I'll bung it down.'

They handled the things so terribly roughly that the tenants in the end took over the removal, for the bailiff and his assistants were more destructive than a herd of wild animals.

The threat of devastation spread panic around, infecting all the families, and the stairs were blocked with furniture, bedding and all the pitiful chattels of the inhabitants. But they got it all down – no one knew how – and out of the house.

And wherever his assistants were busy Dreverhaven barred the door so that no one could get in. Curses and abuse resounded through the whole house – that was fine – that was what he lived for. He climbed to the very top, sweeping the garrets and the attics empty of people, as though he were smoking out vermin from their nests. Wherever he appeared they began to move away, even the most refractory, and none touched him. He wore the ribbon on his chest.

In the meantime, the corner formed by the Lange Baanstraat and Brede Straat was filled with their belongings, and a louder and more threatening sound rose up around the building. For the tenants, once outside, plucked up the courage which the public street and a crowd will give; and they were maddened by the terrible weather, slipping and tumbling over the cobbles, whilst their piles of goods tottered and slid about. From all sides spectators came running, sliding, tumbling; at the corner a tightly packed, threatening crowd collected. Police arrived and formed a cordon.

But the people continued to curse and swear. Also the cries
from the Goudse Singel fed their anger. For there a second
fun-fair was raging; the storm, the frozen rain, the lights,
and the Saturday evening seemed to be driving the people
mad; they jogged around, screaming, quite out of hand. In
sympathy as it were, they also began to lose all sense of
moderation.

The house was empty. Hamerslag stood, dripping with
sweat, by his master; he had excelled himself; Coal-grab,
more spineless and macabre than ever, seemed to be prey
to a lonely St Vitus's dance; his head rolled about as on a
string, his jaws wide open and hungry.

Dreverhaven extinguished all the lights, drew all the curtains back, and then showed himself like a prince behind
the middle window of his office. He was greeted with
shouts; a brick shattered the glass above his head. The police
forced the people back. But a moment later, Dreverhaven
was outside, pressing past the policemen through the on-
lookers and, under a terrific hailstorm, he, himself, looked
up at his house. He pointed to the hole in the window.

'Much too high – rotten shot,' he said.

His freedom from fear silenced the people. No one now
cursed, no one attempted to lay a hand on him. Then he
unlocked one of the store-rooms leading on to the street,
and magnanimously allowed them to stow their things there,
for one night. But a number of them had abandoned their
rubbish, and in furious despair had gone off to the Refuge
for the Homeless. Before all had been stored, with the
floundering, stumbling people skating over the slippery
cobbles, it had become a carnival of hate and bitterness;
the police helped with the things that had been abandoned.
Everything was mixed higgledy-piggledy in the store-room.
Tomorrow would be a great day, with rows to be expected
between the owners who would not be able to know where
to start finding their things. That would mean more police
interference – Dreverhaven was sure of that – and he
chuckled to himself.

He stood looking at the crowd. On his disgusting hat grains of ice had formed, and in the light it looked as though he stood under a canopy of diamonds. The ice was already beginning to melt – it had turned milder – and the water began to drip down from the rim of his hat. But however long he stood there, the knife did not come. The crowd dispersed over the slippery pavements; the police calmly drove the spectators from the crossing : he remained standing; the knife did not come. Then, walking very slowly, he made the round of the neighbourhood, down the Vogelenzang and the Nieuwe Vogelenzang. Having left him, the people had again started to grumble, but when he appeared the voices were stilled. He slowly walked through all the alleys, with names referring to corn and herbs, wheat, bread, flax and hemp; no one molested him, no one hooted at him, no one spoke to him. He reached the horrible Water-hondsteegje, like a grave; in the very poorest street, the Tholenstraatje, which hummed with the poorest of the poor, the usually noisy populace withdrew into their doorways in silence. For wherever he appeared he wore the orange ribbon and badge with the Kingdom's coat-of-arms; he personified the thing most dreaded by the people, the Law. They did not understand it but they bowed to the ground before it.

Dr Schuwagt felt he owed some explanation to the judge. Dreverhaven had him explain that the house needed modernization. And he actually did seem to foster some plan for this. He had the vague intention of collecting all the smoke vents into one chimney, in a corner at the back. The chimney would be high, visible from afar, and vomit smoke like a crematorium.

Dreverhaven did, in fact, break up all the floors in that corner. But the old cross-beams he kept intact, and looking down from above into the depths one obtained the impression of a huge, square well full of gratings, one above the other, gratings with weird-looking, broad bars of ancient wood. The night wind blew through them from cellar to roof, and played over the benumbed strings of these harps its harshest chords. Sometimes, sitting alone in his room, Dreverhaven could hear it howling in the far corner. Then he thought of the three-toned bawling above his head, and was satisfied. Like a Samson of the Law he had, through his strength, crushed his enemies, and now his temple was almost a ruin.

More and more he began to abuse his position, more and more he derived satisfaction from this. He had, of late, a very simple method of collecting a debt. He went to the debtor's house, sat himself comfortably in his best chair, saying that he had not only come to execute a summons, but that he had in his pocket a warrant to take the debtor to prison if he did not pay, a warrant signed by the whole Bench. Then the matter was settled, including costs and everything – and more than that, much too much, as in the end it became pure extortion – then he would look for the geneva bottle and cigar-box; if he saw them he would take them, if not, he just ordered them. But he was very cunning; he did not repeat these tactics too often; and he chose carefully, people who were very stupid and who would not complain to the authorities.

It was bound to happen sooner or later that father and son would meet, on opposite sides, in court. Katadreuffe and Dreverhaven came to plead. The matter was of no great financial importance, but it had interesting aspects and Katadreuffe brought the case to court.

As a rule he did not attend the police-court; that he had arranged with Stroomkoning, who appointed outside representation whilst he did the necessary clerical work. On this occasion he pleaded, himself.

He was rather too early; his case was low in the list. The court was half empty; they were getting near the end; but the proxies kept their seats in the front rows and were revelling in the case of a woman who had been summoned. It was one of those ridiculous cases with which the police-court teems. The woman's small son, playing ball in the street, had hit a neighbour's window; the neighbour had rented the house with the condition 'window breakage for lessee's account', and demanded damages.

Katadreuffe only heard the end of the exchange between the judge and the woman. She asked with haughty self-confidence :

'But then, by law, I can of course pay for the pane of glass by instalments?'

And the judge, dry as dust :

'That you could only do if your small boy had broken the window-pane by instalments.'

And he ordered her to pay the damage with costs, saying, whilst the proxies were quietly splitting their sides :

'Next case.'

The woman departed, half audibly muttering and abusing the judge, calling him an absolute Nero.

Dreverhaven announced the names of the new parties, then stepped from his place, indicating with his head that the proxies should leave – it was still open court, but they went – put away his ribbon and badge and came up to the plaintiff's desk; Katadreuffe went to the other.

Katadreuffe was not in the least nervous in his pleading. He had, although seldom and never against his father, already had to speak here; he, moreover, knew what his father looked like without coat and hat, with his powerful head of granite. He was not afraid of his father, not now even, and he knew what he had to say.

This case also had an absurd side. The plaintiff was a bridegroom who had ordered for his wedding six beautifully shiny black cars. But the garage proprietor had only gone to fetch the bride's grandmother, and then in a broken-down old car, whose engine stalled for good after driving two streets. The six beautiful cars were of course at the same time transporting more lucrative loads; so the plaintiff insinuated. Well, instead of at ten o'clock in the morning they were married at three in the afternoon, the very last to arrive at the town hall, as the garage proprietor had kept them hours talking, with the promise that the cars would be coming any minute. In the end they had to take taxis from here, there and everywhere, and were made the laughing-stock of the neighbours for years. The bridegroom was demanding damages for all this.

The garage proprietor only admitted that he had not carried out the order, brushed aside every insinuation, appealed to *force majeur*, and disputed the various items in the claim.

Dreverhaven pleaded for the bridegroom with his usual slovenly, booming voice. Whether he was interested in the case it was impossible to tell, but at one moment it seemed to amuse him, for although he kept a straight face, a twitch at the side of his nose indicated that he felt the humour of the situation. And his argument went home : one could recognize the advocate with decades of practical experience behind him.

But Katadreuffe's argument also told. He was young and absolutely serious. He did not risk the slippery ice of jokes, as an elderly judge sometimes does not like to hear these from a youthful counsel. He referred to judgements of more or less analogous cases; his argument was sound, particularly on the question of *force majeur* : that morning the garage proprietor had been deprived of his licence.

Neither side won. The judge, eight days later, ordered the parties to appear in person before him for further information and an attempt at a settlement.

Business and Celebration

By the following winter Katadreuffe had made considerable
progress with his studies for his doctorate examination. His
plan of study was just the same as before. He visited the
new professors and he was again exempted from going to
college. The curriculum was far more extensive and it was
therefore necessary for him to rely more on private tutoring, and he therefore had to pay more, but Stroomkoning
had raised his salary. The new work suited him better than
that for his qualifying exam : he was now dealing with live
law and he had an even greater lead over the other students,
having had some experience of law practice. He told his
professors that he was going to try to take his doctorate in
two years (they had very definitely doubted the possibility
of this), and he remained convinced that he could do it.
At least, when no unforeseen circumstances should arise to
check him. He was no longer frightened about his health;
his constitution remained delicate but he felt well, he slept
reasonably, there was no further talk of sleep-walking, and
he had not coughed up any more blood – that must certainly
have come from the stomach. He had completely recovered
his mental equilibrium.

They often happened to talk about Miss Te George.

Stroomkoning would say to him in confidence, referring
to Miss Van Alm :

'She's not the same.'

Then he would sigh for his former secretary, but he never insinuated that Katadreuffe had been the cause of her departure; he limited himself to saying :

'I'll never in the whole of my life get another like her.'

This warmed Katadreuffe, and it was also proof that Stroomkoning was trying to make the best of the new one. She also did her best and was by no means so bad. But she had not got the culture of Miss Te George; you could see at once, in her bearing, in everything, that she was a typist. That inwardly vexed Stroomkoning most of all. For he had flaunted Miss Te George at the meetings in the conference-room; she was so unique; everyone looked at her, and that had so often given him pleasure, for she gave a cachet to his office. And with Miss Van Alm, although her features were by no means plain and her teeth were even beautiful, hardly anybody looked at her, and she did not appear to be following the debates; not even in the most heated exchanges did her expression change; she was an automaton who took notes.

Once Katadreuffe felt a revival of the old pain. Miss Sibculo was the cause. She was still engaged; there were prospects of marriage, but no immediate possibility. Her fiancé was climbing steadily, but slowly. She seemed to have got over her unfortunate affection for Katadreuffe; she no longer made a play of smiles and dimples and sighs, which did not become her. The little face on too short a neck, in itself insignificant, had with the years much improved; it had become somewhat thinner, somewhat paler, somewhat more elegant. And Katadreuffe had quite a liking for her, although he did not show it. He was a good tactician; he seemed to understand that with women as well as men, the merest approach can prove disastrous.

But once Miss Sibculo said that Miss Te George was married, at least a year ago. They did not see one another – they lived too far apart – also they had few common interests, but she had heard it from another. Yes, Miss Te

George still lived here, but she could not remember her husband's name.

That word, 'husband' hurt Katadreuffe, for the moment; he was not jealous and yet he was wounded. He once again saw the tent at the Hook, with the perky little orange, white and blue flag, and that damn fellow crawling out of it on his hands and knees. She was of course Mrs Van Rijn. But he quickly shook it off; after all, it would be crazy to go on brooding about that. If someone like Miss Te George didn't marry – she was no longer so very young – who then?

The office was badly hit by the depression but like most lawyers' offices managed to keep going all right, for the bad times did not affect the legal profession as it did trade. Stroomkoning did not try to economize on salaries – he was the last man to do that – he merely did not refill the vacancies. And it happened that he missed least the two colleagues who had left. De Gankelaar was, for him, less an assistant than an advertisement, and that not to the extent he had anticipated, as this *jonkheer* would not use his title in the practice. Gideon Piaat had given him real support; his encyclopedia knowledge had been irrefutable, and he had earned good money through his criminal practice. Now there were fewer of these, as Piaat was no longer there to attract them to the office. However, Stroomkoning was not too sorry about this; money was not everything to him. and as a specialist in civil law he always regarded criminal law as somewhat inferior. The two remaining colleagues, Carlion and Miss Kalvelage, were the best; it would not be long before he made Carlion a partner. And Katadreuffe was growing into the practice; the flair of an experienced lawyer told him that a fine future awaited him there, only he needed to improve his arithmetic.

In the meantime, he had raised Katadreuffe's salary without meeting any opposition, as Katadreuffe, himself, considered he was entitled to a rise. He was not grasping, but also not too modest; he felt he could now indeed put a higher value on his work. For he began more and more to fill the place of a colleague; Stroomkoning could not have done without both his departed colleagues, had Katadreuffe not taken over the state-aid practice. Up till now the colleagues had had to do this and also divide between them Stroomkoning's state-aid cases. That now all fell on Katadreuffe's shoulders, at least the voluminous clerical work. That went all right; the cases were mostly routine, but they took up time and that he was able to devote to them.

Katadreuffe also gradually became more versed in Stroomkoning's own practice, as he did not leave everything to Miss Van Alm, but sometimes called in his head clerk. In this way, the latter got more insight into the 'big business' which, although shrunken, was still considerable, with the legal work at meetings, arranging settlements, concluding contracts, acting as arbitrator. For some meetings Stroomkoning had Katadreuffe at the small table where, all eyes and ears, he learnt a lot. He saw the big merchants from close up. And those meetings were fascinating. The merchants were business-like and to the point, but they had never had time to cultivate the spoken word, though a few were thus naturally gifted. And none of them had the legal insight, won only through study. Stroomkoning always had to give their ideas proper form. It was then Katadreuffe saw for the first time that the lawyer is an indispensable link in commerce. Foresee the requirements of a contract, at least limit the scope for dispute.

And he learnt still more. He learnt that Stroomkoning was the biggest of the three lawyers in the office; he had to recognize the all-round lawyer in his chief. It was partly due to his age and experience, but still he must have always had the natural disposition for a real lawyer. There was, moreover, his appearance; the grey lion's head with the bristling moustache and his light green eyes, and the convincingly soft growl of his voice; then his quick mind enabled him immediately to pick out the essentials of a debate, and this was helped by his easy, playful manner of dealing with the most heterogeneous characters. He ended by putting everyone at his ease; that was his forte. According to circumstances, he could be nonchalant, serious, boisterous, calm, stimulating, placating, aggressive, conciliatory. And when talking, he had a ready wit, which he could vary to refinement for the cultured and crudity for the cruder.

Katadreuffe found his former estimate of Stroomkoning that of a snotty schoolboy. He felt ashamed of once having wanted not to be like De Gankelaar, nor Countryside, nor Stroomkoning, for whom his immature judgement had been nothing less than absurdly presumptuous. Stroomkoning was a personality; he might hope to become his equal; all the same he still wanted to be *different*, also a personality, but yet different, *greater*.

Katadreuffe had no holiday that summer. He remained at work, steadily and regularly, but he now also took regular recreation. He kept his Sunday afternoons and evenings free, and in the summer he and Jan Maan went once more to the beach at the Waalhaven. Katadreuffe did not go to the Hook again; the memory of it made him ashamed and sad. Thus he limited himself to the other beach, splashed about a bit in the brackish water there and lay on the river-sand in the sun. A whole town of tents had grown up there, and the restricted intimacy of their first discovery had vanished. He did not like it so much; the smell of the Rotterdam people bothered him; the noise they made, however natural, annoyed him; their too close proximity offended him. He was becoming estranged from this lower class – he was climbing; but they were also becoming estranged from him – they were sinking. The depression caused so much unemployment. One could see it in their faces; a new type now came to this far end of the town. They were often ragged and slovenly; it did not embarrass them to strip off torn clothing and exhibit a dirty nakedness. It really affected his olfactory nerves. There were still plenty of healthy, sturdy people about, but the others caused him to feel a slight nausea. He told Jan Maan he would rather stay away.

'Capitalist,' Jan Maan chided.

'Yes,' said Katadreuffe, 'but the people could keep their clothes decent. The dole is better here than in most countries. And there's always been water enough here.'

'Yes,' Jan Maan answered, 'but you don't realize the moral depression of aimlessly wandering around. You're a blind, narrow-minded capitalist. You ought to be standing in their shoes.'

'You don't mean that, Jan.'

'No, I suppose not, and yet I do mean it.'

To give his friend pleasure, and also because he was not too happy about his own attitude, he went in the winter a few times to red Caledonia. And they took 'her' with them, for she was always glad to go. Katadreuffe, however, did not attend the meetings any more; he only went to the Russian films, and they went on a Sunday afternoon as the evening air was bad for her. With the winter, she felt somewhat better – good Heavens, it could go on for many more years – she coughed but did not spit blood; and when the boys walked slowly she was glad to walk the whole way there and back. She was not actually ill; she was just wearing away; it was a proper slow consumption. She had been ill for at least six years now, but she did not talk about it and did not even complain to herself, for, taking everything together, she had had a much better life than the majority.

At Caledonia they saw Eisenstein's films : *Potemkin* and *The General Line*. The audience sat breathless through them, and at the end there was a storm of applause. Katadreuffe, looking around, was astonished that these communists remained, on an average, such respectable Dutchmen. The worst side of it was their abject slogans and a few rough individuals. But 'she' had been right : there must be some good in the principle, otherwise it could not endure – yet it was nothing for him. And his mother, that self-contained, conservative little person, sat calmly here as if in her element. But the people in this hall looked very different from Jan Maan's circle of friends who visited him in his room and whom Katadreuffe recognized by their smell. Jan Maan had blindly fallen in with the riff-raff of the party.

Eisenstein's films carried them away; none of them had ever seen anything so powerful. *The General Line* was sublime.

'The song of the fields,' Katadreuffe said.

They were raised up, they sank down, they were shattered by a rhythm which pulsed through the films like a heart-beat. It was as though they circulated in the very blood of these films. And for a moment, on the way home, Jan Maan triumphed completely over both of them, for here there was no attempt at criticism.

'Those Russians,' he said, 'what fellows!'

'And apparently happy in spite of Lubyanka,' said Katadreuffe, who wanted to run down communism a bit, if only in its historical rise.

They also saw Dzigan's *Sailors of Kronstadt*, and that was equally estimable, as the Russians had now mastered the subtleties of technique. Yet this film did not have the shattering impact of Eisenstein's earlier films; and what greatly irritated 'her', behind the screen there was a thin woman's voice holding forth in Russian and spoiling a great deal of the effect.

These were Katadreuffe's outings, as well as a walk with her in the Oude Plantage Park; otherwise, he did nothing but work. And once, when the weather was bad, he stayed the whole afternoon and evening at home, reading his encyclopedia.

He had now gone right through from U to Z, picking out the essentials; and he had now such control over his thoughts that when he took out a volume he gave no thought to Lorna Te George.

He lived exclusively for his work and the few persons he knew. Those with whom he came in contact after Miss Te George's departure did not arouse any real interest in him;

it was as though his interest in his fellow-men had disappeared with her. De Gankelaar was no longer there to spur him on to a fresh active study of Man. Miss Van Alm left him cold, as did the new office-boy, and even his new landlord, although he was considerably more comfortable with him than in Graanoogst's chilly, sunless room with the bedstead.

And he continued to move steadily towards his goal : success. The enemy had apparently given up the fight. He went on paying off his debt, punctual to the minute, and was nearly through with it now.

In the spring, C. C. & C. again sent young Countryside to Rotterdam. He arrived with his heavy, aromatic cigarettes, his teeth more decayed than ever, with more spots of gold scattered about them, his voice deeper, more tired, the black hair on his hands reaching to his knuckles. There was to be a great celebration for Stroomkoning, who had been a lawyer for forty years. He was giving a party to a few friends, a few clients, and the office. Young Countryside stayed at the Stroomkonings' lakeside villa; Mrs Stroomkoning was again enraptured with him, but he also came a lot to the office, for he showed great interest in Katadreuffe.

Young Countryside was now the senior in his office. Cadwallader was dead, and old Countryside had retired, but two of Cadwallader's sons had filled the empty places. The office was now called Countryside, Cadwallader and Cadwallader, so in abbreviation it could still be called C. C. & C.

Young Countryside was now a few years older and consequently even more dissipated, but he proposed to recuperate his strength on Dutch gin. He looked even more simian than ever, yet remained well-bred, the representative of a great people. He was sorry De Gankelaar had left; he had got on so well with him, whilst the other two colleagues did not appeal to him. But he fastened on to Katadreuffe; he had suddenly discovered him. And he kept him for hours from his work. Katadreuffe had not omitted, while studying, to improve his languages; that was in fact a part of his studies. He had started with English, the most useful language of all here; he had taken conversation lessons and could understand and speak tolerably well. They were thus able to follow one another enough in the superficial subjects chosen by Countryside. And Countryside always finished with an urging, almost pressing request :

'You show me the sights of the town.'

But Katadreuffe knew nothing about the amusements Rotterdam had to offer of the kind Countryside was seeking (for men only) and excused himself, always explaining that he was not free in the evenings.

Stroomkoning did not like the idea of being the focal point of a celebration. He kept the anniversary secret; it was to be a party in the office and for the office. There was to be a dinner for his guests in the conference-room, and, at the same time, a dinner for the staff in the waiting-room.

During the morning the office remained open, and the last client was Mrs Starels. She arrived just about closing time together with the first flowers. She seemed to possess a sixth sense leading her to the intimate parties in this office, like a water diviner to his well.

On this occasion she came for the sole purpose of paying the account, and was therefore allowed in. She did not see Stroomkoning, who had not yet arrived. Katadreuffe typed out the receipt. She had brought her husband, the stevedore, with her; they had become reconciled. The stevedore was a sturdy fellow, no more a gentleman than she a lady. She felt so at home here that she dragged the stevedore into the general office and, pointing at Katadreuffe, said :

'Look, my pet, that is the gentleman who is studying to be a student.'

'Good God, Woman! What on earth do you mean !' said the stevedore whom Katadreuffe left completely cold, except for the thoughts which his wife's enthusiasm for this young man aroused.

He turned round, rather surlily; he had already for some

days now regretted the reconciliation. She pulled him
further along the passage.

'And this is Mr Stroomkoning's office, my pet.'

She had never been in there, but she did not mention this.
Katadreuffe came after them with the receipt. The woman
asked :

'May my husband have a look at Mr Stroomkoning's
office, Mr Katadreuffe?'

They were standing on the broad steps. Katadreuffe
handed the receipt to the stevedore.

'Certainly, madam,' he said, trying to pass them to open
the door.

But madam, with a rapid movement, had quickly
snatched the receipt from her husband's hand.

'That's mine.'

The man turned red.

'Are you crazy? Give it me.'

Angrily he tried to seize the paper but only succeeded
in tearing off a scrap before she put it behind her back.
He swore.

'If you don't give that back double quick. Who pays for
these lovely law-suits of yours, you or me? Who only has
his use when he stumps up?'

He tried once or twice to recover the paper, and then
suddenly all was up again between the two. She screwed
up the receipt and threw it down at his feet.

'There !'

Royally she swept into the general office; he, snorting,
left the house. When Katadreuffe came in with the unfolded receipt she was already sitting at his table with tears
on her eyelashes.

'And now I want *you* to help me, Mr Katadreuffe. That
Miss Kalvelage isn't kind to me . . . I shall never go back
to that man, but *you* must help me from now on.'

'Tomorrow then, madam. The office is now closed; we'll
have a look at it tomorrow.'

So he got rid of her. Shedding little tears from her flashy

eyes, she moved her heavily armoured body through the flowers, outside. Shortly after, he also left.

The dinner that evening was arranged by the proprietor of the restaurant where Stroomkoning used to lunch. The tables were tastefully appointed; he, himself, kept an eye on it all and later, when the dinner started, came to see that everything was in order. At eight o'clock the guests arrived. They had all had a drink together in a bar and were in a festive mood. They sat down at once to dinner.

In the waiting-room, the round table had been laid for the staff, but this time it was no improvised meal; on the contrary, a princely banquet, the menus printed on hand-made paper with hand-painted decorations, the wines in red between the courses. That menu was a masterpiece, with white wine for the fish, claret and Burgundy, and two kinds of Champagne, one to start with and one at the end. And the dinner for the staff was the same as that in the con-ference-room. The whole staff was present with the excep-tion of the office-boy, but Stroomkoning had also remem-bered him. Katadreuffe sat with the three typists, Miss Van Alm, Miss Sibculo and Miss Van den Born; Graanoogst, his wife and Pop. He enjoyed sitting there again with his old landlord and family; he had again placed Mrs Graanoogst and Pop on either side of him. He missed someone, who would at once have lent distinction to the company, but he was not foolish; he expressly did not miss her too much. He was pleased that Mrs Graanoogst did not this time every now and then have to trot off to the kitchen; the cook was there, and the serving was done by waiters. Pop talked to him continuously; for she was still a child but was showing signs of growing up. Suddenly, he saw the woman in this child; he saw it plainly and it gave him a shock. He noticed her coquettish mannerisms, the eyes too attractive to be really attractive, and he thought : her mother must keep a sharp look-out or the daughter will be getting into trouble.

Then, during a silence, Mrs Graanoogst pointed :

'The last time Miss Te George was sitting *there*.'

And so the conversation turned to her – she was the only one of the former staff mentioned – but they did not know anything about her present life; she was married, yes, but what more? And the talk turned quickly to other topics.

None of them had ever sat down to such dishes before, and they found them more interesting than tasty. Katadreuffe took a little of everything; in the end a glass of water tasted best of all. Graanoogst, the gourmand, liked the poultry; he took two helpings of it; the bald patch began to blush, and yet he said to his wife:

'We mustn't be ungrateful, but I'd just as soon eat stew.'

His eyes showed their light melancholy as he refilled his glass.

Katadreuffe looked round the table. Miss Van Alm sat quiet and stiffly; he could never avoid seeing through the girl her predecessor; for her he had not much interest. He liked Miss Sibculo all the more, who, although engaged, was happy and friendly and an asset to the party.

Miss Van den Born had now put in an appearance as a young lady, in a tolerable skirt and actually wearing a ring. For she, too, had got herself engaged; the impossible was, it seemed, possible. Yet during the week she continued to wear the strangest clothing. Quite recently, Katadreuffe had overtaken a very conspicuous couple, someone with a boy's head and plus-fours, and the other with long hair and a cape. The boy's head was Miss Van den Born, the cape her betrothed, a pale, nasty bit of work. It seemed the travesty of a couple, and was antipathetic.

With the warm spring evening it had gradually become close in the waiting-room, when the door into the corridor was opened, and also the door of the conference-room. It was just the time for the speeches and they were now able to follow everything. They heard Carlion speaking with his precise endings; it was not bad and was well-intentioned, but too dry, too business-like, too unadorned. But Miss Kalvelage's speech was an exuberant success; almost a satire, about the profession, about the clients, about herself, about everything. This bodyless little creature displayed a flashing wit which was lisetned to, now in silence, and then greeted with bursts of laughter. The ending, with a few genuinely warm words for Stroomkoning, was in its unexpectedness, in its abruptness, irresistible. Mrs Stroomkoning immediately stood up, enraptured with her, and gave her a kiss.

Then it was Stroomkoning's turn to reply, and he had to honestly acknowledge that Miss Kalvelage's speech had put them all in the shade. But he had the gift of easy speech; he answered each one, his tone and his words were very cordial, and yet modest. He said that if he were now able to speak from his heart (according to the kind words of praise they seemed to consider him a man with a heart), this had come easily to him, not through any merit of his own but through the favour of circumstances. He also referred to the death of Gideon Piaat. He did not mention De Gankelaar.

They thought it was then all over. But no. For young Countryside, who, to everyone's amazement, had announced that he was *not* going to speak – not a syllable – young Countryside surprised all the table by making a final speech in Dutch which, with a terrible accent but otherwise quite intelligible, he successfully put across. And Mrs Stroomkoning, sitting next to him, was then enraptured with him. She impressed a kiss on a cheek of wrinkled old leather.

In the meantime, the sweet course had been served and in the waiting-room spirits rose considerably, particularly amongst the girls, as this variety of sweet things was too delightful. Flans, tarts, ice, chocolates, crystallized pineapple and chestnuts, all exquisitely served. Then Stroomkoning came and said to Katadreuffe :

'Now I'm going to take your place and you mine.'

For he wanted to end the evening with his staff, about most of whom he knew so little that he scarcely remembered their names. He did it in such an unconstrained manner, and also the atmosphere was by now so merry, that there was no question of embarrassment. On the contrary, his arrival increased the general hilarity.

Mrs Stroomkoning beckoned to Katadreuffe to come and sit next to her, at the head of the table, on her left hand. Katadreuffe had no false illusions; he was by nature too sober-minded; he understood that this was just a passing gesture made by the kind of people who are at ease in social intercourse, and above all not too affable, not condescending in their attitude to subordinates. Mrs Stroomkoning sitting in between him and Countryside was enraptured with both.

Stroomkoning's daughter sat on the other side of Katadreuffe. Their children, a boy and a girl, were now grown up, but were still inclined to be delicate; the children of a father past the climacteric; a slight degeneration in their constitutions. The son was called Molyneux after old Countryside; the daughter's name was Leda. Molyneux had not much in the way of brains; he would never be his father's successor; but he had a remarkable talent for drawing which, although lacking originality, and reminiscent of Beardsley, was undeniably good. His art was cosmopolite, in the pre-war sense of cosmopolitism; he was a typical epigone, and remarkably conservative. His sketches were never pornographic, but sometimes so perverse that his healthy-minded mother hid some away and wept over them. He was a decadent, and would not live long. His features were regular, but his eyes were restless and too deep-sunken.

The girl was not sickly; a pretty, silly face, but her look was lack-lustre; only in the evening were her eyes attractive.

Katadreuffe, accepted for the first time in higher circles, coolly and discreetly looked round the table, and saw that the Stroomkonings' friends and clients could also eat otherwise than in 'fortress style'. For here, with ladies present, their first interest was in the conversation; then came the wines, and only after that, the food. This was also a picture that he never forgot. In the meantime Mrs Stroomkoning was telling them that he would shortly become her husband's new colleague; she made everyone, including himself, feel that he sat here not as head clerk but as an advanced student. They accepted him completely, he realized, and he sat there calmly but modestly, the student, the future lawyer. And what he did not realize was that his handsome face did the rest. Leda Stroomkoning stole a covert look at him every now and then.

The party broke up when Stroomkoning returned from the waiting-room. The ladies were taken home, but the men were going to wind up in the Hague, and Katadreuffe must go with them, obviously. The only lady who accompanied the men was Mrs Stroomkoning who drove, her husband next to her, Countryside and Katadreuffe in the back. The car shot off at a great speed, the others racing behind, and in half an hour they arrived. There, in a night-club, the men were surrounded by ladies of the town; Mrs Stroomkoning laughed and encouraged the men :

'Go and dance, I don't mind.'

And she, herself, glided off with a stranger, probably an attaché from one of the embassies. Katadreuffe, who could not dance, said to himself : I must learn to do that; God ! What a lot I have still to learn.

He would learn it because it was necessary, not because he really wanted to. For he did not enjoy this ending to the evening. The glances of the loose women were inclined to make him really angry, but it was necessary to control himself, and he succeeded.

He remained seated and fortunately was kept company by young Countryside who also did not dance, except on one occasion when Mrs Stroomkoning insisted. But it did not go well; he was too well-bred to lose his self-control and appeared to be sober, but he danced like a spineless, black gibbon, his legs moving with a will of their own, until Mrs Stroomkoning, laughing, gave it up. She had the tact not to ask Katadreuffe. So he remained sitting with Countryside drinking his whisky whilst Countryside drank several. He leant over to Katadreuffe and whispered :

'We'll go in a moment. You show me the sights of the Hague.'

It was completely incomprehensible. Here he was, sitting surrounded by tarts, some of them quite attractive, and it apparently meant nothing to him; and it was all the more strange that he continued to regard Katadreuffe as a hardened libertine who knew the night life of every town, and, apparently, even worse places than where they were.

They went to another cabaret, two of the women from the first one accompanying them. But it was exactly the same as before. Katadreuffe noticed the deadly monotony, the torpor of night-life. They were beginning to get tired and soon left, the ladies of the town with them. Then the manager of the establishment came to the door and called out to one of the creatures :

'Mrs Lia, your glass hasn't been paid for. I'll chalk it up to you.'

The girl was no longer young and with a bloated unattractive face. She said :

'Well now, I came in here with eight gentlemen and no one wants to pay for me !'

Katadreuffe heard the cry for help whilst the others were wandering off to their cars and waving the women aside.

He could not bear it, and, in spite of his prudishness, he turned back with the intention of paying for her drink. But Molyneux Stroomkoning forestalled him and was already sorting out the coins in his hand by the light of the doorway. And he looked at her keenly; was she perhaps a subject for a drawing – no she was too common-looking. The girl went off, sobbing gently, and a little drunk.

Then on the way back, Countryside took the wheel, which could have led to a terrible accident. For, at full speed, he insisted on keeping to the left, in the English fashion; and he said with his English obstinacy :

'That doesn't matter, I call *this* the right side.'

Until Mrs Stroomkoning, next to him, simply jammed on

the hand-brake, stopping the car with a jerk, and with her muscular arms, dragged young Countryside from his seat and took his place at the wheel.

Katadreuffe sat silently at the back with Stroomkoning, who also said nothing. Stroomkoning was already thinking of what he had to do tomorrow, or rather today; and Katadreuffe of the indignation of the drunken girl over such male discourtesy.

The Hill

By the summer, Katadreuffe had completed his studies for his law degree. He was absolutely convinced that he would pass. His tutors told him that he had nothing more to learn, but his conviction did not come alone from their assurance. He had a still stronger spur to his belief – the enemy could no longer put a spoke in his wheel. He no longer had to anticipate the horrible eventuality of a bankruptcy. The moral shock which had endangered his matriculation was no more to be dreaded. His debt to the bank was paid off, including all interest and costs. His father could not touch him now.

At this time, his mind was an enormous archive of knowledge, and he knew his way about it. The law clauses were to him like files; he fetched them out of the archive, opened them, and everything lay before his eyes; meaning, historical origin, practical application. It amazed him that such voluminous material could so easily be compressed into the brain-cells, and yet remain legible, without a crease. Every student must experience this; he was no exception. He felt so calm that, up to the end, he kept his Sunday afternoon free.

Once he and Jan Maan made a trip round the port with 'her'. It had not happened for years, and she wanted very much to do it once more, as she had the greatest affection for the water, particularly the water that was Rotterdam.

She stood between her two sons; she had no wish to sit, but stood at the ship's rail. It was a beautiful afternoon. The waves had the majestic roll of the broad river where the wind was unhampered, with valleys and crests, but no spray. There were patches of mist; the river smelt of the sea – it was half sea. And this gave Katadreuffe the thought – he did not utter it – that the sea-water and that from the mountains were eternally wedded at Rotterdam. If De Gankelaar had spoken to him now it would no longer have been a monologue; he would have found a partner, and the exchange of their thoughts would have given depth to the conversation. Katadreuffe was not introspective; he was unaware that he stood at the most important turning-point in his life. He stood on the demarcation line which divides the world of every intellectual. The line is indefinite, a shadowy frontier one crosses unconsciously. Only later, when one has learnt to survey one's own little world, does it strike one how clearly the line is drawn. Katadreuffe was now no longer the intellect that can only greedily absorb, he had also begun to make a return; he was, indeed, beginning to emit light. And the metaphor of the line, like all metaphors, when carried to its logical conclusion is inadequate, for the world it encircled was his own life; what remained on this side was his, like that which lay on the other, and if he crossed the line to take root in a new land, the old territory would still supply him with nourishment. He was, with all his ambition, modest; true ambition goes hand in hand with humility; one cannot desire to achieve something without the realization that one needs to achieve it : whoever says, 'I'm there' is intellectually dead.

The port was not looking its best, as being Sunday, so much of the work had stopped. They sailed past heaps of ore in all colours, gleaming green, or dark-red, or a rusty brown, nothing taken from it, nothing added to it. Over there a large sea-going ship was discharging grain, with four elevators sucking at its hull, the grain streaming so swiftly

into the lighters that it looked like thick, yellow oil. They
lay there, quiet and voracious, with the whole ship in their
power, bleeding it to death.

Then, at the entrance to the Waalhaven, they came upon
an inland sea, with, in the far distance, the aerodrome,
above which flashed insects. Then quite a breeze got up,
and both boys, at the same time, looked at her, at her neck.
She had already drawn her scarf tighter. Did she see their
movement, feel their silent solicitude? She did not show
anything – talk about obstinacy!

Katadreuffe was so positive of his success that he did not
wish to work on the day before the exam. He asked for the
day off and already in the morning went to her and suggested walking to the Park. She would have liked this but
there was so much traffic on a weekday, and as they would
not be able to avoid the main streets she did not feel she
could face it.

So they took the tram. The Park began at the terminus
and they slowly and silently climbed the 'Hill'. It was
reasonably quiet there, with a few unemployed sauntering
about. The day was dark and oppressive, with low cloud
and driving mist, a sky under which Rotterdam-on-the-
water was at its most beautiful.

Then Katadreuffe had the feeling that this was the
moment for which he had been waiting for years; that he
must have seen it in a vision; on the eve of a great new
day in his life no strangling fear, but a gentle melancholy.
He quickened his pace; he shook her hand.

'Mother, mother,' he called, as she had walked on.

She did not hear him but went on and sat down on the
seat ahead.

'Mother apparently won't hear,' he said, and then,
questioningly :

'Mrs van Rijn?'

For he always remembered the hateful quadruped crawling out of the tent at the Hook.

'No,' said Lorna, 'Mrs Telger.'

'Thank goodness,' he sighed.

'Mrs Telger, but for *you* – please – Miss Te George.'

There was a seat close by. They went to sit there, whilst she moved the small child in the pram slowly backwards and forwards. The encounter was much too unexpected; the conversation demanded a very ordinary beginning.

'Do you still live in the Boogjes?'

'No, but my parents are still there and we live quite close to them. It's a long way for my husband, but he cycles over the bridges like I used to; do you remember?'

How could he not remember it?

'I so love that quiet countrified neighbourhood that I persuaded by husband to come and live out there.'

She paused, sensing a question which he did not dare to ask.

'He's an accountant with a Rhine shipping company.'

Things would be all right for her in spite of the bad times, he thought. She was such a lady, she was very little changed. And in the bitter-sweetness of his gladness it surprised him that a man's paradise can lie in something so enigmatical, which is none the less, covered with a skin like his own. He looked at her teeth, sound and white, and the woman presented him with another problem with her moist inviting lips. For he was a man, no mealy-mouthed contemplator; in her presence he was a man. And as if she grasped the perilous nature of his thoughts, she said:

'And you, how are you getting on? I saw at the time about your qualifying exam. How are the studies going?'

'Tomorrow my doctorate begins.'

'Oh, and you'll pass, of course, you always pass.'

'Yes, I can say without undue conceit: yes. Do you find me conceited?'

'No, you don't mean it like that. And I am sure you will go a long way. You'll become a lawyer to start with.'

'Yes, Miss Te George, that's exactly it: to start with. When I'm a lawyer I'm still nothing. This isn't a contra-

diction of the other, this isn't false modesty. Deep down,
I'm convinced that once I'm a lawyer I'll have only just
begun.'

'But you'll go a long way,' she repeated obstinately.

'Perhaps . . . in a certain sense. But at the bottom I'm a
coward. Don't you think I'm gradually beginning to know
myself?'

She gave no answer, every now and then moving the
sleeping child back and forth just a little. He resumed :

'I am possessed with one idea, I'm afraid of all others;
I have a private security service watching me day and
night. Isn't that cowardly? Yes, I'm a coward.'

She did not reply. The conversation was taking a sad
turn. And yet this man fascinated her, even more than
before; his mind was more mature; he would cut a big
figure. He seemed also more gentle, and yet a man.

And after staring straight ahead for a bit she turned
and looked at him, smiling as a woman will, who is fond
of a man yet does not show it – just a suspicion of it, perhaps. She saw him so adult, so proud, chaste, ambitious;
she looked at his hands, now lightly tanned from the few
days of spring sunshine. And she saw him so irresistible,
just because he did not realize it. They both remained
silent, whilst he also looked at her, straight in the eyes,
those eyes which hesitated between grey and blue. He took
in every detail, the elegant instep of the small foot, legs
rather slender, yet breeding showing in the curve of the
calf; the hands in the white gloves with gauntlet sleeves,
rich-looking; auburn hair under the small hat. The whole
figure, calm, compact, slender, too slender, yet not over-
refined. The head, large for a woman, but because she was
tall not too big – just right. A beautiful head, with broad
forehead, smooth, truly feminine. The face that had so
charmed him in its individuality the thin line from the
nostril to the corner of her mouth; that came from an old
grief, something in her life hidden from him. The same
face, not changed in anything at all, only a slight shadow

under the eyes, perhaps what remained of their mutual sorrow.

He now saw her differently. The ruthless vivisection of himself which he had just made brought calm to his look and balance to his words, and with the greatest simplicity he expressed himself, knowing exactly how far he could go :

'I shall never marry anybody else. You were an episode in my life, an outstanding episode, *the* episode, I shall not forget it. I just couldn't.'

Naturally she could not refrain from blushing. She looked straight ahead, and on her features appeared what he had noticed at their very first meeting, on the stairs – something dreamy and half-smiling. He had so honestly, without circumlocution, made a declaration of love of such delicacy that it did not hurt, but rather produced a feeling of sweetness, a subtle joy, like the aftermath of something sweet-smelling that passes and is gone.

Then he found means to turn the conversation :

'Do you see my mother sitting on the bench there with her back to us? Isn't she a fine person, that mother of mine? How well we should get on if only I were different! But it's funny – perhaps it doesn't sound too good to you that I can talk about my mother like this but I can say it to *you* – we don't get on together, and it's not only my fault, it's both our faults; we irritate one another.'

She smiled again.

'You've got character, Mr Katadreuffe; that I knew already. What you now say shows that your mother also has character.'

He pondered :

'Blood relationship sometimes has its dark side. So it is between us two. As long as we don't live together we get on fine. Even then we have our little squabbles, they mean nothing. In any event she's a remarkable woman.'

He did not want to say that he feared he would soon be losing her; that would sound too sentimental.

'Do you often come here?' he asked. 'It's years since I've seen you.'

She continued to move the sleeping child backwards and forwards.

'No, I don't often come over to the north side except to shop sometimes, but not a lot. My husband has had to go to Ruhrort on business and will be away a week. I have been staying with some friends near here, but the week is up tomorrow.'

She said these last words with the old shrewdness, and he smiled back without embarrassment. He understood her well enough.

'I have always thought,' he said, 'that I should meet you again, but here . . . I would like to have a look at the river with you. May I?'

Whilst walking to the parapet she said:

'I am no longer a child. I realize that a moment like this should sublimate everything; for a man at least. Therefore I want to look at the river, standing next to you; it will then look its nicest, though it is always nice.'

They stood together at the parapet. She moved the child back and forth, just a little – at this moment there was nothing of the mother about her. The water rolled under the driving mist and the low cloud. Due west glowed the ruddy fire from a wharf. From a mighty hull on the stocks the hammering resounded on all sides; in a corner, the light flickered. The smoke from the factories could not penetrate the clouds and heavy dark wisps of it hung around in tatters. The mist every now and then provided surprises. What, from a distance, looked like a huge Rhine barge, when it came closer was quite tiny. Over there, a fine, black point protruded out of the mist and grew into a great big steamer, coal black, gliding out of the dock, with its snow-white bulwarks and bridge. Like bitterns in the marshes, the cranes on the quays thrust their beaks upwards and to one side, motionless; but look, there one could see some turning, bending, and picking up supplies floating on the water. As far as the eye could see, left and right, a town in motion – the water a shining conveyor-belt.

'The step-child amongst our large towns,' he said. 'And yet the best and proudest. Don't you agree?'

'I like Amsterdam still better,' she said.

'I don't,' he said. 'Rotterdam to me is *our* town. Just because there's nothing specially Dutch about it. Amsterdam is our national town, Rotterdam our international. I'm all for the international, so I like this town. And it's got that hall-mark from the sea, for the sea knows no frontiers – the sea is the only cosmopolitan in the world.'

'You're becoming quite a philosopher or a poet,' she said, with a serious little smile.

'No,' he said. 'I've got to contradict you again. I only think as much as is necessary for my actions. I'm too sober-minded for a poet.'

'I must go,' she said.

He answered :

'Yes, but I'll be seeing you again.'

'By chance . . .'

'Quite. By chance. I shan't look for you, I'll wait on chance.'

She gave him her hand.

'I'll wait on chance,' he repeated, holding on to her hand for a moment. 'Do you remember our first talk that evening in the office when you were typing a gentleman's agreement? I'll conclude this gentleman's agreement with you – I won't look for you.'

He went to sit with his mother. 'An old acquaintance,' he explained. 'She used to be Stroomkoning's secretary.'

'Was she keeping company then?'

'No,' he said.

And then as he found the words 'keeping company' were wrong in connection with her, he added, 'No, she was not engaged then.'

'Oh,' said his mother, not heeding the correction, 'then you've been a great big ass, Jacob.'

For, with the lightning understanding of a woman who is a mother she had guessed it all, in less than a second. His lying there brooding, that one week at home. She had also seen how they had met just now. That was sufficient, she was able to turn her back on them, as there was not much more to be learnt by an old mother.

Her reproof annoyed him. That was what she always did. She kept silent when he would be glad of a word and, when he wanted silence, she came out with some spitefulness. Always, always, she ended by irritating him. He said so. She answered dryly:

'Then you shouldn't be so stupid . . . Come along home, I'm getting cold.'

They stood for a moment at the point where the Hill descends to the quayside and river.

'You stay true to Rotterdam, Jacob,' she said. 'Rotterdam is *our* town. We are not the people for the Hague.'

'That rotten Hague,' he exclaimed, as his need to express himself violently had not passed. 'What do you think of me, mother! A town of loafers and blighters.'

Then they were friends again, and with gentle abuse of the seat of Government they walked towards the tram.

But the conversation with Lorna Te George, that diamond he hid away, for when it comes to the jewels of his inner life every man is a miser; he looks at them alone in the safe-deposit of his heart, lit up by his memory.

Dreverhaven and Katadreuffe

According to all human reckoning, he was bound to pass his doctorate. He passed it, and he passed it well. That period of his life was thereby concluded. He had never really been a proper student, not having taken part in the life of the university town or colleges – that rich life, which later on, the man who has arrived likes to relive in his thoughts. He did not miss it; his time of study had been directed solely to one end – he had finished with Leiden for good.

He had so urgently begged them not to make any kind of celebration that they respected his wishes. To Stroomkoning he said what he had already earlier thought :

'I've still got to become something; I'm only just at the beginning.'

This mixture of pride and humility had appealed to his chief. But another, equally important reason for this abstention he withheld : the remembrance of that one celebration after his matriculation. He had forced her out of his thoughts – he did not want to conjure her up again. Whenever he thought of Lorna Te George it was in a spirit of gentle, mature melancholy, of the delightful, bitter-sweet atmosphere of their last meeting.

In September he was to be sworn in as lawyer, and then his name would appear on the door-plate, a fourth, the youngest brass plate to shine on the Maas. But his inten-

tions reached further. Stroomkoning was average-adjuster,
but only in name. Katadreuffe wanted to turn his chief's
office into a proper average-adjuster's office. After some time
in the normal practice he would be going to London, to
learn from C. C. & C., and when he had finished there he
would visit the Rotterdam exchange like other nominal
average-adjusters. And he would write a thesis to obtain his
promotion in Leiden. Then he would see what further was
to be done; that he would have to leave to chance, and at
the right time make his choice from the various possibilities
offered, carefully and resolutely.

He again went without a holiday; he did not feel the
necessity. It was different from that other time, with the
formidable matriculation, when he had lived on his nerves.
The law studies had gone so easily; he had completely regained his equanimity; he could go on working without a
break. Moreover, as now he would not much longer remain
head clerk, he had to make the necessary arrangements and
see to it that he chose a suitable successor.

Then he asked the approval of Stroomkoning – the easiest
person in such matters – to take Rentenstein back. For Rentenstein was no fool; he had good enough brains, and knew
the office. Rentenstein could easily come back as chief clerk,
provided a control was kept of the cash, and that Katadreuffe, himself, would do weekly. And if Rentenstein could
no longer attend the police-court, that wouldn't matter as,
when all's said and done, he had also omitted to do this.
He would give Rentenstein more varied work; he loved
teaching, guiding another; well, Rentenstein would now
have to become his disciple.

The sacked Rentenstein came and was very subdued. He
had been filling a junior clerk's job at Dreverhaven's bank.
He looked down and out, but that would improve. Katadreuffe took him back and was tactful enough not to
address him as the other colleagues did, but as 'Mr Rentenstein'.

And Rentenstein was only too glad to accept; it was like

a message from Heaven after the misery of the last few years. He was now divorced from the dreadful little woman. He is certainly improved, thought Katadreuffe, listening to him. He decided to risk this step with an unfortunate, his social feeling coming into play.

When, in August, Rentenstein came to the job, he was shabbily but reasonably dressed, his hair cut short, with the carriage of a man, no longer effeminate, and no dandruff on his collar.

That summer 'she' began to deteriorate more obviously than before. To Katadreuffe it appeared no longer to be a curve – up and down – but a slow, steady downward trend. Perhaps the trip round the port had not agreed with her. She coughed uncontrollably at night, keeping Jan Maan awake with it, but he did not speak about it. Yet there was no deterioration to be noticed in her daily life, in her eyes, or in her will. She still did her handwork, just went to bed a little earlier, and also rested in afternoons; but no one must know this; if anyone knocked she quietly got up from her bed, light as a feather.

Katadreuffe and Jan Maan discussed her condition and already began to make plans.

'You come to my digs, Jan,' said Katadreuffe, 'there's room enough.'

'My heartiest thanks,' said Jan Maan, 'I'll go to my parents. What should I have to do with a Doctor of Law? A nice state of affairs.'

Katadreuffe went white with anger.

'Jan, if you dare to say a thing like that again I'll hit you straight in the face.'

'Now then, calm down. Good God! You're more violent than any member of the Party, and that means something when a communist says so.'

And so they had a grand old row. The misplaced delicacy of his friend maddened Katadreuffe – he couldn't have insulted him more. So they went to drink it off at a local bar.

Then, at the end of August, a letter came for Katadreuffe from the Dean of the Law Society. The Dean invited him to his office. And immediately Katadreuffe felt:
the enemy is not yet dead.

The Dean was head of one of those stately offices which
appear deserted because no client is ever seen there unless
a state-aided one, where all business is done by correspondence because all the clients are regular ones. The Dean
received him in a stately room rather like a church, with
three leaded windows at the back. A Temple of the Law
it was in any case; here there would never be any shouting,
like at Stroomkoning's meetings.

The Dean was sitting at the end of the room. He stood
up, gave Katadreuffe a hand and indicated a chair opposite
him. He had the appearance of a French marquis, small,
very carefully groomed, with a white moustache and a
short white beard. He looked very much like the presiding
judge who had examined Katadreuffe that time; he was,
in fact, an elder brother. He spread a letter in front of him
and screwed a monocle into his eye. And this most pre-
carious armature for the eye – so easily rendered ludicrous when coupled with affectation – suited him extraordinarily well, adding the final touch to the French
marquis. Katadreuffe sat calmly, observing him closely; he
was determined nothing should put him out.

'Against your admission to the bar,' said the Dean, 'objection has been raised by a member of the bar, namely, Dr
Schuwagt. I should say four objections, as it is based on
four reasons. First of all, you are an illegitimate child. Then,
at the moment, you are employed in the position of head
clerk. In the third place, he maintains that you adhere to
communist principles. Finally that you have been twice
bankrupt, and even a third time on the borderline of bankruptcy.'

Katadreuffe took a deep breath. These, then, were the
last trumps of the adversary. He was to be torpedoed just
before reaching harbour. But he kept cool – he was prac-

tised in self-control – he had a quick temper, as had shown on one occasion, but whenever important things were at stake he would never give way to it. He kept cool.

The Dean looked attentively at him; in the expression on the set face opposite no change could be observed. He had not yet finished.

'Let me to some extent reassure you by saying that I am not blind to the fact that these obstacles come from a side which . . . well, let me say, is not to be taken too seriously. And as regards the objections themselves : point one : the question whether you are legitimate or not leaves me completely indifferent . . .'

'I am called after my mother, *meneer de deken*,' Katadreuffe said.

He said it calmly and with spirit.

'Quite so,' went on the Dean, 'we'll leave that out of it. Number two : the objection regarding your present occupation is also of no weight; rather is it an advantage compared with others who come along brand-new from the university, as you have considerable law practice, and only recently Mr Stroomkoning spoke to me about you with the highest praise.'

Katadreuffe remained silent.

'The third objection has more weight. Are you a communist?'

'No.'

'How is it possible they try to hang this on you?'

'Mr Schuwagt or someone else must have watched my movements very closely but drawn the wrong conclusions. Ask the people where I live, or my former landlord, whether they have ever found me with any communist literature, or whether anything of the kind has ever come by post, or whether I have ever had any meetings at home . . .'

'You understand,' interrupted the Dean, 'you are going to swear shortly that as a lawyer you will remain loyal to the Royal Family, obedient to the Constitution, et cetera.

Communism is opposed to all that. In the bar here such a case has never come up, but I believe we should indeed have objection to a communist lawyer.'

'Excuse me, *meneer de deken*, I had not quite finished. With a friend of mine, who is a communist, I have in the past attended meetings, but always more out of curiosity than conviction. I have, moreover, completely broken with it : communism is in any case nothing for *me*. My friend's friends are not my friends. But he has other good qualities and I have never even considered dropping him because of his communism. He is the same : he often calls me jokingly bourgeois and capitalist.'

Katadreuffe saw something of a smile on the face of the Dean. He did not realize that these last few words, in his eyes, cleared him of every suspicion.

The Dean resumed :

'The fourth point is the worst, should it be true . . .'

'I have been bankrupt twice,' said Katadreuffe, 'the third time it did not come off.'

The look of him, his attitude, his deportment had all impressed the Dean. This was a serious matter which could go against him.

'Then your request for admission is without precedent in the Rotterdam bar. Just how is it possible for someone of your age to have been twice bankrupt?'

'The same person who is now advancing these objections procured the three bankruptcies, only the last time he did not succeed. I contracted a debt, in the first place by taking on a shop in the Hague. It was a stupid thing to do, I admit, and I deserved my first bankruptcy. But I owned nothing and it was annulled. Then, on the recommendation of my trustee Mr de Gankelaar, I obtained a job with Mr Stroomkoning, and once I had settled down properly there, the same creditor applied for my bankruptcy. I had thought that my debt was cancelled, and so I deserved that bankruptcy. I should not have been so stupid. The debt was paid out of my salary, my second trustee being Mr

Wever. After that I borrowed money again from the same creditor in order to pay for my studies, and that I was paying off regularly until they suddenly demanded repayment of the lot, and in that way applied for my third bankruptcy. That did not succeed, and I should *not* have deserved a third bankruptcy. Now I have paid all my debts. I can show you the last receipt from the bank, my former creditor. Also Mr Carlion will give you any further information you require.'

'Just one thing,' said the Dean. 'Why did you go back to the bank again for a loan?'

Katadreuffe answered with spirit:

'I wanted to show them I was not afraid of them.'

'And why did the bank give you a further credit?'

'I'm not quite sure,' said Katadreuffe truthfully. 'I have my suspicions, but I would rather not mention them.'

'Oh, it was just an idle question. So you are clear of the bank now?'

'Absolutely.'

The interview was at an end; he could go. And it again struck him how quiet it was here. He now recognized three kinds of quietness: at Wever's, the quiet of a small business, the practice just starting – with the Dean, the distinguished quiet of the élite – at Dreverhaven's the silence of fear. And without any doubt whatsoever, he liked best of all the bustle of Stroomkoning's office.

As he walked back he became certain of two things: firstly, that he would be accepted, and secondly, that it would be absurd to make himself angry over a father whose efforts were all the time becoming weaker and more bungling.

During the first half of September he was sworn in. The Public Prosecutor proposed his admission, coupled with his congratulations; the President of the District Court administered the twin oaths.

And, deep in thought, he walked the whole of the long way from the Noordsingel to the Boompjes. The first autumnal nip was in the air, but light as a feather; it was a beautiful morning. And hardly heeding what he was doing, he suddenly found himself standing on the Boompjes, on the edge of the quay, on a small cobbled space amidst the general turmoil. He was standing right opposite his office, unaware of what force had led him there. And he saw, on the front of the house, four suns nailed up, one large one and three smaller ones underneath. He read: 'Dr J. W. Katadreuffe, lawyer and solicitor.' He did not know how it had happened; he had not given a thought to his own name-plate; the episode with the Dean had, for a short time, robbed him of his normal ever-awareness. Now the name-plate was already up. He sensed the delicacy of a woman there; Miss Kalvelage must have done that. How high above him she already stood. He was only at the beginning.

At that moment, images flashed before him with a perplexing rapidity and clarity. There they were, all the things he still had to know about: he must learn to seize them and hold on to them – the programme for his life. He had never seen more clearly the awful distance between the ordinary man and the gentleman, between the people and the élite, but above all between the former. For the gift of adaptation is greater in women, and at the same time society places less heavy demands on them. The most difficult task in a man's life is to reach that status – not in appearance – in reality.

He must be able to converse about everything, not with book-knowledge from an encyclopedia, but airily. He must know how to start up an interesting conversation amongst men, and differently again, amongst women. He must know his own literature, speak foreign languages with the right accent, know *their* literature – he must be up in the plastic arts, music. He must learn to travel at ease in foreign lands – must be able to discourse on towns, countryside, peoples, their customs and his own discoveries. He must be witty, and above all, live in style, dress without extravagance, but with always the right clothes of the right cut. He must be able to discuss sport and politics, national and international, economy, the exchange, opera, films. He must be able to play cards, dance, talk about good hotels, good food and, above all, good wine. He must be able to lunch as he had seen the business-men lunching in that restaurant, self-contained like a fortress – he didn't like the idea, but he must. And such an awful lot more must happen.

He must become an all-round man – in the big things as in the small, but self-reliant. He should never marry.

And when you looked at it, the encyclopedia could after all help him considerably.

Having reached these heights, in his opinion, he would still be nothing more than one cultured man amongst many, eclipsed by the lustre of the élite. But he would develop a lustre of his own so that people would say : 'Look, look at that man.'

But he would remain loyal to Jan Maan.

That evening, Katadreuffe went for a final reckoning with his father. It was a plan which he had cherished for years : the hour of retribution had struck, but it must be a dignified requital. With a calm step he walked to the poor quarter. On the first floor, light gleamed through chinks in the curtains. Unhurriedly, he walked up the stone stairs, pushed open the first door (a bell sounded in the distance), the second, the third. But inexplicable sounds echoed through the empty building, in a far corner, which had something sinister about them. The evening breeze had got up and was playing on the 'harp' in a whining manner.

All those recent thoughts vanished – he did not understand these sounds; he stood before his father. Dreverhaven sat still, with hat and coat on, but he was not smoking, not drinking; he was awake. The hand of the old ruler risen from the people pointed to a chair. Katadreuffe ignored the gesture.

'I wanted . . .'

Dreverhaven interrupted him.

'Well, Jacob, what has that cad of a father to thank for this visit from his son? Are you after that rascal Schuwagt's job now you've been sworn in?'

He laughed loudly, sarcastically. And this had a queer effect on Katadreuffe – not the laugh, but the words.

'I wanted to tell you, father, that what I said in my anger during my first visit – over caddishness – I withdraw that. I am sorry about it. I have waited a long time to say I was sorry. I will not put it off any longer because at the same time I've come to say . . .'

He stumbled for a moment, for right across this conversation the idea struck him that he did not use the familiar form with his father like he did with his mother : that it would be simply impossible to have done so.

'. . . at the same time to say that this is my last visit to you. You haven't got me down, as you must now well realize. I was sworn in today, as you no doubt know and regret, but I have been sworn in . . . And I have only one thing to add . . . this is my final visit to you – I shall say good-bye to you for good – I no longer recognize you as my father, or anything else – you no longer exist for me.'

A change came over the grey, old stubbled face in front of him. It grew young, it shone, it laughed. Surely enough, after years of cynicism, his father laughed. It was so unrecognizable as to give the son a fright. And he was even more frightened when a hairy, grey monkey's paw was stuck out over the desk towards him.

But the fright at once turned to fury, the dark fury of their related blood. He had all at once forgotten his intention of a dignified requital. And he grew very desperately small – he could have been fitted into a match-box, and yet felt that the *Grote Kerk* was not large enough to contain him.

'What!' he cried, 'now that in spite of all your efforts I have got there, now I should accept your hand and congratulations? Never. Never, from a father who has all my life worked against me.'

Dreverhaven had got up from his chair. His fists, with their grey hair, rested on the desk, the full weight of his body thrown on to them, turning them into an ugly network of veins. He looked like a monster disguised as a man, a grey gorilla. His mouth opened as if to utter a roar . . . and yet . . . and yet . . .

'Or worked for you,' he said slowly, clearly, hoarsely, yet gently.

And it sounded so mysterious – the man at once turned into an enigma.

And Katadreuffe, caught between anger and fear, but with no change in his face, turned and left without another word. His feeling of arrogance began in a curious way to dissipate, yet he would not show it – that amount of pride he retained – he left without a word. Then there it was again, in a far corner of the building, that weird string music giving a lugubrious accompaniment to his departure.

Then, outside, an irrational dejection over his behaviour drove him to his mother.

But the picture and the sound followed him. He saw the monster of a father standing there, opening his mouth and the words issuing from it :

'Or worked for you?'

'Theatrical stuff, pure theatre !' he cried out to himself, 'nothing but theatre from the damned, old rogue; theatre and lies.'

Thus he steeled himself.

And he went home. She was not in, only Jan Maan. His mood was so disturbed that he was about to hurl all sorts of reproaches at his friend. But Jan Maan saw his eyes beginning to flash and said :

'Do you think I'd let her go out on the street? She's with the people upstairs. They have an addition to the family. They wanted her to go and look at the future bourgeois.'

Katadreuffe went and sat at the table. Up till then he had never seen the will. Jan Maan sat opposite reading his seditious pamphlet, his head in his hands. Katadreuffe noticed that Jan Maan was growing grey and bald – the workman ages quickly – but he still had his clean linen and nails; *she* saw to that, *she* took care of those. And Katadreuffe knew that he, himself would go grey early, earlier than his friend. You could see some white hair above his ears, though it was still thick enough – thank goodness he wouldn't be bald – and he was not yet thirty.

He had regained his self-control; the worst was already over, and yet he remained dissatisfied and unquiet. If she came quickly he would talk to her openly. Or, perhaps, once she was there, he would, none the less, keep silent.

Then inexplicably, his dissatisfaction and disquiet turned in a different direction. That programme of what he had to learn, there was something missing from it, something he had omitted. He saw the lacuna, and rather embarrassed, said to Jan Maan :

'Listen, Jan, I should like to go to church for once in a way.'

'Are you crazy? Church? What sort of a church do you mean?'

'Well, a Protestant one, naturally. "She" was brought up a Protestant, although she doesn't go to church. But I would like once to hear a really good preacher. Do you know of anyone?'

Jan Maan was too astonished to get cross.

'You ask a member of the Dutch Godless for a list of preachers ! Do you realize what you are asking and whom?'

'Yes, all right, don't fly up in the air. I only wanted to say . . .'

He stopped.

'Come on, then, tell me. What did you want to say? That you're now a complete capitalist, no doubt? The only thing missing is religion, and you now want that support? Your degree and money in your pocket, and then a bit of the cross as a stick – no doubt you're going to get there swimmingly.'

'You're too silly for words, Jan.'

'Just as well. If we both had the same views we'd long ago have gone our own ways. A bond between two people who have nothing to say to each other is quickly broken.'

'She's staying a long time,' said Katadreuffe.

Jan Maan was already back with his reading-matter. He mumbled :

'Give her time to examine the little worm from top to bottom.'

Katadreuffe mused silently over what he had just been saying. The furrow of thought appeared above his nose. No, it was not true what De Gankelaar had maintained, that religion was a disease of old age; he suddenly felt the need not to use religion as something to lean on – that showed weakness in a man – but to bring God into his life as a thought to which he could always turn.

He was sitting in his mother's place at the table, her big work-basket near her chair on a stool. His hand absent-mindedly stroked the wool. Then he took a hank in his hand; what a pretty colour of green gleaming in the light. He noticed a piece of work she had just begun, but he must not touch that; in fact, he was not allowed to rummage in the work-basket; she had chastised him for it as a child.

Then again he thought how he could bring God into his life, not as a capitalist, but because this was the moment when he was on the point of beginning his journey. There must be no slack stowage in the cargo; everything must be shipshape; now that he checked up he saw that he had overlooked one hold.

Then something whispered in his ear these words :

'Or worked for you?'

But suddenly he found between his fingers the Savings Bank book – this was reality. It must have been lying in the basket and he must have, without realizing it, picked it up. He thumbed the pages; on the last page he saw a largish amount and, turning back to the previous pages, he noticed with surprise the same deposits every month : every month she had taken the money he had given her to the bank. Then, on the first page, he read her will, the hand-writing large and still childish : 'For my son Jacob Willem after my death. Mrs J. Katadreuffe.' And the date. The will.

He put the book back in the basket and stood up. His eyes were blinded – he stepped to the window.

The will, illegal, invalid, unnecessary. The sublime will.

'Damn it all!' he said hoarsely.

For when a man feels strong emotion he does not weep, he swears.

Jan Maan, at the table, heard it and asked :

'Jacob, what's the matter, old chap?'

The name as he spoke it had a biblical ring, a name from the books of the Old Testament. A friend, he felt touched and at the same time had a premonition.

Katadreuffe saw that there were four people in his life and all was sadness.

Jan Maan, his friend, whom he had never been able to wean from his pedestrian and ephemeral affairs and his narrow-minded dependence on the Party. The man who had been able to preserve nothing but a loyal heart in the suffocation of the mediocre.

Lorna Te George, the woman whose warmth he had spurned. He on this side of the river, she on that; that river of the eternal marriage of waters between them. He had stood here, and had remained on the bank like a cowardly Leander. He had contented himself with marriage in imag-ination with a wraith. It had remained spiritual, inhuman.

'Her' – he saw her. The stern, dour woman who had never helped him. But a woman with eyes like coals of fire, the writer of this will. And having lost Lorna Te George, he now stood to lose that woman, whose blood was so similar that they could not get on with one another. For Jan Maan was right; in his naïveté, he had announced a great truth. And how sad that was; how different it ought to have been between him and this woman.

But the fourth person he did not see as a man; he saw

him as a tree. And the tree symbolized at the same time his feeling for the man; it also symbolized *him*. Within that tree was this man and he had grown up together with him, inextricably. In a dark corner of his heart, in the hot tropical jungle stood that tree. But he saw himself fell the teak with his axe; he had felled that man together with himself.

'Jacob, what's the matter?'

And Katadreuffe, so excessively honest, in despair took refuge in a lie. He struck his forehead with his hand.

'Damn it all,' he repeated, 'I've forgotten something I've just got to do. So long. I'll be back in half an hour, tell her.'

Averting his face from his friend, he left the room – Now, in Heaven's name, no meeting on the landing; but no, everything was quiet; only the weak cry of a child, could be heard.

He walked quickly down the stairs and quietly shut the street-door behind him.

ELEPHANT PAPERBACKS

Literature and Letters

Walter Bagehot, *Physics and Politics,* EL305
Stephen Vincent Benét, *John Brown's Body,* EL10
Isaiah Berlin, *The Hedgehog and the Fox,* EL21
F. Bordewijk, *Character,* EL46
Robert Brustein, *Dumbocracy in America,* EL421
Anthony Burgess, *Shakespeare,* EL27
Philip Callow, *From Noon to Starry Night,* EL37
Philip Callow, *Son and Lover: The Young D. H. Lawrence,* EL14
Philip Callow, *Vincent Van Gogh,* EL38
Anton Chekhov, *The Comic Stories,* EL47
James Gould Cozzens, *Castaway,* EL6
James Gould Cozzens, *Men and Brethren,* EL3
Clarence Darrow, *Verdicts Out of Court,* EL2
Floyd Dell, *Intellectual Vagabondage,* EL13
Theodore Dreiser, *Best Short Stories,* EL1
Joseph Epstein, *Ambition,* EL7
André Gide, *Madeleine,* EL8
Gerald Graff, *Literature Against Itself,* EL35
John Gross, *The Rise and Fall of the Man of Letters,* EL18
Irving Howe, *William Faulkner,* EL15
Aldous Huxley, *After Many a Summer Dies the Swan,* EL20
Aldous Huxley, *Ape and Essence,* EL19
Aldous Huxley, *Collected Short Stories,* EL17
Roger Kimball, *Tenured Radicals,* EL43
F. R. Leavis, *Revaluation,* EL39
F. R. Leavis, *The Living Principle,* EL40
F. R. Leavis, *The Critic as Anti-Philosopher,* EL41
Sinclair Lewis, *Selected Short Stories,* EL9
William L. O'Neill, ed., *Echoes of Revolt: The Masses, 1911–1917,* EL5
Budd Schulberg, *The Harder They Fall,* EL36
Ramón J. Sender, *Seven Red Sundays,* EL11
Peter Shaw, *Recovering American Literature,* EL34
Tess Slesinger, *On Being Told That Her Second Husband Has Taken His First Lover, and Other Stories,* EL12
Donald Thomas, *Swinburne,* EL45
B. Traven, *The Bridge in the Jungle,* EL28
B. Traven, *The Carreta,* EL25
B. Traven, *The Cotton-Pickers,* EL32
B. Traven, *General from the Jungle,* EL33
B. Traven, *Government,* EL23
B. Traven, *March to the Montería,* EL26
B. Traven, *The Night Visitor and Other Stories,* EL24
B. Traven, *The Rebellion of the Hanged,* EL29
B. Traven, *Trozas,* EL44
Anthony Trollope, *Trollope the Traveller,* EL31
Rex Warner, *The Aerodrome,* EL22
Thomas Wolfe, *The Hills Beyond,* EL16
Wilhelm Worringer, *Abstraction and Empathy,* EL42

ELEPHANT PAPERBACKS

Theatre and Drama

Linda Apperson, *Stage Managing and Theatre Etiquette,* EL430
Robert Brustein, *Dumbocracy in America,* EL421
Robert Brustein, *Reimagining American Theatre,* EL410
Robert Brustein, *The Theatre of Revolt,* EL407
Stephen Citron, *The Musical from the Inside Out,* EL427
Irina and Igor Levin, *Working on the Play and the Role,* EL411
David Wood, with Janet Grant, *Theatre for Children,* EL433
Plays for Performance:
   Aristophanes, *Lysistrata,* EL405
   Pierre Augustin de Beaumarchais, *The Barber of Seville,* EL429
   Pierre Augustin de Beaumarchais, *The Marriage of Figaro,* EL418
   Anton Chekhov, *The Cherry Orchard,* EL420
   Anton Chekhov, *The Seagull,* EL407
   Euripides, *The Bacchae,* EL419
   Euripides, *Iphigenia in Aulis,* EL423
   Euripides, *Iphigenia Among the Taurians,* EL424
   Euripides, *The Trojan Women,* EL431
   Georges Feydeau, *Paradise Hotel,* EL403
   Henrik Ibsen, *A Doll's House,* EL432
   Henrik Ibsen, *Ghosts,* EL401
   Henrik Ibsen, *Hedda Gabler,* EL413
   Henrik Ibsen, *The Master Builder,* EL417
   Henrik Ibsen, *When We Dead Awaken,* EL408
   Henrik Ibsen, *The Wild Duck,* EL425
   Heinrich von Kleist, *The Prince of Homburg,* EL402
   Christopher Marlowe, *Doctor Faustus,* EL404
   The Mysteries: Creation, EL412
   The Mysteries: The Passion, EL414
   Luigi Pirandello, *Six Characters in Search of an Author,* EL426
   Sophocles, *Antigone,* EL428
   Sophocles, *Electra,* EL415
   August Strindberg, *The Father,* EL406
   August Strindberg, *Miss Julie,* EL422

European and World History

Lee Feigon, *Demystifying Tibet,* EL211
Mark Frankland, *The Patriots' Revolution,* EL201
Lloyd C. Gardner, *Spheres of Influence,* EL131
Raul Hilberg, et al., eds., *The Warsaw Diary of Adam Czerniakow,* EL212
Gertrude Himmelfarb, *Darwin and the Darwinian Revolution,* EL207
Gertrude Himmelfarb, *Victorian Minds,* EL205
Thomas A. Idinopulos, *Jerusalem,* EL204
Allan Janik and Stephen Toulmin, *Wittgenstein's Vienna,* EL208
Ronnie S. Landau, *The Nazi Holocaust,* EL203
Clive Ponting, *1940: Myth and Reality,* EL202
Scott Shane, *Dismantling Utopia,* EL206
Alexis de Tocqueville, *Memoir on Pauperism,* EL209
John Weiss, *Ideology of Death,* EL210

ELEPHANT PAPERBACKS

American History and American Studies
Stephen Vincent Benét, *John Brown's Body,* EL10
Henry W. Berger, ed., *A William Appleman Williams Reader,* EL126
Andrew Bergman, *We're in the Money,* EL124
Paul Boyer, ed., *Reagan as President,* EL117
Robert V. Bruce, *1877: Year of Violence,* EL102
Philip Callow, *From Noon to Starry Night,* EL37
David Cowan and John Kuenster, *To Sleep with the Angels,* EL139
George Dangerfield, *The Era of Good Feelings,* EL110
Clarence Darrow, *Verdicts Out of Court,* EL2
Floyd Dell, *Intellectual Vagabondage,* EL13
Elisha P. Douglass, *Rebels and Democrats,* EL108
Theodore Draper, *The Roots of American Communism,* EL105
Joseph Epstein, *Ambition,* EL7
Lloyd C. Gardner, *Pay Any Price,* EL136
Lloyd C. Gardner, *Spheres of Influence,* EL131
Paul W. Glad, *McKinley, Bryan, and the People,* EL119
Sarah H. Gordon, *Passage to Union,* EL138
Daniel Horowitz, *The Morality of Spending,* EL122
Kenneth T. Jackson, *The Ku Klux Klan in the City, 1915–1930,* EL123
Edward Chase Kirkland, *Dream and Thought in the Business Community,*
    1860–1900, EL114
Herbert S Klein, *Slavery in the Americas,* EL103
Aileen S. Kraditor, *Means and Ends in American Abolitionism,* EL111
Irving Kristol, *Neoconservatism,* EL304
Leonard W. Levy, *Jefferson and Civil Liberties: The Darker Side,* EL107
Thomas J. McCormick, *China Market,* EL115
Walter Millis, *The Martial Spirit,* EL104
Nicolaus Mills, ed., *Culture in an Age of Money,* EL302
Nicolaus Mills, *Like a Holy Crusade,* EL129
Roderick Nash, *The Nervous Generation,* EL113
William L. O'Neill, ed., *Echoes of Revolt: The Masses, 1911–1917,* EL5
Gilbert Osofsky, *Harlem: The Making of a Ghetto,* EL133
Edward Pessen, *Losing Our Souls,* EL132
Glenn Porter and Harold C. Livesay, *Merchants and Manufacturers,* EL106
John Prados, *The Hidden History of the Vietnam War,* EL137
John Prados, *Presidents' Secret Wars,* EL134
Edward Reynolds, *Stand the Storm,* EL128
Richard Schickel, *The Disney Version,* EL135
Edward A. Shils, *The Torment of Secrecy,* EL303
Geoffrey S. Smith, *To Save a Nation,* EL125
Bernard Sternsher, ed., *Hitting Home: The Great Depression in Town and*
    Country, EL109
Bernard Sternsher, ed., *Hope Restored: How the New Deal Worked in Town*
    and Country, EL140
Athan Theoharis, *From the Secret Files of J. Edgar Hoover,* EL127
Nicholas von Hoffman, *We Are the People Our Parents Warned Us Against,*
    EL301

Norman Ware, *The Industrial Worker, 1840–1860,* EL116
Tom Wicker, *JFK and LBJ: The Influence of Personality upon Politics,* EL120
Robert H. Wiebe, *Businessmen and Reform,* EL101
T. Harry Williams, *McClellan, Sherman and Grant,* EL121
Miles Wolff, *Lunch at the 5 & 10,* EL118
Randall B. Woods and Howard Jones, *Dawning of the Cold War,* EL130